90 Miles 2.0

THE CULPRIT OF COMMUNISM IN THE AMERICAS

Jose L. Gonzalez

Published by: AR PRESS
Roger L. Brooks, Publisher
roger@americanrealpublishing.com
americanrealpublishing.com

EXT. BEACH – DAY

A deserted beach, crystal blue water, and sand purer than sugar fill the frame.

WAVE AFTER WAVE RUSH ASHORE.

CREDITS ROLL.

MUSIC FADES IN, A CUBAN BOLERO

CAMERA TILTS UP AND ZOOMS BACK TO A WIDE ANGLE OF THE SHORELINE.

                                        DISSOLVE TO:

CLOSE UP: Pieces of a raft float aimlessly in the water.

                                        CUT TO:

VIDEO FOOTAGE OF BALSEROS CLIMBING ABOARD A COASTGUARD SHIP.

CLOSER ANGLE ON COAST GUARD PERSONNEL AS THEY GAFF THE DEAD FLOATING NEAR THE BOAT.

FADE IN VOICE OVER (V.O.) OF TV commentator.

COMMENTATOR

At approximately 5:00 a.m. this morning, a Coast Guard cutter found the remnants of a raft adrift near mile marker 4. Thirteen Cubans were picked up earlier today close to the island of Dry Tortugas. Unfortunately, two of the rafters (apparently two young women in their twenties) didn't make it.

MUSIC/A Cuban bolero and Images

FADE OUT TO BLACK.

FADE IN PRESENT DAY MIAMI.

CUT IN SALSA MUSIC

CUT IN A MONTAGE OF MIAMI:

A beautiful aerial shot of the city of Miami. The skies are clear, and the sun is shining on a warm summer afternoon. Multiple shots of the city reflect the tempo and lifestyle in South Florida. People are shopping at Bayside with towering modern skyscrapers in the background. The skyline is only beset by good-looking people just about everywhere. Two seductively dressed women walk by and flirt with a handsome young man. The young man flirts back.

EXT. AT BAYSIDE MAIN ENTRANCE – DAY

The parking attendant drives up in a fire engine red Ferrari convertible, the hottest car you've ever seen. The YOUNG MAN gets in and speeds off, laying down some serious rubber.

EXT. NEAR EXCLUSIVE CORAL GABLES NEIGHBORHOOD IN FRONT OF A MAJESTIC RESIDENCE – DAY

The young man drives up and the security gates open. He drives through.

EXT. FRONT DOORS – DAY

A servant opens the car door for the young man who jumps out and hustles inside the house.

CREDITS END

THE MUSIC FADES

INT. FOYER – DAY

The young man walks in. A party is in progress (una quinceañera).

A MIDDLE-AGED MAN greets him at the door.

> PEPE
> ¿Que pasó mijo? Why are you late?
> (What happened?)

> JUAN
> Nada, PEPE… el tiempo se me fue volando. (Nothing, PEPE, time just flew by.)

> PEPE
> I think you're in the dog house!

> JUAN
>
> Okay…okay.

The young man rushes upstairs.

We see A MONTAGE OF THE PARTY.

INT. LIBRARY — DAY

Pepe is sitting in his chair smoking a Cuban cigar and sipping a scotch. He's taken a load off and has checked out from the party. On his lap is an old photo album. He opens it and starts to reminisce. At about the third page, he stops and focuses on an 8 x 10.

HIS POINT OF VIEW (POV)

A picture of a beautiful YOUNG WOMAN posing for the photographer. She's smiling and very sophisticated.

BACK ON PEPE

He's distraught. The more he focuses on the picture, the closer he comes to tears.

> PEPE
> (thinking)
>
> I'd give my right hand just to hold you
> once again…

Suddenly, the double doors to the library open, and a beautiful YOUNG WOMAN (Lucia) runs in. She is stunning and amazingly similar to the one in the photograph.

LUCIA
Daddy, what are you doing in here? I've
been looking all over for you.

She walks over to him and sits on the armrest of his chair.

PEPE
I just needed a break.

She picks up on his mood.

LUCIA
What are you looking at?

PEPE
Some old pictures.

LUCIA
Let me see.

He hands her the album. Lucia sees the picture he's worshipping.

LUCIA
You miss Mom?

PEPE
Very much.

Lucia can't take her eyes off the picture.

LUCIA
She was so beautiful.

PEPE
Just as you are!

> LUCIA
> How old was she when she—?

Pepe interrupts.

> PEPE
> Too young.

He takes the album away from Lucia and puts it in a desk drawer.

Juan barges in. He's in a playful mood.

> JUAN
> Where is the party girl? Or should I say
> the old maid?

> LUCIA
> Funny…very funny!

Juan, not as perceptive as Lucia, continues to joke around.

> JUAN
> Why haven't you heard? Brad Pitt is
> outside looking for you.

> LUCIA
> A comedian, how original.

Finally, Juan catches on.

> JUAN
> What's up? Why the sad faces?

Pepe looks at Juan, then at Lucia. He reaches out to both of them for a hug. They hug. The warmth and love for one another fills the room.

PEPE

Sorry for taking you away from the
party. Go on and have some fun.

LUCIA

Sorry hell? It's time to fess up.

Lucia is determined to finally get the whole story of how her mother
died.

LUCIA

You promised that when I turn fifteen
you'd tell me everything.

PEPE

And I will—right after the party.

LUCIA

The party? Give me a break!

PEPE

What about our guests?

LUCIA

They can wait!

A difficult moment for PEPE.

JUAN

I think it's time.

Juan grabs a chair and sits next to Pepe and Lucia. Lucia slides on to
the ottoman across from him. A poignant silence settles in. Pepe fights
back tears.

PEPE
Your mother was so beautiful.

JUAN
How did she die?

PEPE
It should have never happened. It was
all my fault.

Lucia takes Pepe's hand and holds it as if to say, "No, it was no fault of yours." Pepe takes a deep breath, reaches across the desk, opens a drawer, and pulls out several old pictures from an album. As he points to one of the pictures, he speaks.

PEPE
She was my reason for living.

CUT TO THEIR POV OF THE PICTURE

ALICIA, Lucia's mother, is standing with Pepe behind FIDEL CASTRO and other MEMBERS of the Cuban Revolutionary Party.

PEPE'S V.O.

> It all began in Union City, New Jersey, around 1957. Your mother and I were not married, but we had talked about it on several occasions. Here (pointing to one of the pictures) we were having lunch with Castro and several members of the Cuban Revolutionary Party.

CAMERA FOCUSED ON THE PHOTOGRAPH FADES BACK IN TIME.

EVERYONE IN THE PHOTOGRAPH COMES TO LIFE.

A very young Fidel Castro is sitting at the head of the table with several colleagues. Pepe is standing directly behind Fidel with Alicia. The group is talking and carrying on.

PEPE'S V.O.

> The man sitting to Fidel's right was your grandfather, JOSE MARTINEZ. ROBERTO Martinez, your grandfather's younger brother, my uncle, was the guy giving the victory sign. And your great uncle LUIS who died while still in Cuba is the man sitting to the left of Fidel.

As Fidel and the group of colleagues prepare for another photograph, Fidel stops the picture taking process and switches his plate with Ramon's plate.

FIDEL
No quiero que cuando el publico vea esta fotografía piensen que yo soy un cerdo comiendo. (I don't want people to see this picture and think that I am a pig eating.)

Flash, the camera goes off. The group resumes eating their meal and Fidel gets his plate back. Alicia goes back to the kitchen.

CASTRO AND COLLEAGUES IMPROVISE DURING PEPE'S V.O.

RESUMES TELLING THE STORY.

PEPE'S V.O.
It was 1956 when we started organizing the Cuban revolution. Your mother loved politics. She was always involved in many activities. A group of us gathered at a hotel with Fidel to discuss strategy and fund raising.

PEPE'S V.O. CONTINUED
As you know, our objective was noble… we wanted to overthrow Batista's dictatorship. He was a ruthless criminal, corrupt and a thief. We had quite a following thanks to your mother. That year we received contributions from several US companies, US citizens, and many wealthy Cuban families.

CLOSE ON TONY ALVAREZ

PEPE'S V.O. CONTINUED
For example, Tony Alvarez, an engineer whose family owned twelve independent sugar mills just west of Havana.

CLOSE ON ERNESTO CARBONEL

PEPE'S V.O. CONTINUED
Another dear friend, Ernesto Carbonel, owner of the largest freight forwarding company in Havana.

CLOSE ON RUBEN AND ENRIQUE GARCIA

PEPE'S V.O. CONTINUED
And yes, how can I forget Ruben and Enrique Garcia, the owners of the largest tobacco plantation in Cuba?

CLOSE ON RAMON MOREJON

PEPE'S V.O. CONTINUED
By 1957, we had stockpiled guns, ammunitions, and other supplies needed for the war against Batista. Keeping track of all the progress was the job of Ramon Morejon, a recent political science graduate from the University of Havana.

CLOSE ON FIDEL CASTRO

PEPE'S V.O. CONTINUED
(somewhat sarcastic)

And oh yes, last but not least our fearless leader, Fidel Castro also known as dirt ball (bola de churre) who was born in Biran, Cuba August 13th, 1926.

PEPE'S V.O. FADES OUT AS THE CONVERSATION AT THE DINING ROOM TABLE FADES IN.

INT. CAMERA PULLS BACK ON DINING ROOM – DAY

The group laughs at a joke interpreted by PEPE.

JOSE

Caballeros, me parece que esta reunión debía de comenzar. Enrique, por favor danos el reporte de Tesorería. (Gentlemen I don't want to spoil the party, but I believe the meeting should begin. Enrique, please give us the Treasury report.)

FIDEL

Buena idea. Silencio por favor. (Good idea. Silence please.)

CLOSE ON ENRIQUE AS HE TURNS TO ERNESTO.

ENRIQUE

Trajiste los libros contables? (Did you bring the accounting records?)

ERNESTO

Si, están en mi maletín. (Yes, they're in my briefcase.)

Ruben gets his briefcase and gives it to Enrique.

CAMERA FOCUSES ON A LEATHER BRIEFCASE THAT NOTICEABLY BEARS THE INITIALS OF ERNESTO CARBONEL (EC).

CLOSE ON ENRIQUE AND ERNESTO.

Enrique places the case on top of the dining room table, opens it, and pulls out the necessary documents for his report. He clears his throat.

ENRIQUE

Muchas gracias por su atención. Les informo que a partir de Agosto 30, tenemos en depósitos exactamente $75,155.67. (Thank you for your attention. As of August 30th, we have raised $75,155.67.)

The group celebrates. Fidel takes a puff from his Cuban cigar.

ENRIQUE

La semana pasada recibimos una donación grandísima de una compañía petrolera Norte Americana en Cienfuegos. (Last week, we received a sizable contribution from the US Oil Company in Cienfuegos.)

                    FIDEL
         Menos mal que los gringos sirven para
         algo. (I'm glad to see these Yankees are
         good for something.)

Fidel relights his Cuban cigar.

                   ROBERTO
         Al pasó que vamos, la victoria será nues-
         tra. (At this pace, victory is ours.)

CLOSE ON FIDEL CASTRO.

                    FIDEL
         Me gusta que pienses así Roberto, pero
         cuidado en quien confías. (I like the way
         you think, Roberto, but be careful who
         you trust.)

CLOSE ON ROBERTO.

                   ROBERTO
         Solamente confío en nosotros. (I only
         trust us.)

BACK ON CASTRO.

                    FIDEL
         Bien, muy bien… (Good, very good.)

By now everyone has finished their meal. Pepe is the first to pick up
his plate and head toward the kitchen. Jose follows close behind.

INT. KITCHEN – DAY

ROSA is standing in front of the kitchen sink washing and rinsing dirty dishes and glasses. Alicia, young and beautiful, is drying them as Rosa hands them to her. Pepe unloads his dishes in the sink. Jose does the same.

ROSA

Are they ready for dessert?

PEPE

I think so.

Jose takes a cigar from his cigar box and lights one up.

JOSE

The truth is the food was fabulous.

Jose walks over to Rosa and gives her a peck on the cheek. Rosa kisses him back. Pepe gently grabs Alicia by the waistline. She looks back at him.

ROSA

I'm glad everyone enjoyed the meal.

PEPE

The black beans and rice were great!

Jose laughs at Pepe.

JOSE

I think you love your mother's cooking.

Alicia comes to the rescue.

ALICIA
I think everyone loves Rosa's cooking.
Wouldn't you say, Jose?

Jose's reply is with body language.

ROSA
In this family, everyone has a healthy
appetite.

Roberto comes into the kitchen.

ROBERTO
Do you have another one of those cigars
you gave Fidel?

JOSE
Sure, here.

Jose opens a kitchen cabinet, pulls out a cigar box, opens it, and offers
his brother a cigar. Roberto helps himself to several cigars. Jose walks
over to the dining room door and peeks through the crack to verify
that no one else is coming back into the kitchen. The group in the
kitchen is curious about Jose's actions. Jose turns to the group and
cautiously speaks.

JOSE
Quickly listen to me. You have to be
very careful and watch what you say
during these meetings…especially when
Fidel is present.

ROBERTO
Why?

JOSE

We need to be prudent. I don't trust everyone in the room.

ROBERTO

If you are referring to Fidel, you're wrong. He is a sincere and trustworthy friend.

JOSE

Roberto, my experience tells me even friends turn on each other.

ROBERTO

Are you paranoid or just crazy?

JOSE

No, I'm being prudent. I was warned last week by an old military buddy. He discovered that meetings are being held, to which none of us get invited. Why?

Roberto is now upset. Luis walks into the kitchen. As Roberto leaves the kitchen, he turns to Luis.

ROBERTO

Your father has lost touch with reality. I don't know what's wrong with him.

Roberto rushes out, upset and annoyed with Jose.

LUIS

What's wrong, Papa?

> JOSE
> Nothing son, nothing. We'll talk later.

Rosa recognizes that a change in topic is needed.

> ROSA
> Everyone, out of the kitchen. Now, let's go! Desert is almost ready. It'll be right out with it.

CAMERA PANS TO ALICIA AND PEPE.

Alicia opens the oven and pulls out a deep dish of arroz con leche. The smell breaks through the tension in the kitchen.

> PEPE
> Mmm, that smells delicious!

Pepe prepares the countertop where Alicia places the hot dish. Jose and Roberto leave the kitchen.

CLOSE ON PEPE AND ALICIA.

> PEPE
> When are you going back to Havana?

> ALICIA
> I'm leaving Saturday morning.

> PEPE
> Good, then let's have dinner tomorrow.

> ALICIA
> Pick me up at eight?

PEPE

You bet!

Pepe gives Alicia a peck on the cheek and leaves the kitchen.

INT. LIVING ROOM – DAY

The group has moved from the dining room to the living room. PEPE straggles into the living room.

ENRIQUE
We anticipate that by the end of the month, we'll have more than $100,000.

FIDEL
Not bad.

(a beat)

Before I forget, I want Ernesto and Ruben to return to Cuba next week.

ERNESTO
Why, what's up?

FIDEL
I need you to pick up some documents from our gambling friends in Havana.

JOSE
What documents? You mean the bribe from the mob, don't you?

FIDEL
Yes, that's right.

>   JOSE
>   Fidel, this could be a problem for us.
>   Why don't we—

Fidel interrupts.

>   FIDEL
>   I don't care whose money it is. Money
>   is money. We need it for the revolution.

>   JOSE
>   If we accept money from the mob, we'll
>   be no different than Batista.

Fidel stands. He's furious, looking directly at Jose.

>   FIDEL
>   Let's make something perfectly clear
>   here and now. Nobody, but nobody, has
>   the right to question my judgment.

He catches himself before exploding.

>   FIDEL
>   Please, don't misunderstand me. Let's
>   never forget why we're all here.

>   (several beats)

>   We must remain united!

An eerie silence fills the room.

>   FIDEL
>   Do you understand?

Fidel turns to Ruben and Ernesto.

FIDEL

I need your cooperation and support.
Do I have it?

RUBEN

Yes.

ERNESTO

We'll leave for Havana tomorrow.

CUT TO:

EXT. THE CITY OF HAVANA – DAY

The downtown streets of Havana look prosperous. Cars, trucks, buses seemingly going in every direction. Billeteros are selling lotto tickets at every street corner. The streets are crowded with people.

A 1956 Ford Fairlane, a cream puff of a car, stops at the red light. As the camera zooms in on the driver, we see Ernesto in the driver's seat. Ernesto is smoking nervously. The light turns green.

CAMERA FOLLOWS THE CAR AS IT TURNS RIGHT AT THE CORNER

The car comes to a stop. Ernesto exits the car with his leather brief-case. He feeds the meter and looks around, orienting himself to the numbering of the buildings. He walks up the steps of a building and directly to its front door.

Ernesto knocks on the door using an unusual sequential knock. The door's peephole opens. A person's eye is visible behind the door. A few seconds pass. The door is unlocked and opened from the inside by an old lady. He enters the foyer which is dark and humid. The old lady closes the door behind him. Ruben walks into the foyer from an adjacent room. They greet each other.

INT. HALL – DAY

Ruben and Ernesto walk down the hall.

> RUBEN
> I'm glad to see you made it.

> ERNESTO
> It was easy…maybe too easy.

> RUBEN
> Don't worry, Fidel has things under control.

> ERNESTO
> Yeah, but dealing with the Mob gives me the creeps.

> RUBEN
> Come on, let's get it over with.

INT. OFFICE – DAY

Ruben leads Ernesto down the hall into an office. Ernesto closes the door behind him, leaving the old lady outside. Ernesto puts the briefcase on top of a conference table. Ruben pulls the keys from a floor safe just behind the desk.

                    RUBEN
Let's see what those mobsters think of
Fidel.

Ruben unlocks the briefcase. Ernesto opens it.

                    ERNESTO
Holy shit!

                    RUBEN
Coño!

Their faces light up.

ERNESTO AND RUBEN'S POV

The briefcase is full of money ($100 bills). They're speechless.

                    RUBEN
I guess Fidel was right.

                    ERNESTO
Batista is history!

Ruben shuts the briefcase.

                    RUBEN
Okay, do you have Fidel's instructions?

He pulls two envelopes out of his pocket.

                    ERNESTO
Here they are.

They open the envelopes, read the instructions, and with a cigarette lighter, light up both sets of instructions. Ernesto speaks as the instructions burn.

ERNESTO

I must leave immediately.

RUBEN

I have several things to do before I can return to New Jersey.

ERNESTO

Be careful. Don't take any chances. If you don't hear from me by nine tonight, leave without me.

(a beat)

See you later.

Ernesto closes the briefcase, takes the keys from Ruben, and heads out. Ruben escorts him to the front door. The old lady is waiting in a chair by the door.

EXT. FRONT OF THE BUILDING – DAY

Ernesto walks quickly out of the building and toward the car carrying his briefcase. He opens the car door, throws the briefcase on the passenger seat, and gets in.

RUBEN'S POV THROUGH THE PEEPHOLE.

Ernesto cranks up the car and drives off. Ruben shuts the peephole.

EXT. FRONT OF BUILDING – TWO CARS BACK FROM ERNESTO's VEHICLE – DAY

An unmarked car with three men inside watch Ernesto drive off. They crank up their car and begin following Ernesto.

EXT. DOWNTOWN STREETS OF HAVANA – DAY

Traffic is backed up, and Ernesto's car is caught up in stop-and-go traffic. Several cars are blowing their horns trying to persuade traffic to move quicker. Ernesto has not noticed he's being followed. The unmarked car pulls up directly behind Ernesto's car.

EXT. INSIDE ERNESTO'S CAR – DAY

He is uncomfortable and fidgety.

EXT. ON THE CAR FOLLOWING ERNESTO – DAY

The three men watch Ernesto's every move. One of the three men exits the car and walks toward Ernesto's car around the passenger side.

BACK ON ERNESTO'S CAR.

The traffic in the lane next to Ernesto loosens up temporarily. The car with the remaining two men pulls up alongside Ernesto. They are so close to Ernesto's car that no human being can walk between the cars. Ernesto notices how close they are. He has eye contact with the two men. Cold chills run down Ernesto's back. He senses something is terribly wrong,

Ernesto reaches for his revolver beneath the car seat. The traffic is still not moving in either lane. Perspiration is pouring from Ernesto's forehead. Ernesto cradles the .38-caliber revolver across his lap. The driver adjacent to Ernesto purposely opens his car door, slamming it against Ernesto's car, denting and scratching both vehicles. The man begins to yell obscenities at Ernesto. Ernesto puts his car in park and grabs his gun. Suddenly, several shots ring out. At point-blank range, the man on foot has shot Ernesto through the car window. Blood spackles the interior of the car. Ernesto falls forward against the car horn.

The killer finishes breaking the car window then reaches in and steals Ernesto's briefcase, with the horn blasting. The traffic remains at a standstill. The man with the briefcase hustles back to his car and gets in. Tires squealing, they pull in front of oncoming traffic and do a U-turn, knocking over a fruit stand and almost running over several pedestrians. The car hauls ass in the opposite direction.

BACK TO FRONT OF THE BUILDING WHERE RUBEN PREVIOUSLY MET ERNESTO.

The car with the three men pulls up.

INT. BACK OFFICE – DAY

Ruben is sitting at the desk, giving instructions to the old woman. Someone knocks on the front door with the identical knock Ernesto used earlier.

RUBEN

What the hell?

Ruben, leery about the knock on the front door, reaches into his desk drawer and pulls a .45-caliber pistol.

INT. HALLWAY AND FOYER

Ruben walks out of the office and down the hall with the old lady close behind. Ruben opens the peephole. He sees a man he does not recognize pointing a gun directly at his head. Ruben panics and shuts the peephole. As he turns around, the old lady jams a large butcher knife into Ruben's gut. The old lady smiles cynically as she jams it in even further.

OLD LADY

Por hijo puta! Maricon. (You son of a
bitch! Scumbag!)

Ruben drops the .45 and falls to his knees. The old lady opens the door. The men who followed and killed Ernesto are standing at the door. She invites them in.

THE KILLER

Good job, Grandma.

CLOSE ON RUBEN.

Ruben is still alive. He bleeds profusely as he tries to hold his guts in.

BACK IN THE FOYER WITH THE OLD LADY.

The old lady turns her trophy over to the three men.

OLD LADY

He's all yours.

The killer raises his gun, pointing at Ruben's head. He's about to pull the trigger when he re-aims it at the old lady.

THE KILLER

Por traidora! (You traitor!)

The killer fires two rounds in the old woman. She falls dead to the ground. The killer now aims at Ruben.

THE KILLER

Come mierda! (Now is your turn, you dirt bag!)

BLAM! BLAM! ERNESTO AND RUBEN ARE HISTORY.

INT. NEW YORK CITY HOTEL ROOM – NIGHT

Fidel Castro, with a view of Manhattan behind him, is sitting, smoking a cigar, and drinking a cognac. The telephone rings. Fidel answers.

FIDEL

Hello?

V.O. A MAN'S VOICE.

A MAN

Picadillo. (Your hamburger is done.)

FIDEL

Con huevos o con arroz? (With eggs or rice?)

A MAN

Con los dos. (With both.)

FIDEL

Muy bien! (Good!)

Fidel hangs up the phone and takes a puff from his cigar.

CUT TO:

INT. SOVIET EMBASSY, HAVANA, CUBA – NIGHT

A hand hangs up the phone. The camera pans up to reveal Che Guevara together with two Soviet diplomats.

CHE GUEVARA
Everything is right on track.

(a beat)

Let's talk about the arms shipment.

Cut in sound:

A BATTLE FIREFIGHT in process.

DISSOLVE TO:

SCENES OF CASTRO IN LA SIERRA MAESTRA BATTLING BATISTA SOLDIERS.

DISSOLVE TO:

On the screen "JANUARY 1, 1959."

Fidel Castro, on top of a Sherman tank, as he arrives triumphantly into the city of Havana. The celebration is in full swing, and thousands of Cubans are dancing, waving the Cuban flag, and kissing the soldiers that arrive with Fidel.

CLOSE ON FIDEL AND SEVERAL MEMBERS OF THE LIBERATING ARMY. Fidel is wearing a large crucifix.

> SOLDIER
>
> Since when do you wear a crucifix?

> FIDEL
>
> We only get one chance at first impressions, so we must be very careful how we present ourselves. These are very religious people.

Fidel waves to the crowds.

CUT IN FOOTAGE OF BATISTA'S ESCAPE FROM CUBA.

As the camera pulls back, we realize that this footage is being watched on television at Jose and Pepe's house in Union City, New Jersey, the same living room where the meetings were held to organize the revolution. Sitting around the television are Pepe, Jose, Luis, Roberto, Tony, Ramon, and Enrique. As the group watches the news reel, Pepe speaks.

> PEPE
>
> I think we've made a grave mistake.

> ROBERTO
>
> Give Castro a chance.

> JOSE
>
> A chance? A chance to do what? You want him to kill us the same way he killed Ernesto and Ruben?

Roberto is steaming.

ROBERTO

Bullshit, and you know it! We have no proof that Castro did it. It was Batista's men!

JOSE

(very sarcastically)

Then explain why Castro never tried to hunt down the bastards who killed our colleagues and stole the money (getting hot!). Explain that to me. After all, Money is money.

LUIS

Look, we all have our doubts and rightfully so, but the facts are that Fidel Castro is our new leader. What the hell you want to do? Kill him?

Enrique jumps in.

ENRIQUE

I think he's dirty as sin, and I don't trust the son of a bitch. I plan to find out who killed Ernesto and Ruben.

TONY

Gentlemen, please calm down. Don't forget we're responsible for what's happened.

> (a beat)

> Let's cool it for six months and see what materializes.

CUT TO:

INT. PRESIDENTIAL PALACE IN HAVANA, CUBA – DAY

Castro's soldiers are evacuating the palace, disposing of people and things.

FADE TO BLACK.

ON SCREEN "SIX MONTHS LATER."

EXT. TOBACCO FACTORY ESTABLISHING SHOT – DAY

INT. ENRIQUE'S OFFICE AT THE TOBACCO FACTORY – DAY

Enrique is at his desk. A picture of him with his deceased partner Ruben sits on his desk. Enrique is looking at the picture, reminiscing. The phone rings.

> ENRIQUE

> Hello?

> RAMON

> It's me!

> ENRIQUE

> What's up?

                    RAMON

I got it!

                    ENRIQUE

You got what?

                    RAMON

I've got proof that Castro's secret police
(G-2) is responsible for murdering
Ernesto and Ruben.

                    ENRIQUE

Don't say another word. I don't trust
these phones.

                    (a beat)

Meet me at El Encanto for lunch.

                    ENRIQUE

I can't. I have a meeting with other
tobacco producers at the Presidential
Palace in a few minutes.

                    (pause)

I'll meet you for dinner tonight at 9:00
p.m. at the Tropicana.

                    RAMON

Okay, but be careful. I've heard rumors
we could be next.

                    ENRIQUE

See you tonight!

Enrique hangs up the phone, gets his coat and walks out of the office.

EXT. ESTABLISING SHOT OF THE PRESIDENTIAL PALACE – DAY

INT. THE PRESIDENTIAL PALACE – DAY

Enrique is walking down the hall on the way to his meeting. Just outside the meeting room, a security guard approaches him.

> SECURITY GUARD
> Mr. Garcia?

> ENRIQUE
> Yes.

> PALACE GUARD
> Fidel Castro has asked me to escort you to his office immediately.

> ENRIQUE
> Why? What for?

> SECURITY GUARD
> I don't know. I'm just following orders, sir.

Enrique is ushered to Fidel's office. As they approach the double doors of Fidel's private office, Che Guevara is leaving Castro's office with his personal bodyguard. Enrique notices that El Che is carrying Ernesto's briefcase.

CLOSE ON THE BRIEFCASE.

It's identical. The briefcase has Ernesto's initials, EC.

BACK ON ENRIQUE IN SLOW MOTION.

Enrique recognizes the briefcase. The initials burn a deep wound in his soul. Outraged, Enrique lunges at Che and pins him against the wall. In a split second, both Enrique's escort and El Che's bodyguards restrain him. Castro hears the commotion outside his office and hurries out. Che Guevara pulls out his .45 caliber and is about to blow Enrique's brains out when Castro intervenes.

> FIDEL
> What the hell is going on here?

> CHE GUEVARA
> This asshole went crazy. I'm going to kill
> this son of a bitch.

> FIDEL
> Hold on! Hold on!

> (pauses)

> Goddammit…Enrique, what's your
> problem? What's wrong with you?

Enrique foams at the mouth.

> ENRIQUE
> The hell with you and El Che! You killed
> Ernesto.

> FIDEL
> What are you talking about?

Enrique points at the briefcase and struggles to break free.

ENRIQUE

That's Ernensto's briefcase!

Fidel realizes that the cat is out of the bag. He signals to the body-guards to bring him inside. The bodyguards drag Enrique into Fidel's office. The doors shut.

INT. FIDEL'S OFFICE – DAY

Fidel speaks without hesitation in cold blood.

FIDEL

Shoot the son of a bitch.

ENRIQUE

You'll pay for this! You'll...

BLAM! BLAM!

El Che holsters his .45.

CHE GUEVARA

We should eliminate the rest of your friends as soon as possible.

FIDEL

Not so quick...We have to be careful how we dispose of them. We can't afford any more mistakes.

(pause)

Dump his body at the railroad yard.

CHE GUEVARA
Why there? They'll find him there.

FIDEL
Just do as I tell you…

The bodyguard and the escort pick up Enrique's body and carry it out the door.

EXT. ESTABLISHING SHOT OF JOSE'S HOUSE – DAY

INT. JOSE'S HOUSE IN HAVANA – DAY

A newspaper is on top of the coffee table in the living room.

CAMERA ZOOMS IN ON THE HEADLINES.

"Tabacos Cubanos' President Shot to Death."

The camera pulls back to reveal Jose, Pepe, Roberto, Tony, Ramon, and Luis sitting around the living room coffee table.

PEPE
First Ernesto and Ruben. Now Enrique.
Which one of us is next?

LUIS
Patience, patience. There are still many
anti-Castro supporters trying to under-
mine the revolution.

                    JOSE

Are you blind? Or are you just stupid?
Batista didn't have anything to do with
this.

                  ROBERTO

I agree…What motive would Batista
have? He's living in luxury with everything he stole.

                    LUIS

Since when did Batista need a motive to
kill someone?

                    JOSE

Stop the bullshit, won't you? You didn't
believe the article, did you?

Jose stands up and starts pacing around the room.

                    JOSE

Two things are clear. One, Enrique,
Ernesto, and Ramon were murdered by
the same element that has ostracized
us from the revolution. Two, Fidel has
changed everything. We need to find
out who is supporting his every move.

                    PEPE

I was advised that the Shell Refinery
Project was canceled.

                    TONY

I heard that several American companies
have had their assets confiscated.

PEPE

Well, if it's not the Americans and us, then who is supporting this animal?

RAMON

What really worries me is what's happening in government. They're prohibiting all professionals, regardless of who you are, from leaving the island.

TONY

Are you sure about that?

JOSE

Yes, it's true. Several friends have had to falsify their passports to get out.

PEPE

We need to do something.

LUIS

What if Castro finds out?

PEPE

Then we take other measures.

LUIS

Surely, you're not thinking about—

ROBERTO
(interrupting)

Gentlemen, I think we are overreacting. Maybe Fidel is trying to stabilize things, get a grip on government.

JOSE

Stabilize my ass! You don't stabilize a country by nationalizing the banks, the oil industry, and who knows what else.

(angry)

And meet with him? Ernesto met with Fidel. Look what happened to him.

The discussion is now heated and tempers are flaring. Pepe attempts to discretely change the subject.

PEPE

Settle down now. Maybe we should take some time off?

TONY

Yeah, Varadero is nice this time of year. We need to get away from Havana.

Both Luis and Jose are still fighting mad.

PEPE

Great idea. You guys take some time off. Dad and I will sort things out with Fidel.

Jose looks at Pepe and reads between the lines.

FADE TO BLACK.

ON THE SCREEN: "1960."

DISSOLVE TO:

EXT. ALICIA'S HOUSE IN HAVANA – NIGHT

Pepe and Alicia arrive from a dinner date. They pause at the front door.

ALICIA

Would you like a cup of coffee?

PEPE

Sure.

Alicia unlocks the door, and they enter the house.

INT. ALICIA'S LIVING ROOM – NIGHT

ALICIA

Make yourself comfortable. I'll have it ready in a minute.

Alicia proceeds to the kitchen but they continue to talk to each other. Pepe sits down on the sofa.

PEPE

Have you had any luck getting a visa?

ALICIA

No. They keep telling me, "Next month."

PEPE

I know. They've been telling me the same thing for over a year.

ALICIA
Have patience. We'll get ours.

PEPE
I don't think so. They have no intentions
of letting our families leave.

Alicia comes out of the kitchen with a tray and two cups of coffee.

ALICIA
Did you come here to talk about your
visa?

PEPE
Sorry, honey, I didn't mean to ruin our
evening. You know you're my passport
to heaven.

Alicia puts the tray on the coffee table. She sits on the sofa next to him. Pepe forgets the coffee is there. His attention is focused on Alicia.

ALICIA
Didn't you want coffee?

PEPE
Not as much as I want you.

Pepe's face is inches away from Alicia's. He hovers over her, exploring, anticipating their touch. Gently, Pepe caresses her. He holds Alicia closer to him until that moment of magic when their lips touch and they lose all sense of reality. Passionate love begins. Pepe undresses her. First the blouse, then her dress. Alicia unbuttons Pepe's shirt, then dives into his pants, unzipping them, reaching for his...

DISSOLVE TO BLACK.

ON SCREEN "1961."

EXT. VARADERO BEACH, CUBA – NIGHT

It's a moonlit sky, and we can barely see Pepe's silhouette with three other men hustling to put branches, sand, and brush on top of a raft and what appears to be provisions for a trip.

CLOSE ON PEPE, LUIS, TONY, AND RAMON.

Suddenly, along the beach and not too distant from the shoreline, they hear the sound of a patrol boat. They freeze. The men see a glimpse of a spotlight scouring the beaches with blinding intensity. At the same time, but from the opposite direction, a foot patrol of Cuban soldiers is heard. They seem to be walking directly toward them.

PEPE

Pierdanse! (Scatter!)

The men scatter. The foot patrol leader sees the patrol boat and walks toward the shoreline.

PATROL LEADER

Capitán, no he visto nada. (Captain,
I've seen no trace of the men.)

(pause)

Parece que la información que nos dio
el G-2s no servía. (I believe the secret
police gave us bad information.)

As the soldiers take a breather, CAMERA PANS TO REVEAL WHERE EACH MAN IS HIDING.

Tony is totally buried in the sand, with his nose barely visible on the surface. He is lying less than fifteen feet away from one of the Cuban soldiers.

Ramon is in the water, grabbing on for dear life to a huge rock. He's trying to keep the waves and current from carrying him out to sea and exposing him to the Cuban patrols.

Pepe has climbed a coconut tree and has a bird's eye view of the entire situation.

Luis has hidden in the tall grass by the sand dunes. He's motionless.

CAMERA PANS DOWN LUIS'S BACK, STOPPING ON HIS ASS. Several crabs with huge claws are crawling on his thigh and butt.

CUT TO CLOSE UP OF LUIS. Cold sweat is dripping from his forehead.

CAPTAIN

> Busquen bien por toda esta área. Esos gusanos tienen que estar por aquí. (Search this area thoroughly. Those traitors are around here somewhere.)

LEADER

> Si, Capitán. (Yes, Captain)

The boat revs up and resumes its search as the foot patrol heads in the opposite direction. After the coast is clear, Pepe slides down the coconut tree. He quickly surveys the area and whispers.

PEPE

Tony…Ramon…Luis! Where the hell
are you, guys?

From the sand directly in front of him, Tony pops up, scaring the shit
out of Pepe.

PEPE

Cabron, don't scare me like that.

Tony giggles.

Ramon walks up. He's visibly in pain. A close up on him reveals multiple barnacle cuts on his chest, arm, and abdomen from the thrashing
he took against the rocks. Pepe takes off his shirt and uses it to help
Ramon stop the bleeding.

TONY

Are you okay?

RAMON

I'll live.

TONY

Where the hell is Luis?

PEPE

I don't know.

TONY

Luis, stop playing around, where are
you?

Faintly from behind the dunes.

> LUIS
Over here, guys! Help me!

Tony and Pepe run toward the sand dunes where they find Luis covered with large sand crabs ready to make a meal out of Luis.

> TONY
Holy shit!

> PEPE
Luis, don't move a muscle.

> LUIS
Yeah, sure. Easy for you to say.

Pepe turns to Tony.

> PEPE
Hurry, get me several leaves.

> TONY
You got it!

Tony runs toward a fallen coconut tree limb. He pulls several leaves, rushes back to Pepe, and hands them over.

> PEPE
Like I said before, don't move a muscle.
Okay?

> LUIS
Sure, just get these flesh-eating flatheads
off my ass.

With the skill of a surgeon, Pepe takes one of the leaves and passes it between the claws of a crab. The crab tenaciously snaps its claw and latches onto the leaf. Pepe lifts the crab off Luis's butt and heaves it into the water. Pepe repeats the process until all the crabs are off his back except for one. The last crab has latched onto Luis's butt and won't let go. Pepe gets this crab to latch onto a leaf with its other claw, but the crab refuses to let go of Luis's butt. Finally, Tony uses his cigarette lighter to light a fire under the claw holding on to Luis. The crab lets go, and Pepe heaves it into the water as well. Luis gets up, brushing off the sand and sweat. He feels his butt.

LUIS

Thanks, man!

PEPE

Thanks for what?

LUIS

Thanks for literally saving my ass.

They share a good laugh.

PEPE

Okay, you guys, listen up. We meet here
next Tuesday at midnight. Anyone late
stays behind. If we miss the forecasted
winds and currents, we'll all be fish bait.

LUIS

Do you really think we'll make it?

PEPE

You bet your ass we will! If you have any
doubts about going, don't show up!

TONY

You said each one of us could bring one
person. Right?

PEPE

Right, but make sure you bring someone that can take care of themselves.

RAMON

Pepe, when can we tell our families
about our trip?

PEPE

No sooner than thirty minutes before
departure. Any sooner would be too
risky.

A Cuban coast guard helicopter flies by at very low altitude, scaring
the daylights out of all of them.

PEPE

Okay, let's get out of here.

LUIS

Remember the code word, LANCHA.
This will confirm our trip twenty-four
hours before departure.

As they walk into the woods, they discuss tonight's anniversary party.
Fidel Castro is having the first Revolution Anniversary Party at the
Presidential Palace.

LUIS

Are you going to Fidel's party tonight?

TONY

No, not me. I can't stand the sight of that son of a bitch.

PEPE

Luis and I will both be there. I think the secret police has their eye on us, so we're going.

RAMON

I'll see you there!

The men scatter into the darkness of night.

FADE TO BLACK.

EXT. FIDEL CASTRO'S PRESIDENTIAL PALACE – NIGHT

An establishing shot of the Presidential Palace.

The entire area is heavily guarded and cordoned off by military personnel. The soldiers are dressed in either black tie or combat fatigues. They all bear, at a minimum, a side arm. Several foreign-looking limousines arrive. The limos bear flags from different foreign countries (the Soviet Union, North Korea, North Vietnam, China, etc.). Guests are dressed to the max. Simply put, this is more than just another black-tie affair.

INT. THE PRESIDENTIAL PALACE (STEADYCAM SHOT) – NIGHT

As we follow some of the guests inside, we observe that absolutely everyone is stopped by soldiers just inside the main entrance to verify their invitation, credentials, and a weapons search. Above them is a huge banner hung across the main entrance. The banner reads "Welcome to the First Anniversary Party of the Cuban Revolution." The camera continues to follow the guests after they've been checked. Pictures of Fidel Castro are strategically located throughout the palace ballroom.

As the camera follows the guests, a multitude of people, all impeccably dressed, are enjoying champagne and hors d'oeuvres inside. Soft classical music comes from a black grand piano sitting at the back of the ballroom. As the camera continues to follow, it focuses on an incredibly gorgeous lady. We notice that a tall man whose back is to camera is talking to this beautiful woman. As the camera pans around them, we reveal their identities, Alicia and Pepe.

CLOSE ON PEPE AND ALICIA.

PEPE
You look absolutely stunning.

ALICIA
You're in love.

PEPE
Yes, I'm in love with you.

ALICIA
I feel a little dizzy.

PEPE
Why? Are you ill?

ALICIA
No, not ill just dizzy. I'm sure it will all
go away soon enough.

Alicia keeps him at bay. She's saved by a waiter who offers them champagne from his tray full of glasses.

PEPE

If it continues, you need to go to the doctor.

ALICIA

In due time, Pepe. All in due time.

Pepe unknowingly smiles and takes a sip from his champagne glass.

PEPE

Should we break the news to the family?

ALICIA

What news?

PEPE

About our engagement, of course.

Alicia is surprised to see that PEPE has not caught on.

ALICIA

Of course, let's announce our union.

PEPE

Some great help you are.

(kidding)

Let's do it before I change my mind.

Alicia smiles from ear to ear, pleased with Pepe's innocence and decision.

Pepe, in a very gentlemanly manner, escorts Alicia toward the back of the ballroom.

INT. BALLROOM BY THE BLACK GRAND PIANO – NIGHT

A group of three very sophisticated and distinguished couples are standing by the grand piano, sipping champagne and discussing current events.

> ROBERTO
>
> Well, what do you think of the revolution now?

> JOSE
>
> (in a patronizing manner)
>
> My dear little brother, let's not discuss this topic here and now.

> ROBERTO
>
> Why? Have you changed your mind?

> JOSE
>
> No, there are ladies present.

Roberto is quickly getting hot. Rosa intervenes without hesitation.

> ROSA
>
> Is politics all you two know? I can't believe that you're such opposites.
>
> (a beat)
>
> Now both of you behave and stop arguing about this dammed revolution.

A mulatto Cuban officer approaches the group. He addresses Jose.

OFFICER

Are you Mr. Jose Martinez?

JOSE

I am.

OFFICER

I have orders to place you under arrest.
Please turn around.

The officer pulls his handcuffs from his belt. Tension fills the air. Everyone is ready to explode. Roberto grabs his balls with his cupped left hand in defiance.

ROBERTO

Arrest these!

The Cuban officer (Oscar) starts laughing uncontrollably as Jose embraces him.

JOSE

It's been a long time.

OSCAR

Yes, it has.

ROBERTO

Where the hell have you been?

OSCAR

In Angola.

Oscar embraces Ramon and, finally, Luis.

                    JOSE
Angola? What for?

                    OSCAR
As a military advisor.

Jose looks at Roberto as if telling him "I told you so." Still talking to Oscar, Jose speaks.

                    JOSE
Why are we spending money and send-
ing soldiers to Angola when we need
all the help we can right here? Can you
explain that to me?

                    ROBERTO
He can't. It's not his job to explain
Castro's strategy or decisions.

Pepe and Alicia walk up. Pepe escorts Alicia directly to his mother (Rosa's) side. They break the tension building between Roberto and Jose.

                    PEPE
Hello, everyone.

Oscar comes over to Pepe and greets him with a hug.

                    OSCAR
I haven't seen you in years. Why, look at
you, you're all grown up.

PEPE
Thanks for the vote of confidence. Now
everyone, please listen up.

(pause)

I hate to break up this reunion, but I
have a very important announcement to
make.

The group settles down and gives Pepe and Alicia their undivided
attention.

PEPE
Alicia and I are engaged. We're getting
married November 2nd.

Pepe pulls a beautiful diamond ring from his vest and places it on
Alicia's ring finger, surprising everyone, including Alicia.

ALICIA
It's beautiful.

ROSA
I'm so happy!

Rosa turns to Alicia and gives her a kiss and a hug, then turns to PEPE
and gives him a mother's hug.

ROSA
Congratulations, son! I hope you're both
very happy.

ALICIA
I'm sure we'll all be.

Suddenly, the Cuban national anthem begins to play. Again, Alicia is interrupted and not allowed to finish her announcement.

INT. AT THE MAIN ENTRANCE OF THE BALLROOM – NIGHT

The crowd starts clapping, and an entourage of soldiers in fatigues opens a path through the crowd for the guest of honor, Fidel Castro. A few steps behind him follow Che Guevara, Raul Castro, and other dignitaries. As the anthem continues to play, the guests join in the singing of the Cuban national anthem.

INT. BALLROOM HEAD TABLE – NIGHT

Fidel and the dignitaries stand by their seats at the head table. They all salute the Cuban flag at the end of the anthem and take their assigned seats.

INT. JOSE AND PEPE AT THE PARTY – NIGHT

Jose turns to his son and whispers.

> JOSE
> Are you sure this is what you want?

> PEPE
> I love her, Papa. I wouldn't have it any
> other way.

> JOSE
> Fine, son, but tell me something: Is this
> where you've been spending most of
> your evenings?

PEPE

No, Papa, not at all.

JOSE

Then where have you been?

A serious tone takes over the conversation.

PEPE

Can we talk about this later?

JOSE

Fine, make sure you come sometime tomorrow to our house. I want to know what you're up to.

CUT TO:

EXT. BASEBALL STADIUM – DAY

A game is in progress. A baseball is smacked over the fence for a home run. The crowd goes wild. The camera pans to reveal Pepe, Tony, and Luis at the game.

CLOSE ON PEPE, TONY, AND LUIS.

PEPE

Things are getting pretty sticky.

LUIS

What are you talking about?

PEPE

Dad wants to know what's going on. He
knows something up.

LUIS

Should we leave on Tuesday instead?

PEPE

If the weather permits.

The crowd stands. Several fans boo the umpire's call. Pepe looks
around, searching for Ramon.

PEPE

Where the hell is Ramon?

TONY

I don't know. I was just wondering the
same thing.

LUIS

It's not like him to be late.

(a beat)

I'm sure he's okay. I'll go see him tonight
and bring him up to speed.

CUT TO:

INT. A TORTURE CHAMBER – DAY

Ramon is naked from the waist up and tied to a chair. He's being
interrogated by several soldiers. The stitches on his chest and abdomen from the thrashing he took against the barnacles and rocks at

the beach are visible. Ramon's father and mother have also been detained and are strung up to wooden posts like wild animals ready to be slaughtered directly in front of Ramon. The soldier smoking a cigarette pulls out an eight-inch blade from his boot and walks over to Ramon. First, he puts out his cigarette on Ramon's barnacle wounds and stitches. Ramon screams in pain. Then he takes his blade and starts opening Ramon's stitches, one by one. As the stitches pop open, Ramon grimaces in pain.

SOLDIER

Ramonsito, my dear boy, tell me how
you got those nasty cuts. What were you
doing?

The soldier pops open another stitch, this time trying to inflict more pain.

SOLDIER

What are you up to?

Ramon spits on the soldier face. The soldier raises his blade to Ramon's throat, almost cutting it.

SOLDIER

I'm going to teach you a lesson, you bas-
tard. Something I learned a long time
ago.

The soldier walks over to Ramon's father and begins to carve him up good. He grabs an ear and cuts it clean off. Ramon's father screams in pain. The soldier continues and slices off the other ear. The scene is gut-wrenching. Ramon is screaming at the top of his lungs, begging the soldier to stop. The soldier turns to Ramon.

SOLDIER

Let's not ignore Mamacita.

He signals to one of the other soldiers to start doing his thing. The other soldier walks over to Mamacita and rips off her clothes. A naked Mamacita screams, begging for mercy. The soldier lowers his pants and starts sodomizing Ramon's mother. Mayhem reigns.

Ramon, screaming at the top of his lungs, working to free himself, begs.

RAMON

Stop! Stop! Please Stop! I'll tell you anything you want to know, but please stop.

The soldier acknowledges Ramon's plea and turns around. He grabs Ramon by the hair, jerking his head back almost to the breaking point.

SOLDIER

Cabronsito, if you lie to me, you are going to beg me to kill you. Comprendes?

RAMON

Si, si, I understand, but please let them go.

The soldier pulls up a chair to listen to Ramon's confession.

DISSOLVE TO:

INT. JOSE'S HOUSE – THE BEDROOM – DAY

Rosa is dusting off a recent family picture. The picture shows Jose, Luis, Pepe, and Rosa. Rosa sets the picture down and continues to dust the rest of the furniture. Unexpectedly, she finds a drawer partially opened. A garment is keeping the drawer from closing properly. As Rosa opens the drawer to put the clothing article back in the drawer, she finds a black portfolio. She takes it and opens it. As she reads what's inside, we CLOSE ON ROSA. Rosa's expression is one of horror and disbelief. She calls Jose immediately.

ROSA

Jose, Jose, come see this!

JOSE

What is it?

ROSA

Jose, por favor. Come here!

Rosa's voice trembles. She is shaking with fear. Jose approaches Rosa. He takes the portfolio from Rosa and examines it. A closer look by Jose triggers a similar reaction.

JOSE

I can't believe this. Where did you find
this?

ROSA

In Luis's drawer.

JOSE

Jesus Christ! How can this happen?

He starts pacing, holding the portfolio in one hand, scratching his head with other. He stops, he starts again, and he stops.

                    JOSE
I'll take care of this. Not a word to
anyone.

                    ROSA
What are we going to do?

                    JOSE
I don't know yet. I need time to think.

                                    CUT TO:

INT. PRESIDENTIAL PALACE – CASTRO'S OFFICE – NIGHT

Fidel is smoking a cigar and across his desk are two Soviet officers. A
translator is also present. The dialogue between Castro and the Soviet
officers is in Russian.

            FIDEL'S TRANSLATOR
When should we expect delivery?

Translator translates.

            SOVIET OFFICER 1
Fifteen missiles with thirty warheads
will arrive in approximately fifteen days.
Will the missile bases be ready?

Translator translates.

                    FIDEL
Absolutely!

A Cuban officer, Castro's aide, knocks on the door and interrupts the meeting. He approaches Castro and whispers a message regarding a note he carries.

FIDEL
Don't bother me with such details. Tell Raul to take care of this matter immediately.

CUT TO:

INT. RAUL CASTRO'S QUARTERS – NIGHT

A beautifully decorated suite with the best that money can buy. From the entrance you can see two bodies making passionate love in the bedroom. The sounds of lust and pleasure fill the air. As the camera slowly zooms closer, we are able to see the bare backside of Raul Castro, who is sadistically sodomizing his sex partner, a young black man. There's a knock on the door.

RAUL
Jesus Christ!

The knocking gets harder.

RAUL
Ya voy coño, ya voy. (I'm coming, dammit, I'm coming.)

He quickly puts on his pants and opens the door.

MESSENGER
Excuse me. Fidel ordered me to inform you of this matter immediately.

The messenger hands Raul the note. Raul reads it and turns to his lover on the bed.

RAUL

Get lost! (Pierdete!)

He turns to the messenger.

RAUL

I'll get dressed. We'll leave immediately.

BACK TO:

INT. FIDEL'S OFFICE – NIGHT

The two Soviet officers are just leaving. Castro's aide gives a box of Cuban cigars to each of them.

FIDEL

Tell these Ruskies that the Americans
are bigger cowards than they are.

The translator looks at Fidel in dismay. Fidel laughs at the translator's reaction and with a cynical smile says.

FIDEL

Tell them whatever you want. Just get
them out of here.

The translator makes up his own translation and escorts the Soviet officers out. As the double doors open, Raul comes in closely followed by the messenger.

RAUL

Fidel, this is a very delicate matter. How
do you want me to handle it?

Raul has the note in his hand, pointing to a specific paragraph. Fidel closes the doors to his office.

FIDEL

Handle it the same way you handled all
the others.

(he pauses several beats)

Wait, wait, a minute. Let me have the
pleasure of getting to the bottom of this
myself. Bring Roberto to me. And yes,
don't forget to bring his brother. What's
his name?

Castro snaps his fingers trying to remember the name of Roberto's brother.

RAUL

Jose!

FIDEL

That's him. Bring them both to me.

EXT. JOSE'S HOUSE – DAY

Rosa is in the kitchen when somebody knocks on the front door.

ROSA

Coming. Coming.

As Rosa opens the door, five soldiers push their way through and into the house. They enter without identifying themselves or requesting permission.

> ROSA
>
> Hey. What's going on? What do you want?

The sergeant who remained by the front door turns to Rosa.

> SERGEANT
> Where is Jose Martinez?

The other soldiers can be heard taking the house apart. Rosa is scared.

> ROSA
>
> He's not here. He went to the grocery store.

Rosa's humility turns into anger.

> ROSA
>
> Stop and get the hell out of my house now! I said he's not here! Get out!

The soldiers ignore ROSA. Jose, always known for his great timing, walks in the front door with grocery bags in each hand.

> JOSE
> What's going on here? What do you think you're doing?

The sergeant immediately grabs Jose. The grocery bags drop to the floor.

SERGEANT
Fidel has summoned you.

JOSE
Why? For what reason?

Without an explanation, the soldiers cuff Jose and throw him into the waiting van. Rosa is horrified. They haul Jose off as Rosa stands in shock by the front door. As the van pulls away, Pepe arrives and sees his mother vanquished and crying.

PEPE
What's wrong, Mama? What happened?

Rosa bawling uncontrollably.

ROSA
They just took your father.

PEPE
Who? Where?

ROSA
Soldiers, they just took your father. Oh,
God. Something is wrong. Something is
terribly wrong.

Pepe's worst thoughts cross his mind. He tries to control his emotions. Pepe comforts his mother with courage and poise.

PEPE
Don't worry, I'll find him. I'll find out
where they've taken him. Everything
will be fine, you'll see.

FADE TO BLACK.

FADE IN.

INT. ROBERTO'S OFFICES IN DOWNTOWN HAVANA – DAY

You can tell from these offices that Roberto is an attorney and a professional in good standing. As he sits at his desk reviewing a file, a similar group of soldiers storm in and surround Roberto at his desk.

SOLDIER

Roberto Martinez?

ROBERTO

I am.

TENSION FILLS THE AIR

SOLDIER

We have orders to arrest you for committing crimes against the revolution.

A beat as the news settles in.

SOLDIER

Let's go.

Roberto turns to his secretary on the way out.

ROBERTO

Don't worry. I'll be all right. Call PEPE now.

The soldiers shove Roberto right out of his office and into the waiting elevator. Roberto is confused and bewildered.

EXT. ESTABLISHING SHOT OF THE PRESIDENTIAL PALACE – DAY

A van stops at one of the side entrances. Soldiers take Jose out of the van and into the palace. Within seconds we see another van arrive. Roberto is taken out of this van and also escorted by soldiers into the palace.

CAMERA PULLS BACK TO REVEAL THIS IS OSCAR'S POV

Oscar, the mulatto officer from the revolutionary party, has observed the entire process. He's concerned. He decides to follow Roberto and Jose into the palace.

INT. PRESIDENTIAL PALACE – DAY

Oscar follows the escorts through the hallway and directly to Fidel's office. The double doors to Castro's offices burst open. In go both Roberto and Jose, escorted by the soldiers. Just a few feet away outside the opened double doors is Oscar—sizing up the situation.

INT. CASTRO'S OFFICE ENTRANCE/FOYER – DAY

Castro welcomes Jose and Roberto.

> FIDEL
> Bienvenidos, colegas de la revolución.
> (Welcome, colleagues of the revolution.)

Raul Castro, sitting on the sofa, stands up. They all walk into Fidel's office.

                    ROBERTO
          Porque nos traes con tanta prisa? (Why
          did you bring us here? What's so urgent?
          Are we under arrest?)

The double doors to the office are slammed shut.

OSCAR'S POV IS CUT OFF.

INT. OUTSIDE CASTRO'S OFFICE – DAY

After thinking a few seconds, Oscar decides to stick around and find
out what's happening. He enters the administrative offices directly
across the hall and starts visiting with several workers. Every chance
he gets, he glances over to Fidel's offices, waiting for something to
happen.

EXT. ALICIA'S HOUSE – AFTERNOON

Pepe arrives at Alicia's house. He gets out of the car, walks up to the
front door, and knocks. There is no answer. He knocks again, this
time a little harder. Finally, Alicia opens the front door.

                    ALICIA
          What are you doing here?

                    PEPE
          We're in trouble. Fidel just picked up
          my father and Roberto.

                    ALICIA
          Why?

PEPE

Dad warned me about that. He said if Castro picked him up, for me to take Mom and disappear, perhaps go to the US. He said not to wait for him or endanger anyone trying to save him.

ALICIA

Come in, come in.

INT. ALICIA'S LIVING ROOM – AFTERNOON

Pepe enters the house and sits on the sofa. Alicia sits next to him.

ALICIA

What are you going to do?

PEPE

Mom says she's not leaving without Dad.

Pepe is nervous. Perspiration drips from his nose and forehead.

ALICIA

You don't think Castro is—

Pepe puts his index finger over Alicia's lips, silencing her momentarily.

PEPE

I know what you're going to say. Please don't.

(a beat)

Do you trust me?

ALICIA

Of course! What kind of question is
that?

(a beat)

I trust you with my life!

Pepe gets up and starts pacing the room. He notices baby clothes on
top of the dining room table.

PEPE

Who is this for?

Alicia briefly hesitates. She can't maintain eye contact with PEPE.

ALICIA

It's for a friend. She's having a baby.

PEPE

Do I know her?

ALICIA

I don't think so.

(changing the subject)

Please, Pepe. Stop this! Tell me what's
going on.

PEPE

Okay, listen closely. Luis, Ramon, Tony,
and I are stealing a boat and leaving for
Miami tomorrow.

ALICIA

Are you crazy?

PEPE

Just listen to me.

(a beat)

Look, Castro already killed Ernesto, Ruben, and who knows how many other people. My dad knew he was on the list. That's why we tried so hard to get visas for the whole family.

ALICIA

You are crazy!

PEPE

The fact is my father could be dead by now, and he left me with specific instructions that I must follow.

ALICIA

You're leaving your father behind?

PEPE

Of course not! From Miami, I can get those visas through Spain or Mexico and get him out.

ALICIA

If anyone finds out, we'll all be shot!

Pepe reaches for Alicia, takes her in his arms.

PEPE
I want you to come with me.

A moment of silence. Alicia is devastated. She struggles to make a decision. Internally, she wants to go but realizes she can't risk the life of her unborn child. She's pregnant with PEPE's baby. She withstands the temptation to reveal anything and finally finds the words to answer.

ALICIA
I can't…I just can't! Better said…I won't!

Pepe holds Alicia close to him.

PEPE
Why? Why not?

Alicia breaks away. She is about to start crying.

ALICIA
How can you be so selfish? You can't expect for things to happen exactly the way you want.

PEPE
What do you mean?

ALICIA
I'm definitely not going!

Alicia is trying hard to hide her innermost feelings. She portrays someone she's not. Pepe is surprised at her reaction.

PEPE
But I thought…Since—

Alicia turns around and interrupts Pepe.

ALICIA

I want you to leave. I don't want to discuss this matter any further.

PEPE

But how can you be—

Alicia interrupts again. She walks to the front door, opens it.

ALICIA

I want you to leave right now!

Pepe, in total disbelief, walks toward her. Alicia points the way out. Frustrated and angry, Pepe leaves, slamming the door on the way out.

CUT TO:

BACK IN THE PRESIDENTIAL PALACE JUST OUTSIDE FIDEL'S OFFICE.

The doors to Fidel's office opens, and out comes Jose and Roberto, escorted by several soldiers. Oscar hears the commotion and turns around.

OSCAR'S POV

Both Jose and Roberto are handcuffed and are being hastily escorted down the hall.

BACK ON OSCAR.

Oscar realizes what's about to happen. Terror begins to flow through his veins.

BACK ON OSCAR'S POV

One of the soldiers escorting the prisoners draws his .45-caliber pistol from his holster. They turn at the end of the hall and enter a room. Oscar cautiously follows the prisoners from afar. The door is slammed shut.

BACK ON OSCAR.

In total anxiety, Oscar searches for a way to stop what he fears might happen. Before he can organize a thought, two shots ring out. Oscar's knees buckle; his stomach cramps up. He finds it hard to breathe. Two more shots are fired. Oscar looks around to see if someone reacts to the sound of the gunshots. To his amazement, everyone continues as if nothing happened.

INT. PALACE HALLWAY – DAY

Oscar backtracks away from the room and heads for the nearest exit.

EXT. PALACE SIDE ENTRANCE – DAY

As Oscar exits the palace, he pauses. He looks for a phone booth, finds one and goes inside.

INT. PHONE BOOTH – DAY

Oscar is hyperventilating. He puts a nickel in the pay phone and starts to rotary dial. He screws up. He hangs up and starts all over again. Finally, he makes the call.

V.O. ROSA

Hello.

OSCAR

Rosa?

V.O. ROSA

Si!

Rosa picks up on Oscar's urgent tone of voice.

V.O. ROSA

Si, Oscar, what is it?

OSCAR

Something terrible happened.

INT. ROSA ON THE TELEPHONE IN HER LIVING ROOM – DAY

Rosa's eyes open wide, her worst fear has become reality. She's afraid to breathe or make a sound.

OSCAR

Jose and Roberto have been shot!

Rosa goes into shock. She starts shaking. Not a word comes forth from her mouth.

BACK ON OSCAR.

OSCAR

Are you there? Did you hear what I said?

Rosa can't speak. Oscar can hear her breathing, her meltdown starting.

                    OSCAR
         Rosa, I know you can hear me. Listen
         and do exactly as I say. Get Pepe and go
         to my house immediately.

Rosa hangs up the phone. Oscar, frustrated, curses and hangs up as well. He turns around to leave the phone booth, and a soldier is standing there waiting. It startles him. He opens the booth door, nods to the soldier and leaves. The soldier enters the booth to make a call.

EXT. THE ENTRANCE TO TONY'S APARTMENT – DAY

Pepe arrives at Tony's place. Just as Pepe gets ready to knock on the front door, Tony opens it.

                    TONY
         I heard they picked up your father and
         uncle, and now they're looking for you.

                    PEPE
         Shit, those traitors are on a rampage.
         Things are worse than I thought.

Pepe enters Tony's apartment.

                    TONY
         I also heard Ramon is dead.

                    PEPE
         What?

                    TONY
         The rumor is that Ramon and his family
         are all dead!

PEPE

We can't wait till tomorrow. I think we
should leave tonight.

TONY

What about the weather?

PEPE

The weather won't matter if we're dead,
will it?

(a beat)

We can't wait any longer. Where's Luis?

Tony grabs Pepe's arm.

TONY

Pepe, sit down. We've got to talk.

PEPE

Sit down? What's your problem?

TONY

Please sit down.

Pepe reluctantly sits down. Tony takes his time.

PEPE

Get it out, man. What the hell is it?

TONY

The same person who turned in your
father turned in Ramon, Ernesto…You
know…our whole group.

                    PEPE
Yeah, and I'd like to get my hands on
the son of bitch that did it.

                    TONY
It's Luis.

                    PEPE
What? What are you saying?

                    TONY
He's a snitch, a Fidelista. He works for
the secret police (G-2).

Pepe is in denial.

                    PEPE
My brother? You're nuts, man!

The news starts to settle in.

                    TONY
He's responsible for everything that's
happened.

                    PEPE
Bullshit! YOU'RE FULL OF SHIT!

Pepe is outraged, steam blowing out his ears. Tony speaks very
carefully.

                    TONY
That's why we almost got caught at the
beach, remember? He turned us in.

Pepe lunges at Tony, grabbing him by the jacket.

> PEPE
> You're mad! Who's the asshole that's feeding you this crock of shit?

Tony pushes Pepe away, demanding respect.

> TONY
> Get your hands off me!

Pepe lets go.

> TONY (CONT'D)
> Listen to me!
>
> (a beat)
>
> We've been friends a long time. Does that mean anything to you?

Pepe searches for answers.

> TONY
> Come with me. I'll prove it to you.

Tony leads Pepe into his bedroom.

INT. TONY'S BEDROOM – DAY

Tony pulls from under a wooden chair a big manila envelope. He hands it to Pepe. Pepe opens it. Inside is the portfolio with negatives and pictures that JOSE and Rosa had found in Luis's drawer. He pulls out several pictures. Stunned by what he sees, he sits on the edge of the bed. By the look on his face, he's trying to sort things out, trying to control his emotions.

PEPE
How can this be? How could he do this?

Tony sits next to Pepe.

TONY
Pepe, we can't change what's happened.

(a beat)

We should try to leave as soon as possible. If not, we'll be dead by morning.

Pepe stands up, his frustration and temper both starting to show.

PEPE
My own flesh and blood... Why would he do it?

Pepe starts for the door. Tony grabs him and slams him against the wall.

TONY
Pepe, snap out of it! Goddammit, don't bail on me now.

Tony shakes Pepe like a rag doll.

                    TONY
Forget Luis! I need you. Your mother
needs you. Alicia needs you.

                 (several beats)

If we aren't careful, we won't be around
to get rid of this nightmare.

Finally, he regains his composure. Tony slowly lets him go.

                    PEPE
Okay. Okay, you're right.

                  (a beat)

Give me paper and pencil.

                    TONY
What for?

                    PEPE
I need to leave Mom and Alicia
instructions.

Tony gives him paper and pencil. Pepe begins to write.

                    PEPE
We'll leave tonight!

EXT. ESTABLISHING SHOT OF JOSE AND ROSA'S HOUSE
– NIGHT

INT. IN OSCAR'S CAR – NIGHT

Oscar is driving up to the house. As he arrives, he notices an unmarked
car staking out the place.

OSCAR'S POV

Two members of the secret police sitting in a car across the street from the house.

BACK IN OSCAR'S CAR.

He decides not to stop and drives by the house and around the corner. As he makes the turn, he notices a uniformed police officer in the alley.

OSCAR'S POV

A police officer smoking a cigarette leaning against a telephone pole.

Again, Oscar continues driving further up the street and finally brings his car to a stop a half a block away from the police officer in the alley.

OSCAR'S POV FROM HIS REAR VIEW MIRROR.

The back of Rosa's house and the police officer in the alley.

EXT. OSCAR'S CAR – NIGHT

After casing the situation for a minute from his car, Oscar gets out of the car and approaches the police officer in the alley.

EXT. IN THE ALLEY – NIGHT

The policeman is still smoking and leaning against the telephone pole.

                              OSCAR
             Buenas noches.

The police don't acknowledge or greet Oscar. He continues to walk closer to the officer and repeats himself.

OSCAR

Buenas noches, companero!

The policeman turns, recognizes Oscar's uniform, and salutes.

POLICE

Good evening, sir.

OSCAR

At ease, at ease. Do you have a cigarette?

POLICE

Yes, sir.

As the policeman reaches for his cigarettes, Oscar grabs him and shoves him back with tremendous force against the telephone pole, jamming one of the stirrups into the policeman's back. The officer goes into shock. His body shakes as if a million volts of electricity flow through his body, an expression of horror on his face. His chest is soaked in blood, and the tip of the stirrup protrudes from his uniform. Finally, the policeman dies. Oscar pulls him off the telephone pole and hides him behind a fence.

EXT. REAR OF THE HOUSE – NIGHT

Oscar runs across the alley and enters Rosa's house through the back door.

INT. INSIDE THE HOUSE – NIGHT

OSCAR
(softly)

Rosa, Rosa…

Oscar hears someone crying in the house. He follows the sound trail. As he searches for Rosa, he avoids every light and window he passes. Frequently, he checks on the car sitting out front to make sure no one has seen him or is heading toward the house. Oscar enters the bedroom. Rosa is crying on the bed.

OSCAR

Good Lord, Rosa.

Oscar approaches her carefully.

OSCAR

Please, Rosa, please stop crying.

Rosa looks as you would expect, just having lost her husband. Oscar comforts her, holding her close and pleading with her.

OSCAR

You have to be strong, Rosita.

ROSA

What for? So that son of a bitch can kill
us too?

OSCAR

Don't think like that, Rosita. Think of
Pepe, Alicia…

Rosa is nonresponsive. Oscar seems to be running out of words. Time is precious now.

                    OSCAR
Come on, you're coming with me.

                    ROSA
No, why?

                    OSCAR
It's not safe for you here.

                    ROSA
Safe? Ha! No one is safe on this godfor-
saken island.

                    OSCAR
Where is Pepe?

Rosa loses it. In a fit of rage, she starts throwing things and yelling obscenities about Fidel Castro. Oscar tries to restrain her, which is next
to impossible. In fear of her being heard by the secret police outside,
Oscar slaps Rosa. She breaks down crying again.

                    ROSA
                  (in tears)

You think they got Pepe too?

                    OSCAR
No, if they did, the secret police would
not be parked outside.

Rosa takes a long look at Oscar.

                    OSCAR
Take a look.

Oscar dims the lights and slowly opens a Venetian blind.

POV OF OSCAR AND ROSA FROM THE HOUSE.

> V.O. OSCAR
> See that white car across the street?

> V.O. ROSA
> Yes.

> V.O. OSCAR
> That's them.

BACK ON OSCAR AND ROSA.

> ROSA
> What do we do now?

> OSCAR
> I've got to get you out of here. My car is
> out back. Let's go find Pepe.

EXT. ALICIA'S HOUSE – NIGHT

Pepe is at the front door. He pulls two white envelopes from his jacket. Pepe knocks on the door.

INT. ALICIA'S FOYER – NIGHT

Alicia opens the door, but there's no one there. She looks around and notices two envelopes stuck to her screen door. She takes the envelopes.

ALICIA'S POV OF THE ENVELOPES.

One envelope reads, "Dear Alicia." The other says, "Dear Mom & Dad. Love, Pepe." Alicia opens the envelope addressed to her.

> PEPE'S V.O.
>
> My loving Alicia,
>
> It's hard for me to understand why you refused to come with me. I know you love me as much as I love you. For now, I accept your decision, but please know that I will return for you when you're ready to join me. I will contact you as soon as I get to Miami. I'll miss you and think of you every day. Please be ready to leave soon. With all my love and devotion.
>
> Pepe

Alicia is instantly in tears, grieving.

INT. PEPE'S CAR – NIGHT

Pepe and Tony are going down a residential street.

> PEPE
> How much farther?

> TONY
> Just a few blocks.

> (a beat)

> You know, this fellow used to be my father's personal bodyguard. He's in great shape. Why, Pablo can probably row us all the way to Miami.

> PEPE

Sure, but can he be trusted?

> TONY

Relax, Pepe, he's like a brother to me. I
know his life story.

> PEPE

Where is he from?

> TONY

He was born in New York City, educated at Annapolis, and his parents were
from Pinar del Rio.

> PEPE

Did I hear you say NYC?

> TONY

Yes, NYC. They were killed last year in a
very unusual accident in Santiago.

> (a beat)

Turn here.

Pepe turns the wheel.

> TONY

Pablo should be waiting around the
corner.

As they turn the corner, a tall, well-built man is waiting with a small
duffel bag. Pepe stops the car.

EXT. BY PEPE'S CAR – NIGHT

                    TONY
          Get in!

INT. PEPE'S CAR – NIGHT

                    PABLO
          Hola, Tony.

                    TONY
          This is Pepe.

                    PABLO
          Pleased to meet you, Pepe.

                    PEPE
          You speak English very well.

                    PABLO
          Thank you. I went to American schools.

                    TONY
          So did I, but my accent is awful.

Pablo and Pepe shake hands. Pablo's grip is like a vice. Pablo is HUGE. He barely fits in the car. This guy wears a size G for *gorilla*. Pepe turns around smiles at Tony, cranks the car up, and drives off.

INT. PEPE'S CAR AS THEY DRIVE

                    TONY
          Pablo, you remember the plan, don't
          you?

                    PABLO
         You bet!

                    PEPE
         What's in the duffel bag?

                    PABLO
         Lifesavers!

Pepe looks at Pablo kind of funny.

                    TONY
         Will both of you relax? I know you don't
         trust each other yet, but I know you
         both trust me, remember me.

                    PEPE
         All right, all right!

                    (a pause)

         If anything goes wrong tonight and
         we get separated, remember we'll meet
         at the Spanish Embassy in forty-eight
         hours.

                    PABLO
         I'm ready.

As PEPE continues to drive, a serious tone takes over the conversation.

                    TONY
         God help us!

EXT. ESTABLISHING SHOT OF THE TROPICAL JUNGLE – NIGHT

The car drives into frame.

Pepe slows the vehicle down to a crawl and turns off the headlights. He enters a gravel road. The vehicle coasts to a stop.

INT. PEPE'S CAR – NIGHT

> PEPE
> We're here. Let's go!

The men get out of the car.

EXT. FOLLOWING AND LEADING TONY, PABLO, AND PEPE ON THE BEACH – NIGHT

Together, they start walking through the tropical jungle and past some tall palm trees. The ground turns to sand, and we recognize that this is the same beach where the guys were almost caught by the beach patrols. It is dark, and only the moonlight illuminates the beach. Pepe leads Pablo and Tony through the darkness, closer and closer to the place where the raft is buried. Suddenly, we hear the cranking of an automatic rifle. Pepe freezes, then slowly turns toward the sound.

PEPE'S POV LOOKING DOWN THE BARREL OF A NERVOUS AK-47.

> SOLDIER
> On your knees, gusano (you traitor)!

EXT. ON PABLO AND TONY BEHIND PEPE – NIGHT

Tony and Pablo freeze behind Pepe. They can barely see the tip of a rifle pointed directly at Pepe's head. The soldier is uneasy and nervous. It's evident that the soldier hasn't seen Pablo or Tony.

EXT. ON SOLDIER / BEACH PATROL – NIGHT

The soldier is a young man in his late teens. Neither Pablo nor Tony is visible from where he stands.

> SOLDIER
> Are you deaf? I said on your knees, you
> son of a bitch.

BACK ON PABLO AND TONY.

Pablo seems to relax. He starts walking toward the light.

BACK ON PEPE WITH THE SOLDIER.

Pablo walks up behind Pepe. The young soldier's eyes open wide when he sees Pablo. The soldier eases off the trigger and begins to lower his weapon.

> SOLDIER
> What the hell are you doing here?

> PEPE
> Do you two know each other?

> PABLO
> Yeah, I guess you could say that. He's
> my brother!

Pepe breathes easier. Tony walks out from behind the bushes.

TONY

Hi, AUGUI! I thought I recognized your voice.

AUGUI/SOLDIER

What's going on?

Augui shoulders his rifle to hug his brother Pablo.

EXT. ON PABLO, AUGUI, TONY, AND PEPE – NIGHT

PABLO

Look, I couldn't tell you anything. I was sworn to secrecy. Besides, I didn't want to jeopardize your life or our escape.

AUGUI

My life, your escape?

(several beats)

Oh, I see. You're the guys we're looking for.

PEPE

Holy shit.

PABLO

You know about our escape?

AUGUI

Me and every other patrolman on this beach. Why, we've had your raft staked out for weeks.

Pablo turns to Pepe and Tony. Tony a bit worried.

> TONY
> Don't worry. We had a little problem
> with Pepe's brother.

> PABLO
> I'd say.

> PEPE
> It's taken care of.

> PABLO
> I sure hope so.

> AUGUI
> Why are you leaving? I thought—

Pablo interrupts.

> PABLO
> Never mind what you thought. I'm not
> staying here to fight for these commies.

> AUGUI
> But—

> PABLO
> No buts, just listen.

Pablo grabs his brother by the shoulders to straighten him out.

PABLO

I don't like what's happening here. It's not what was promised. More people are getting killed now than during the revolution. And look at you, where is your freedom, your future? No thanks, I want control over my life.

The engine of a patrol boat is heard in the background.

CLOSE ON AUGUI.

AUGUI

Get down, quick.

A spotlight finds Augui. The intensity of the light is blinding. The BOAT CAPTAIN calls out over a megaphone.

BOAT CAPTAIN

Who goes there?

AUGUI'S POV

Looking directly into a blinding spot light.

AUGUI

It's me, sir. Private Serra.

V.O. CAPTAIN

Why aren't you at your post?

AUGUI

I thought I heard a noise over here, so I decided to investigate it, sir.

> V.O. CAPTAIN
>
> And what did you find?

> AUGUI
>
> Nothing, sir.

> V.O. CAPTAIN
>
> Private Serra, if you leave your post again without calling in on the radio, you'll be serving the rest of your tour in Siberia. DO I MAKE MYSELF CLEAR?

> AUGUI
>
> Yes, SIR!

> V.O. CAPITÁN
>
> Carry on!

The boat resumes its patrol. The spotlight leaves Augui as he turns and wipes perspiration from his forehead. Augui whispers to Pablo.

> AUGUI
>
> Get out of here!

Pablo whispers back.

> PABLO
>
> I'll be back for you.

Tony, Pablo and Pepe retreat into the jungle. They regroup back by the car.

EXT. AT PEPE'S CAR – NIGHT

TONY

What do we do now? No boat, no provisions, nothing.

PEPE

I'm thinking! I'm thinking!

PABLO

I know where we can steal a boat.

PEPE

The Port of Mariel?

PABLO

Exactly!

TONY

What are we waiting for?

PEPE

Let's go.

They pile into the car.

EXT. ALICIA'S HOUSE – NIGHT

Oscar and Rosa are knocking on Alicia's front door. Rosa is wearing a
shawl over her head, concealing her face. Alicia looks through the side
window before opening the door.

After a beat

THE DOORS OPEN.

                    ALICIA
             Come in, Rosa. Come in!

They quickly enter the house.

INT. ALICIA'S LIVING ROOM – NIGHT

                    OSCAR
             Where's Pepe?

                    ALICIA
             I don't know. He left here hours ago.

                    ROSA
             Where did he go?

Alicia hesitates. After several beats, she picks up the envelope left by
Pepe.

                    ALICIA
             Pepe asked me to give you this.

Alicia hands Rosa the letter. Rosa opens it. She reads it. Tears begin
to fall from Rosa's eyes. She hands the letter to Oscar. Alicia consoles
Rosa while Oscar reads the letter.

                    OSCAR
             That's the best thing he can do.

                    ALICIA
             He asked me to go with him.

CLOSE ON ROSA AND ALICIA.

Rosa is sobbing.

ROSA

He did?

ALICIA

Yes, but I couldn't.

ROSA

Couldn't or wouldn't? You know how much he loves you.

ALICIA

We couldn't risk the danger.

(several beats)

And yes, we love him too!

Rosa's eyes light up.

ROSA

We? Are you pregnant?

Alicia nods her head.

ALICIA

Pregnant!

The expression on Rosa's face instantly changes. Oscar's jaw drops wide open.

ALICIA

Please don't be angry with me. I couldn't tell him. He would have never left. Fidel would have caught him and killed him for sure.

Alicia starts crying.

> ALICIA (CONT'D)
> Oh God, why didn't I tell him?

Rosa hugs Alicia. The tender touch of a mother comforts her.

FADE TO DARKNESS

EXT. THE PORT OF MARIEL – NIGHT

CAMERA PANS TO A SIGN "BIENVENIDOS EL PUERTO MARIEL" ("WELCOME TO THE PORT OF MARIEL")

CAMERA PANS TO Pepe, Pablo and Tony lying on the ground, hiding behind trees just over a ridge overlooking the port's entrance.

THEIR POV

The marina is full of all kinds of vessels.

CAMERA PANS RIGHT. There is one patrol boat docked close to the main entrance. Two well-armed soldiers patrol on foot up and down the piers. Another soldier sits in the guardhouse at the port entrance.

BACK ON THE RIDGE WITH PEPE, TONY AND PABLO.

> PEPE
> Okay, Pablo, let's see your stuff.

Pablo takes a bottle of scotch out of his duffel bag. He takes a huge gulp and then sprinkles some booze on his neck arms and shirt. When the guards aren't looking, he gets up and starts walking toward the guardhouse. Tony whispers.

TONY
Don't forget to stagger.

CLOSE ON PABLO.

Pablo starts to carry on as if he had drunk the island dry. He belches and then starts singing like most inebriated drunks do.

PABLO
Muuulata! Que nalgas tienes, que rico
cuerpo tú tienes.

The soldier sitting in the guardhouse hears the commotion and stands up. He brushes sand off his butt and cautiously walks toward Pablo.

EXT. ON THE GUARDHOUSE – NIGHT

GUARD 1
Hey, niche. What's your problem?

Pablo in an unbelievable performance continues his act and gets closer and closer to the guard.

GUARD 1
Stop right there!

BACK ON PABLO.

Pablo stops after staggering a few times.

PABLO
I'm celebrating my birthday.

> GUARD 1

Fine, but not here. Go home and sleep it off.

> PABLO

Right after I finish what's left of this.

Pablo points to the bottle half-empty.

> PABLO

Would you like a drink?

EXT. BACK ON THE GUARDHOUSE – NIGHT

> GUARD 1

No, not while on duty.

The guard looks around to see where the other guards are.

> GUARD 1

C'mon, get out of here before you get me in trouble.

Pablo is persistent but careful.

> PABLO

If you have one little drink with me, I promise I'll go quietly.

> GUARD 1

One drink?

Pablo raises his index finger.

PABLO
My word of honor!

EXT. PABLO AND THE GUARD TOGETHER – NIGHT

The guard looks around again and then shoulders the rifle as he approaches Pablo. Tony and Pepe watch Pablo's every move. Pablo hands the bottle to the guard. The guard lifts the bottle to take a swig, but before he starts to swallow, Pablo jams the rest of the bottle down his throat, killing him instantly. The guard falls dead on the ground. Quickly, Pablo drags the body into the guardhouse. He signals to Pepe and Tony to come down. Pepe and Tony sprint to the guardhouse. Tony, the last one in, closes the door behind him.

INT. GUARDHOUSE – NIGHT

TONY
What's next?

PEPE
See if you can find the key to the gunboat.

Tony turns around and starts hunting for the keys on a key rack hung on the back of the door. Pepe is keeping an eye out in case of trouble. Pablo is cannibalizing arms and ammo from the dead guard. Pablo gives Pepe the pistol.

PABLO
Here take this. I'll take the rifle.

Pepe turns to Tony.

PEPE

Hurry up!

Pepe continues to keep a sharp look out for the other guards walking the peer. Tony goes through the keys as fast as he can. Finally!

TONY

Got them! Now what?

PABLO

Give me the keys.

(a beat)

Let's make a run for the boat.

PEPE

Hold up. What about the guards?

PABLO

Screw 'em! I'll spray them with the AK
a few times.

Suddenly, the sound of several trucks coming up the road is heard. They all turn to see what's coming.

PEPE

Shit, we'll never make it now.

PABLO

It's now or never.

(a beat)

You guys head for the boat. I'll cover
you.

In a moment of truth, Pablo loads a round in the chamber. So does Pepe.

PABLO

Ready? A la una, a las dos, y a las TRREEESSSS! (One, two, and three!)

Pablo, Tony and Pepe bolt out of the guardhouse, firing a hail of gunfire at the guards by the pier. Pablo hits one of them. The guard hits the water with his finger still firmly on the trigger, unleashing a wrath of bullets all over creation. The second guard runs for cover. Pablo stops to take refuge behind several large crates. Tony dives behind a forklift as bullets ping and pong around him. By now, Pepe is in the boat, cranking the motor and trying to get it started. The engine turns once, twice, finally it kicks in. *VAAArrrooommmm!*

PEPE

(at the top of his lungs)

C'mon. Let's go.

Pablo, about fifty feet from the boat, does a JIMMY BROWN (better than in the Dirty Dozen), zigzagging, dodging gunfire as he leaps and makes it to the boat in one piece.

The vehicles coming up the road stop at the front gate. Soldiers pour out the back and rush for cover. They direct their fire at the patrol boat.

Pablo cuts the lines loose and mans a .30-caliber machine gun on the bow of the boat. He whip-pans it around and starts firing. The thunder of the fire-breathing machine gun hurls round after round toward the soldiers by the truck. Several soldiers are cut down. Suddenly, *KKAAABOOOMMMM!* One of the trucks goes up like the Fourth of July. Pablo continues to fire at the guard by the pier, pinning him down.

Tony is scared to death. He feels a chilling breeze go down his spine. It feels as if death has come for him. Finally, he gathers enough courage to run toward the boat.

CLOSE ON TONY.

IN SLOW MOTION: Tony is running as fast as humanly possible. His entire life is flashing before his eyes. The boat has drifted about ten feet away from the peer. Both Pablo and Pepe are cheering him on. As he approaches the pier, he leaps, reaching for the boat with all his might.

Suddenly, a burning sensation tears at his back. One round has penetrated his lower back, blowing a hole clean through the front of his chest. A second round (the killer) penetrates the middle of his back, never to be seen again. Tony hits the deck of the boat lifeless, bouncing like a rubber doll.

Pepe revs the engines and throttles the boat to top speed, leaving the pier behind. Pablo continues to pump round after round of the .30-caliber at the pier, killing more soldiers and destroying several boats in the process. The patrol boat disappears into the night.

FADE TO BLACK.

EXT. ESTABLISHING SHOT OF ALICIA'S HOUSE – NIGHT

INT. ALICIA'S LIVING ROOM – NIGHT

CLOSE ON OSCAR.

OSCAR

Don't worry, I'll hide Rosa where nobody will find her.

(a beat)

What about you? What are you going to do?

ALICIA

I'll be fine. No one thinks of me as a threat.

The telephone rings. Alicia answers the phone.

ALICIA

Hello!

V.O. LUIS

Hola, it's Luis.

ALICIA

¡Luis! ¿Qué pasa? How are you doing?

Alicia, surprised, turns to Rosa and Oscar. Rosa reacts as if she's seen a ghost. Immediately, she grabs paper and pencil and frantically starts writing something for Alicia.

V.O. LUIS

I'm doing fine. How about you?

ALICIA

I'm okay.

Rosa finishes writing the note and shows it to Alicia.

ALICIA'S POV OF ROSA'S NOTE.

> Don't tell him where Pepe is!
>
> Don't tell him we're here!
>
> Don't trust him!

V.O. LUIS

Have you seen Pepe or Mom?

Alicia is puzzled by Rosa's note. She decides to cooperate with Rosa.

ALICIA

No, I haven't seen either of them. But if you see Pepe, tell him I need to talk to him.

V.O. LUIS

Anything I can help you with?

ALICIA

No, it's just a personal matter. Pepe owes me an explanation.

V.O. LUIS

It sounds like he's in trouble.

(a beat)

I'll tell him to call you as soon as I see him.

ALICIA

Thanks!

V.O. LUIS

Talk to you later.

ALICIA

Bye!

Alicia hangs up the phone. Rosa breathes a sigh of relief.

ROSA

Sit down, Alicia. You too, Oscar. I have
some explaining to do.

Rosa prepares Alicia and Oscar for the bad news.

ROSA

I have terrible news, and I don't know
where to begin.

ALICIA

What do you mean?

OSCAR

It's about Luis?

Rosa is searching for the right words and teary-eyed.

ROSA

Luis works for the secret police! He is a
traitor.

Emotions break through Rosa's words. Oscar, outraged, interrupts.

OSCAR

I knew it! I knew he couldn't be trusted.

                    ROSA
I'm so ashamed.

                   ALICIA
Don't be ashamed. It's not your fault.

Alicia kneels in front of Rosa. Oscar realizes he needs to keep a cool head.

                   OSCAR
Alicia is right. Don't blame yourself.
We'll deal with it.

                    ROSA
How?

Oscar comes over and sits on the other side of Rosa. He puts his arm around her.

                   OSCAR
Don't worry. I've got it all worked out.

Oscar turns to Alicia.

                   OSCAR
You know, Luis is on to you. You're
taking a huge risk by staying here. You
need to come with us.

                   ALICIA
Where are you going?

                   OSCAR
In time, you'll know. What's important
is that we need to do a disappearing act.

Alicia nods affirmatively.

EXT. SOMEWHERE IN THE MIDDLE OF THE CARIBBEAN – DAY

It's early morning. The sun is peeking over the horizon. As the camera pans down, we see the patrol boat adrift, out of fuel, with Pablo, Pepe and Tony inside. Pablo is slumped over the steering controls, sleeping from pure exhaustion. Pepe also sleeps. He has Tony's head cradled on his lap as he tries to comfort the man. Tony is pale white, lifeless. His eyes are open, pupils dilated frozen. His chest is soaked in blood.

The humidity and heat have begun to decompose Tony's body. A disgusting smell emanates from Tony. Several large sharks are thrashing about the boat, their dorsal fins visible from time to time. The commotion in the water awakens Pablo. He raises his head, turns around, and contemplates the heartbreaking scene of Pepe holding Tony. He walks over to them and gently closes Tony's eyes. Pepe wakes up. He looks down at Tony. Realizing the pain, he starts bawling.

                    PABLO
          C'mon, Pepe, keep it together. We've
          got a long way to go, partner.

Pablo embraces Tony and Pepe simultaneously. Tears can't be denied. After SEVERAL BEATS, Pablo speaks.

                PABLO (CONT'D)
          C'mon, get up. Help me with Tony.

                    PEPE
          What are you going to do?

PABLO

His body is decomposing rapidly. We
have to get rid of it.

PEPE

You mean throw him overboard?

PABLO

We have no choice.

Pepe gets up. Together they lift Tony and place him across the transom of the boat. Tony is stiff as a board. Pepe and Pablo say the Lord's Prayer. The sharks thrash about, seemingly knowing what's about to happen.

As the Lord's Prayer is said, we get SEVERAL AERIAL SHOTS OF THE BOAT AT SEA.

V.O. PABLO and PEPE TOGETHER

For yours is the kingdom, the power,
and the glory, forever and ever. AMEN.

Pablo and Pepe push Tony's body overboard. Immediately, the sharks go into a frenzy as they devour Tony's remains. Pepe can't bear the sound and torment of what is taking place. He covers his ears and shuts his eyes in agony and despair.

DISSOLVE TO:

INT. OSCAR'S HOUSE – DAY

It's early in the morning. The cocks are singing their usual morning song. Rosa is awake, sipping on a cup of coffee and sitting in a rocking chair by the coffee table. Oscar walks in with several bags of groceries.

OSCAR

Good morning.

ROSA

You sure were up early this morning.

OSCAR

I know, I had to go to the store early cause by 10:00 a.m. the shelves are bare. Besides, I don't want to be seen buying all these things. People aren't stupid, you know.

(a pause)

OSCAR

Did you see the paper this morning?

ROSA

Yes, I read it.

OSCAR

It looks like they got away.

Rosa gets up walks toward the counter where Oscar put the grocery bags. She takes the groceries out.

ROSA

How are we to survive on this?

(a beat)

We need milk, eggs, bread!

Alicia walks into frame. She is showing and noticeably very pregnant.

                              OSCAR
                I used all of the food stamps I had.

                               ROSA
                Por favor, this girl is three months preg-
                nant. She needs proper nutrition.

                              OSCAR
                Maybe I can scrounge something up at
                the base.

                               ROSA
                Go now, before those shelves are empty
                too.

Rosa looks at Oscar with eyes that communicate telepathically.

                              OSCAR
                All right, all right, I'm going.

Oscar puts his jacket back on and starts out the door.

BACK ON THE BOAT DRIFTING AT SEA.

The sun is bright. It must be a hundred degrees, and there's not a cloud in the sky. The ocean is smooth like glass, reflecting every ray of light. The boat is at a distance, still drifting. There is no wind, no current, nothing—only unbelievable heat.

ON SCREEN "THREE DAYS LATER."

The camera zooms in on the boat. Pablo is lying across the transom, dangling an arm over the side, touching the water. Not a sound can be heard. It's so quiet and still, it's scary. The dorsal fin of a shark breaks the water. The ripples carry across the back of the boat where Pablo's arm hangs, and it's in the water.

The camera begins to pull back.

CUT TO:

INT. A US COAST GUARD HELICOPTER IN FLIGHT – DAY

The pilot and copilot are talking about last night's football game.

> PILOT
>
> Man, I still can't believe those Packers. They sure kicked ass last night.

> COPILOT
>
> I think they pulled that game out of their ass.

> PILOT
>
> Hell, the Dolphins couldn't stop my grandmother.

The radar starts beeping.

> PILOT
>
> What is it?

> COPILOT
>
> Radar indicates a vessel at two o'clock, sir.

> PILOT
>
> Reconfirm.

A beat passes.

> COPILOT
> Yes, sir, we've got a vessel.

> PILOT
> Radio it in. Let's take a look.

EXT. ON COAST GUARD CHOPPER – DAY

The copilot starts jamming the airways, notifying headquarters of what's in process. The chopper makes a forty-five-degree turn and dives toward the horizon.

BACK INSIDE THE BOAT.

Pepe is totally dehydrated. He's lying half-conscious on the floor of the boat. Pablo is barely awake, still on the transom. The sound of a helicopter is faintly heard creeping in. Pablo, realizing what he hears, struggles to sit up. He gets to his feet. He searches the sky for the sound of the chopper but can't see a thing. He goes to his duffel bag. From the bag, he pulls an American flag. He takes the flag and hooks it onto the boat's flagpole, only upside-down. With his last rush of adrenaline, he runs the flag up the pole. Pablo whispers.

> PABLO
> Please, God. Let it be. Please let it be!

Pepe wakes up.

BACK INSIDE THE HELICOPTER.

PILOT

Holy mother of God…that's a Cuban patrol boat.

COPILOT

Yeah, but do you see what I see?

PILOT

Sure, as hell do!

POV OF CREW IN HELICOPTER.

The patrol boat flying the Stars and Stripes upside-down. Pepe waves at the chopper. The helicopter hovers over the boat.

BACK INSIDE THE HELICOPTER.

PILOT

This is a new one for me.

COPILOT

What if it's a trap? Who knows…maybe they're trying out another one of their tricks?

The pilot checks out the boat from the helicopter.

PILOT

I don't think so. The crew is not in uniform, and they look more dead than alive.

COPILOT

I only see two men aboard.

PILOT
Affirmative. This is unbelievable!

COPILOT
A sign of desperation.

PILOT
The price of freedom.

The copilot nods.

PILOT
Let's pick them up! Lower the hook.

CUT TO SEVERAL SHOTS OF PEPE AND PABLO'S RESCUE.

EXT. THE HELICOPTER FLIES INTO THE HORIZON WITH PEPE AND PABLO ABOARD – DAY

DISSOLVE TO:

ESTABLISHING SHOT OF THE IMIGRATION OFFICE IN MIAMI.

INT. IMIGRATION OFFICE BULLPEN – DAY

Immigration employees are working everywhere, processing refugees. Pepe and Pablo are escorted into a holding tank (a large cell). They're wearing orange immigration duds.

INT. GLASS OFFICE NEXT TO BULLPEN – DAY

AGENT SANDERS
Are those two ready for questioning?

ASSISTANT
Yes, sir.

Jack turns to another agent in the room.

AGENT SANDERS
You ready to play bad guy again?

AGENT BOB
Ready and willing!

AGENT SANDERS
Okay. Bring the first one in.

An assistant approaches the holding tank. He takes Pepe out. The agent leads Pepe to a glass office where he's asked to sit at one end of the table. Inside are the agents, apparently ready to interrogate Pepe. Bob, dressed in a typical polyester suit, sits across the table from Pepe.

AGENT SANDERS
Okay, Mr. Martinez, let's start from the
top. Do you speak English?

Speaking with difficulty partly due to his chapped lips.

PEPE
Yes, I attended an American school in
Havana.

AGENT SANDERS
Good, then let's get down to business.
How did you get that Cuban gunboat?

PEPE
We stole it from the Port of Mariel.

AGENT BOB

Bullshit! You're lying. You don't expect
us to believe that crap, do you?

PEPE

Mister, I don't know who you are, and
frankly, I don't care. But when you talk
to me, make sure you do it with respect,
the same way I speak to you.

Agent Bob, furious, springs out of his chair and approaches Pepe.
He's about to explode inches away from Pepe when Agent Sanders
intervenes.

AGENT SANDERS

Easy, Bob, easy! Give this fellow a
chance to explain.

Bob backs off.

AGENT SANDERS

Please, Mr. Martinez, we need a detailed
explanation for our records. You need to
cooperate with us.

Pepe, cool as a cucumber, directs his response at Sanders.

PEPE

I am cooperating. I'm telling you the
truth. Look, let me explain.

Several beats pass as Pepe gets comfortable in his chair.

PEPE (CONT'D)
Three of us stole the boat from the port
of Mariel. But one of us didn't make it.

CUT TO:

INT. INSIDE THE IMMIGRATION HOLDING TANK – DAY

Pablo is sitting on a bench as four more detainees are escorted into the tank. They're wearing the same uniforms as Pablo and Pepe. An immigration agent locks the cell behind them.

DETAINEE 1
Got a cigarette?

PABLO
No, I don't smoke.

DETAINEE 1
Are you Cuban?

PABLO
Yeah, I'm from Guantanamo.

DETAINEE 2
That's where I'm from.

The four Cubans introduce themselves, get friendly with Pablo. Pablo points to Pepe in the glass office.

PABLO
My partner and I stole a gunboat from
Mariel.

One of the detainees recognizes Pepe.

                    DETAINEE 3

I know that guy. Wasn't his father Jose
Martinez?

                     PABLO

Not wasn't, is!

                    DETAINEE 4

No, was. The right tense to use is was.

                     PABLO

What do you mean?

                    DETAINEE 4

Don't you know? Castro shot his father
and uncle. The rumor was they were
conspiring to overthrow Castro.

                     PABLO

Are you sure?

                    DETAINEE 4

Of course, I'm sure, I dumped their
bodies along with several others behind
EL MORRO Castle. They're at the
bottom of the bay.

Pablo is speechless. All kinds of thoughts cross his mind.

INT. AT JOSE AND ROSA'S HOUSE – DAY

Luis is in the house with several soldiers. They're turning the house
upside-down searching for leads.

LUIS
Continue searching. I'm sure we'll find
something.

As the soldiers continue their search, Luis walks over to the piano. On top of the piano are pictures of the family. One of the pictures was recently taken at the Revolutionary Anniversary Party where Jose, Ramon, and Oscar are all together. He picks up a picture.

LUIS POV

The group of men enjoying the moment.

3/4 ON LUIS

He ponders, focusing on Oscar. His intuition takes over.

                    LUIS
Sergeant, if you find anything, call me
at the precinct immediately.

                    SERGEANT
Yes, sir!

Luis flies out of the house with the picture frame under his arm.

EXT. MAIN ENTRANCE TO MIAMI'S IMMIGRATION
OFFICES – DAY

Pepe and Pablo exit dressed in plain clothes. They start down the steps.

                    PEPE
We made it!

At the bottom of the steps, Pepe takes a deep breath and turns to
Pablo.

                    PEPE
Thank you, Pablo. I would've never
made it without you.

                    PABLO
Don't mention it.

                    PEPE
You know, we make a pretty good team.

                    PABLO
I think so.

                    PEPE
You have a place to stay?

> PABLO

No.

> PEPE

Why don't we stay together?

> PABLO

Okay, but no funny stuff, all right.

They share a laugh.

> PEPE

Should we take the bus?

> PABLO

Do you know where you're going?

> PEPE

No. Does it matter?

Pablo giggles.

> PABLO

Tony warned me about you.

> PEPE

We made it this far, didn't we?

> PABLO

I'm going have to have a talk with Alicia
when we get back.

They put their arms over each other's shoulders. Pepe can barely reach
Pablo's shoulders. As they walk toward the bus stop, Pepe and Pablo
kid with each other.

PEPE

Listen, one of the agents in there told
me that we can get jobs on the beach,
maybe as busboys.

PABLO

You'll never make it as busboy.

PEPE

What are you talking about? I used to
be the head busboy at the Tropicana.

PABLO

Sure, you were. This I've got to see.

PEPE

Miami Beach, here we come!

EXT. ESTABLISING SHOT OF THE PRESIDENTIAL PALACE
IN HAVANA – DAY

INT. OSCAR'S OFFICE – DAY

Oscar is sitting behind his desk. There's a knock on the door.

OSCAR

Come in!

Luis enters the office closely followed by two military policemen
(MPs). The two MPs start coming around the desk. Oscar's instinc-
tively makes a run for it. He grabs a letter opener and jams it into the
leg of the MP closest to him. He shoves the second MP back against
Luis, knocking them both down. Like a cat, he leaps out the window,
crashing through the glass and down onto the street below. Luis draws
his pistol and hurries to the window.

LUIS'S POV

OSCAR IS RUNNING DOWN THE STREET.

                              LUIS
            Get that son of a bitch. I want him alive.

The other MP takes off after Oscar. The MP flies through the window and onto the street as did Oscar. The chase is on through the streets of Havana.

EXT. THROUGH THE STREETS OF HAVANA – DAY

A montage of chase scenes through the streets of Havana.

Pedestrians are getting run over by Oscar running at full tilt. Cars are screeching to a stop to avoid hitting the MP. Suddenly the MP stops and draws his weapon.

                              MP
                   Halt! Or I'll shoot!

People scatter as the MP fires a warning shot straight up in the air. Oscar doesn't even look back. Oscar, like an NFL running back, continues to barrel down the street.

POV OF MP.

There's no sight of Oscar. Oscar lost him.

BACK ON MP.

                              MP
                   Shit!

EXT. BACK ENTRANCE OF A MIAMI BEACH HOTEL – NIGHT

Pablo and Pepe are getting off work. Their aprons are filthy and greasy. Their perspiration has soaked their armpits and the middle of their backs. Pepe wipes the sweat off his brow.

>PEPE
>
>Boy, that was a hell of a day.

>PABLO
>
>Piece of cake. Imagine cutting sugar cane back home.

>PEPE
>
>I guess you're right.
>
>(pause)
>
>I wonder how Mom and Dad are doing?

Pablo doesn't respond. His face turns pale (imagine that on a mulatto). Pepe is perceptive. He picks up the vibes.

>PEPE
>
>What's the matter, Pablo? What is it?

Pablo does not respond.

>PEPE
>
>Are you ill? Do you need an aspirin or something?

Pablo still doesn't respond.

                    PEPE
        Look, whatever the problem is, I'm sure
        we can work it out.

Several beats pass.

                    PEPE (CONT'D)
        C'mon, talk to me.

Pablo is searching for words to break the news to Pepe. With a stone face, he speaks.

                    PABLO
        You father is dead!

Pepe misses the meaning of what Pablo just said. Several beats pass.

                    PEPE
        What did you say?

                    PABLO
                 (carefully)

        Your father and uncle are both dead.

Pepe's knees buckle. His throat tightens up.

                    PEPE
        How?

                    PABLO
        Castro shot them for treason.

The facts sink in. Pepe's soul is in pain. His eyes swell up. Tears begin to run down his face.

PEPE

When did you find out?

PABLO

As soon as we arrived, at the immigration office.

Pepe looks at Pablo with despair, then anger.

PEPE

From who?

PABLO

From those men we met in the holding cell.

PEPE

How can you be sure? Why do you trust them?

PABLO

They saw the bodies. They dumped them into Havana harbor.

Pepe is holding back the pain. It is a gut-wrenching moment.

PEPE

Why? All we ever did was help that son of a bitch!

Pablo embraces Pepe, trying to comfort him. Pepe is sobbing.

PEPE

Tony, my uncle, my father... Christ. So many people have died—

PABLO
(interrupting)

It's not easy, Pepe. I know how you feel.

(pause)

I too lost my parents in a similar way.

PEPE
What about my mother?

PABLO
Nothing was said.

PEPE
Are you sure? Tell me the truth.

PABLO
No, Pepe, I swear, nothing was said.

(a beat)

C'mon, let's go home.

Pepe and Pablo help each other walk down the alley behind the hotel and head home.

EXT. ESTABLISHING SHOT OF OSCAR'S HOUSE – DAY

Oscar drives up. Swiftly he gets out of the car and into the house.

INT. OSCAR'S LIVING ROOM – DAY

Rosa is sitting, writing a letter. Oscar flies in through the front door winded and scared. He peeks out the window to see if he's been followed. He begins to close every Venetian blind he finds open. Rosa looks at him, wondering what's wrong. Alicia, already showing a huge belly, comes out of the kitchen. Oscar is short of breath.

                    OSCAR

They know!

                    ROSA

Who knows?

                    OSCAR

Luis…Castro…everyone! (He catches
his breath.) Luis and a couple of MPs
came to arrest me at the office.

                    ROSA

Why?

                    OSCAR

Who knows why? For the same reasons
they took Jose?

                  (a beat)

I think I lost the MP following me, but
I can't be sure.

                    ALICIA

What now?

Oscar is still gasping for air.

                    OSCAR

We've got to leave right away. I know
just the place we can hide.

                    ALICIA

Where?

OSCAR
A little shack near Port Mariel.

ROSA
What about her baby?

ALICIA
I'm strong. I'll make it.

Rosa turns to Oscar. She hands him an envelope. It's a letter from Pepe.

OSCAR
How did you get this?

ROSA
Stop worrying. My sister works at the Post Office. She smuggled it to me this morning.

Alicia is glowing.

ALICIA
I knew he would write. He'll find a way to get us out.

OSCAR
You can't write back.

ROSA
Why?

OSCAR
That's the first place they'll monitor. They'll track us down.

> ROSA
>
> My sister will help us. They'll never see or know of any letters.

> OSCAR
>
> No. That's out of the question.

> ROSA
>
> C'mon, Oscar, don't be unreasonable. Pepe needs to know where we are.

> OSCAR
>
> If that letter gets into the wrong hands…

> ALICIA
>
> I'll let you read the letters before I mail them.

Oscar mumbles to himself.

> ROSA
>
> What did you say?

> OSCAR
>
> Nothing.

Oscar turns to Alicia, giving his consent.

> OSCAR
>
> Okay, but I see every letter, every line.

Alicia kisses Oscar on the cheek.

> OSCAR
>
> Now let's get out of here.

EXT. ESTABLIHING SHOT OF THE MIAMI BEACH HOTEL WHERE PEPE AND PABLO WORK – DAY

INT. A PRIVATE VIP BALLROOM – ENTERTAINMENT IN PROCESS – DAY

A poker table is in the center of the room. Five men and one woman are sitting around the table. A high-stakes game is in process. Pepe serves drinks to the patrons at the table. Pablo is serving hot hors d'oeuvres and delicacies that would please a king's palate. One of the guests sitting at the poker table is being loud and rude. He's smoking a cigar. As smoke spills from his breath, he talks about his life, his accomplishments.

> MR. THOMPSON
> Yeah, I used to own several businesses
> in Havana. I had a great relationship
> with Batista until the poor bastard was
> pushed out.

He pauses to take a puff from his cigar. The dealer deals a new hand.

> MR. THOMPSON
> Things are different there now. It's
> no longer the paradise it once was.
> All Havana is good for now is average
> whores and good cigars.

> V.O. DEALER
> How many?

MR. THOMPSON LOOKS AT THE HAND HE WAS JUST DEALT.

                    MR. THOMPSON
          I'll take two.

Cigar smoke billows from Mr. Thompson's mouth.

                    MR. THOMPSON (CONT'D)
          It's a shame... That country used to be
          my favorite playground.

Pepe, having heard enough, is about to lose it. The bullshit coming out of this man's mouth is enough to piss off Mother Teresa. As he comes around the table, the lady at the table (MRS. FISCHMAN) picks up on Pepe's intentions. She reaches for Pepe's arm, stopping him.

                    MRS. FISCHMAN
          It's not worth it, son.

Pepe and Mrs. Fischman have eye contact. No other words need to be spoken.

                    MRS. FISCHMAN
          Please bring me a vodka tonic.

Pepe resumes doing his work.

                    PEPE
          Yes, ma'am...

The dealer turns to Mr. Thompson again.

                    DEALER
          Your call, Mr. Thompson.

MR. THOMPSON
I'm out.

Mr. Thompson folds his cards on the table. Pepe heads toward the bar. Pablo is now standing at the bar, folding some napkins.

PEPE
Did you hear what that dickhead said?

PABLO
Who? Wild Bill Hickok?

PEPE
Yeah.

PABLO
Who cares?

PEPE
(HOT!)

Average whores and good cigars, huh?

PABLO
Take it easy, Pepe. If you listen to the bullshit, it'll drive you crazy.

PEPE
I'll fix him.

Pepe turns to the bartender.

PEPE (CONT'D)
Give me two vodka tonics.

Pepe cools his jets a bit and then puts the two drinks on his tray. He takes them toward the poker table. Pablo watches his every move. Pepe serves one of the drinks to Mrs. Fischman.

                         PEPE
            Here you are, ma'am.

                    MRS. FISCHMAN
            Thank you.

Pepe walks over behind Mr. Thompson.

                         PEPE
            May I get you something to drink, sir?

                    MR. THOMPSON
            Yeah, get me one of those Cuba libres.

Pepe, cool as a cucumber, tilts his tray and casually drops the other vodka tonic on top of Mr. Thompson. Mr. Thompson ejects from his seat.

                    MR. THOMPSON
            Jesus dammed Christ, man! What are
            you, an idiot?

Pepe takes his serving tray and slams Mr. Thompson in the head and then on the nuts. Mr. Thompson bends over. Pandemonium breaks out. The dealer pushes an alarm button on the side of the table. Mr. Thompson takes a swing at Pepe, missing but causing two cards hidden in his sleeve to fly out and fall to the floor. Everyone notices the cards. Mr. Thompson freezes halfway between angry and embarrassed. Silence covers the room like a blanket. Pepe picks up one of the cards. Several beats pass.

> MRS. FISCHMAN
> I believe you're the one that can't be
> trusted, Mr. Thompson. You owe ev-
> eryone here an apology, not to mention
> your winnings!

Mr. Thompson is speechless. Two security guards barge into the VIP room. The dealer points to Mr. Thompson. The two guards grab Mr. Thompson and escort him out.

> SECURITY 1
> Let's go, asshole.

The headwaiter signals to Pepe, calling for him. Mrs. Fischman (the only one left sitting at the poker table) stands and approaches Pepe.

> MRS. FISCHMAN
> You'll need a new job now.

Pepe, embarrassed, doesn't say a word.

> MRS. FISCHMAN
> Come see me tomorrow afternoon at
> 2:00 p.m. I might have something for
> you. Here is my card.

Mrs. Fischman gives Pepe her card and casually walks out of frame.

EXT. ESTABLISHING SHOT OF OSCAR'S HIDEOUT / A SHACK IN THE MIDDLE OF NOWHERE – NIGHT

Rosa, Alicia, and Oscar walk toward the front door.

INT. THE SHACK – NIGHT

They enter. Alicia has gotten bigger every day and can barely walk. She heads straight for the sofa. She takes her shoes off and starts fanning herself with a magazine from the coffee table.

> ALICIA
>
> I thought we'd never make it.

> OSCAR
>
> We should be safe here for a while.

Alicia feels her own belly.

> ALICIA
>
> I don't know if I can hold out much longer. This baby is either huge, or I've been pregnant longer than I thought.

> ROSA
>
> It's okay, honey, we brought everything we need in case the baby comes early.

> OSCAR
>
> Listen up, ladies. Here are the rules we'll follow.

He catches his breath and unloads a backpack from his back.

> OSCAR
>
> Everyone stays indoors during daylight hours. No one leaves this shack without my permission. Not even to the post office. Is that understood?

ALICIA

Por favor, Oscar, we're not in the army.

OSCAR

We must be careful. I'm sure we're on every Most Wanted poster between El Cabo de San Antonio and La Punta de Maisi. (These are the two most extreme eastern and western points on the island of Cuba.)

Rosa, trying to lighten the moment, salutes Oscar.

ROSA

Yes, sir.

Alicia giggles.

OSCAR

Very funny... It's good to see you all still have a sense of humor.

Rosa inspects the shack.

ROSA

On what days does the maid come?

Oscar doesn't find Rosa's humor funny.

ALICIA

Relax, Oscar, don't worry so much.

The group settles in.

EXT. AN OLD APARTMENT BUILDING IN MIAMI – NIGHT

Pepe and Pablo walk in the main entrance.

INT. INSIDE THE APARTMENT BUILDING – NIGHT

Pepe and Pablo are both sweaty and tired. They start walking up the stairs when suddenly Pepe stops.

> PEPE
> I'll check the mail.

He turns around and goes back down to the mailboxes. Pablo continues up the stairs.

> PABLO
> Why? All we get are bills.

Pepe opens the mailbox, and sure enough, a bunch of bills fall out. In between the bills is a letter from Cuba. Pepe lights up like a Christmas tree. He starts opening the letter as he goes up the stairs, stumbling and almost falling on his face. Pepe is excited.

> PEPE
> Pablo, we got a letter from Alicia.

INT. PEPE AND PABLO'S EFFICIENCY – NIGHT

Pablo is looking at an empty refrigerator. Pepe walks in and sits at a table with a couple of unmatched chairs. He starts reading the letter.

> V.O. PEPE
> My Dear Pepe,

SWITCH OVER TO:

V.O. ALICIA

I miss you terribly, and I hope you're well when you receive this letter. I'm sure the news about your dad and Roberto made it to Miami. I'm sorry I'm not there for you, especially during this moment of sorrow. I wish I could console and comfort you this very moment.

I've been living with your mother and Oscar almost since you left. We had no choice since the government has been pursuing us for obvious reasons. Recently, we moved to a place you once played in as a child. Oscar told me to tell you that we're at the old house where you fell off the roof and sliced your chin open.

I hope you can get us out soon. We all miss you terribly. Don't worry about us. Oscar is doing a great job of keeping us safe. All four of us are fine and healthy even though we're sometimes having difficulty getting the essentials. I love you, and I look forward to the day when I can hold you in my arms again.

Forever your loving wife, Alicia.

ALICIA'S V.O. ENDS.

CLOSE ON PEPE.

He pauses thinking.

> PEPE
>
> All four of us?

CLOSE ON PABLO.

Pablo raises his eyebrows.

BACK ON PEPE.

He rereads the last two sentences. Suddenly, it dawns on him.

> V.O. PABLO
>
> Well, well, well…you're going be a father.

Pepe can't believe it. He is momentarily gagging, speechless.

> PEPE
>
> I'm going to be a father!

> PABLO
>
> Yeah, I know. Isn't that great?

> PEPE
>
> I can't believe it. I'm going to be a father!

> PABLO
>
> I know. You said that already.

Pepe suddenly realizes why Alicia decided not to come with him on the boat. He stops celebrating.

PEPE

Alicia was pregnant… That's why she refused to come with me.

(pause)

It all makes perfect sense now.

PABLO

Congratulations!

Pepe walks over to Pablo and gives him a bear hug. Exuberant is an understatement.

PEPE

Pablo, I'm going to be a father!

PABLO

Yeah!

PEPE

We've got to get those special visas as soon as possible. We've got to get them out.

PABLO

Don't worry. The embassy said they'll be ready in a few weeks.

INT. FIDEL CASTRO'S OFFICE – DAY

Fidel is having his boots polished by a shoeshine boy. The doors to his office are open, and Luis is being escorted in by two MPs. Luis has a troubled look.

> LUIS
>
> Did you want to see me, sir?

> FIDEL
>
> Yes, come in, sit with me for a minute.

Fidel signals the shoeshine boy to leave and flips him a coin. Luis is still standing by the door.

> FIDEL
>
> Sientate! (Sit down!)

Luis sits down cautiously across from Fidel.

> FIDEL
>
> Do you know why you're here?

> LUIS
>
> Yes, sir.

> FIDEL
>
> Tell me why.

> LUIS
>
> Because I haven't found Oscar, Alicia, or Rosa.

Fidel acknowledges Luis's statement by patronizing him.

> FIDEL
>
> Good...I'm glad we're communicating clearly.

(a beat)

When should I expect them here?

LUIS
By the end of this week, sir.

Fidel, disappointed with his response, moves closer to Luis. He gets in Luis's face. Fidel exhales cigar smoke directly at Luis's face and whispers.

FIDEL
You only have forty-eight hours to find
them. Do I make myself clear?

Luis acknowledges. Perspiration falling from Luis's forehead. Fidel backs away.

FIDEL
Now get the hell out of here before I
change my mind.

Luis stands and hurries out the door without saying a word.

EXT. BRIDGE TO STAR ISLAND ON MIAMI BEACH – DAY

It's a beautiful day. The sun is shining on a hot and steamy afternoon. Pepe gets off the Metro Bus and walks across the bridge. Finally, he makes it to the guard gate. Drenched in perspiration.

PEPE
Excuse me.

The guard opens the glass window to his air-conditioned post.

> GUARD
>
> Can I help you?

> PEPE
>
> I came to see Mrs. Fischman.

> GUARD
>
> Is she expecting you?

> PEPE
>
> Yes, I'm supposed to meet her at 2:00
> p.m.

Pepe pulls Mrs. Fischman's card from his shirt pocket and shows it to the guard.

> GUARD
>
> What's your name?

> PEPE
>
> Pepe Martinez.

The guard checks a list of names of expected visitors on his clipboard.

> GUARD
>
> Yes, here you are.
>
> (a beat)
>
> You may go in.

> PEPE
>
> Thank you!

Pepe ducks under the gate and walks on in.

EXT. ESTABLIHSING SHOT – MRS. FISCHMAN'S MANSION – DAY

What a place! An unbelievable house on the ocean. Pepe walks up to the bronze gates. He notices a surveillance camera tracking his every move. He pushes a button. A servant answers.

> SERVANT
> Can I help you?

A little impatient.

> PEPE
> I'm Pepe Martinez, I came to see Mrs. Fischman. She's expecting me.

> SERVANT
> Please come in.

The gates are electronically opened. Pepe steps through the gates and walks up to the front doors where a butler is waiting for him.

> BUTLER
> Please follow me.

INT. MRS. FISCHMAN'S MANSION – DAY

Pepe follows the butler into this incredible house. Together they walk past the most beautifully decorated rooms filled with priceless works of art. They reach the back of the house, where it opens into a huge pool and deck area facing Biscayne Bay. Mrs. Fischman is sitting under an umbrella, sipping tea.

> MRS. FISCHMAN
> I'm pleased you could make it.

                    PEPE
Thank you for inviting me.

                    MRS. FISCHMAN
Can Sam (the butler) get you something
to drink?

                    PEPE
A cold glass of water would be nice.

Pepe stares, overwhelmed by the beauty of his surroundings.

                    MRS. FISCHMAN
Sure we can't offer you something else?

                    PEPE
No, thank you.

Sam acknowledges and leaves to fetch the water. Pepe sits across from
Mrs. Fischman.

                    PEPE
You have a beautiful home.

                    MRS. FISCHMAN
Thank you, but let's dispense with all
the formalities.

A beat passes as Pepe is surprised by her directness.

                    MRS. FISCHMAN (CONT'D)
I have a job for you. It's a dangerous job,
but it pays very well.

                    PEPE
I'm listening.

Mrs. Fischman takes a puff on a cigarette.

MRS. FISCHMAN

I know all about your family in Cuba.

(a beat)

How your father was murdered and the disappearance of some of your friends. I also know that you and your fiancée are expecting a child.

Pepe is floored. He has no idea how she knows all this information.

PEPE

How do you—

Mrs. Fischman interrupts.

MRS. FISCHMAN

I believe I should ask the questions here.

Pepe backs off and listens.

MRS. FISCHMAN

Let's just say that I work for the US government and that we have vital interests in Cuba.

Mrs. Fischman takes a sip from her tea.

MRS. FISCHMAN
If you successfully complete what we ask of you, we'll guarantee safe passage for your mother and fiancée out of Cuba and pay you $50,000 dollars.

Pepe's eyes light up. He can't believe his ears.

MRS. FISCHMAN
Will you take the job, Pepe?

PEPE
(without hesitation)

Yes, of course, what do I need to do?

MRS. FISCHMAN
Do you remember that Air Force base you and your father built for Castro back in 1960?

PEPE
You mean the one in San Cristobal?

MRS. FISCHMAN
Yes!

(several beats)

We need to visit and inspect that base with your help.

Pepe realizes the danger involved.

PEPE
What you're asking of me is suicide.

MRS. FISCHMAN
Believe me, Pepe, those are not our
intentions. You will be escorted by
America's best on this mission. Besides,
I don't believe you have any options, do
you, Mr. Martinez?

Mrs. Fischman stands and gives her back to Pepe. Several more beats pass.

PEPE
Are you saying that I'll never get those
visas I applied for?

MRS. FISCHMAN
Let me put it this way, Pepe—would you
like to return to work as a busboy and
continue to struggle, or would you like to
get your family out during this lifetime?

Mrs. Fischman turns to Pepe. He's getting frustrated.

PEPE
I believe you know the answer to that
question.

MRS. FISCHMAN
Good then! We have an agreement.

(a brief pause)

Now there is one very important condition to our accord Pepe.

PEPE
And that is?

>   MRS. FISCHMAN
> You must keep our pact and discussion
> totally confidential. You will not discuss
> it with anyone, including your best
> friend, Pablo.

Again, Pepe is surprised by Mrs. Fischman's information.

>   MRS. FISCHMAN
> Do we have an agreement, Mr.
> Martinez?

>   PEPE
> You have my word.

>   MRS. FISCHMAN
> Fine, I want you ready as soon as I call.

She hands him an envelope that has been sitting on top of the table all along.

>   MRS. FISCHMAN
> Read this when you get back to your
> apartment. I have arranged employment
> for both you and Pablo. Now I must ask
> you to leave. I have other pressing mat-
> ters to tend to.

Curiosity overwhelms him. He is about to speak when Mrs. Fischman ends the conversation.

>   MRS. FISCHMAN (CONT'D)
> I've already said enough.

Mrs. Fischman extinguishes her cigarette in an ashtray on the table.

MRS. FISCHMAN (CONT'D)

Will you be ready when I call?

PEPE

Yes! I'll be ready.

The butler brings in the water. A close up on the glass as we dissolve to:

EXT. THE SHACK – DAY

Another scorching day. The heat waves come up from the ground.

INT. THE SHACK – DAY (3 MONTHS LATER)

Alicia is sweating profusely. She is in obvious pain, holding her lower abdomen.

ALICIA

Why am I feeling these contractions? My baby is not due for at least another month.

ROSA

Calm down. Take it easy. This heat can be overwhelming.

Rosa wipes the sweat off Alicia's forehead. Alicia breathes deeply. She's trying to relax.

ALICIA

Rosa, I need you to promise me something.

ROSA

Not now, Alicia, c'mon, calm down. You need to rest.

ALICIA

Rosa, please this is very important to me.

ROSA

Okay, honey, okay, what is it?

ALICIA

Promise me that no matter what happens, you'll take care of the baby first.

ROSA

Are you going crazy on me?

Alicia gets a firm grip on Rosa's arm.

ALICIA

Listen to me! No matter what happens, you will take care of the baby.

(a beat)

Promise me...

Rosa trying to appease Alicia.

> ROSA
>
> Of course, we're going to take care of
> the baby. Now stop this nonsense. You
> need to save your energy. You need to
> rest.

Alicia squeezes Rosa's arm harder, almost cutting off her circulation.

> ALICIA
>
> Promise me. Dammit!

SEVERAL BEATS PASS

Alicia is locked on to Rosa waiting for an answer.

> ROSA
>
> Yes, Alicita…I promise.

Alicia releases Rosa's arm, leans back on the chair, and takes a deep breath. She fans herself with a hand fan.

FADE TO BLACK.

ON SCREEN "APRIL 12TH, 1961." FIVE DAYS BEFORE THE BAY OF PIGS INVASION.

EXT. HOTEL – MIAMI BEACH, FLORIDA – NIGHT

Pablo and Pepe are tending bar at a nightclub. The place is packed with women. The phone at the bar rings. Pablo picks up.

> PABLO
>
> Bellagio's Bar and Grill!

He pauses to listen.

PABLO

Sure thing, one second.

Pablo turns to Pepe.

PABLO

Pepe you've got a call.

Pepe finishes mixing a drink and serves it to a patron. He walks over to the phone.

PEPE

Hello?

MRS. FISCHMAN

Hello, Pepe, it's me.

Pepe can barely hear who's on the other end. The music is blaring.

PEPE

Who?

Pepe takes the palm of his free hand and covers his bare ear.

PEPE

Could you please speak a little louder?

MRS. FISCHMAN

It's me, Pepe. Mrs. Fischman!

PEPE

Oh hi, Mrs. Fischman. Sorry about the
noise, it's just that it's very busy tonight.

MRS. FISCHMAN
It's time, Pepe. You need to be at Nick's Cabaret at 1:00 a.m. Two of my assistants will meet you in the VIP room.

Pepe looks at his watch.

POV OF THE TIMEX—it's 11:31 p.m.

PEPE
Okay, I'll be there.

MRS. FISCHMAN
Don't be late!

PEPE
All right, all right, don't worry…

Pepe hangs up the phone. The bar is packed with patrons.

PABLO
C'mon, Pepe, give me a hand.

Pepe hurries over to help Pablo. They crank out the drinks.

PABLO
Who was it?

PEPE
My date tonight.

PABLO
A date?

PEPE

Yeah, what's wrong with that?

PABLO

What about Alicia?

PEPE

What are you my conscience or something?

A beat passes as Pablo looks at him kind of funny.

PEPE (CONT'D)

Can you cover for me tonight?

PABLO

What are you saying?

PEPE

What are you deaf?

PABLO

I can't believe this…

Pepe pushes Pablo to make a decision by gesturing "Well?"

PABLO

Okay!

PEPE

Thanks, I knew I could count on you.

PABLO

Does your date have a sister, a friend, someone?

                              PEPE
          Not tonight, but I'll check on it. This
          girl is a real beauty.

                             PABLO
          I bet.

EXT. EL TROPICANA NIGHTCLUB IN HAVANA – NIGHT

INT. EL TROPICANA – NIGHT

Luis is alone sitting at a table, enjoying the show. He's about to finish a cigarette when, out of the corner of his eye, he catches a glimpse of a man wearing a red-and-black armband staring at him. The armband reads "July 26." Luis recognizes the armband. It's identical to the armbands worn by Castro's death squads. Luis avoids eye contact. He wipes his lips dry after taking a sip of water and calls for the waiter. The waiter approaches the table.

                              LUIS
          Where are the restrooms?

                            WAITER
          Down the hall and to the right. You
          can't miss them.

                              LUIS
          Thanks.

Calmly, Luis gets up from the table and walks toward the restrooms.

INT. RESTROOMS AT EL TROPICANA – NIGHT

As he enters the restrooms, a soldier coming out startles him. He collects himself and goes inside. He approaches the urinals acting as if he's going to unzip and pee. Patiently, he stands at the urinal. The last man in the restroom leaves. Immediately, Luis zips up and goes to the restroom window. He tries to open it. The window handle breaks off. Quickly, he goes to one of the stalls and takes a bunch of toilet paper, wrapping it around his right hand. He goes back to the window and breaks it with his paper wrapped fist. He climbs out onto the ledge and jumps, cutting himself in the process.

EXT. BACK ALLEY – NIGHT

Luis lands in the alley on top of several garbage cans making a terrible racket.

BACK ON THE ARMBANDED SOLDIER.

The sound of the garbage cans alerts the assassin. He decides to follow Luis into the restrooms.

INT. RESTROOMS AT THE TROPICANA – NIGHT

The assassin enters the restroom, searching for Luis. He finds the broken window. He realizes Luis is on to him and bolts out of the restroom and into the alley, looking for Luis.

EXT. BACK ALLEY – NIGHT

By now, Luis has gotten a good start.

ASSASSIN'S POV LOOKING DOWN THE ALLEY at LUIS.

Luis is a block and half up the street, barely visible to the assassin.

ON LUIS.

Luis turns around and sees the assassin in full stride on his tail. Panic strikes. Running as fast as he can, Luis turns the corner and starts looking for a place to hide. He tries to open several doors to apartment buildings and then to cars parked on the street, but they're all locked. He resumes running down the block. By now, the assassin has a lead on him and is gaining ground fast.

CLOSE ON ASSASSIN.

In a relentless pursuit, he blows by pedestrians, knocking several of them down.

BACK ON LUIS.

Luis turns the next corner, seemingly going around in circles. He sees a little café and decides to go in.

INT. CAFÉ – NIGHT

Luis storms in through the front doors and hustles out the back.

EXT. REAR OF CAFÉ – NIGHT

As Luis exits the rear of the café, he notices a manhole cover on the street. He opens it and quickly climbs down.

INT. STREET MANHOLE

As he pulls to close the heavy manhole cover, he catches a finger between the iron cover and the steel rim, smashing it to bits. The pain is excruciating. The blood gushing from his finger stains both his shirt and pants. Out of breath and with his skin almost falling off his finger, he manages to keep calm, very quiet, and totally still.

EXT. CLOSE TO THE MANHOLE COVER AT THE REAR OF THE CAFÉ – NIGHT

Within seconds, the assassin bursts out the rear door of the café. He stops for an instant, searching for Luis. Suddenly, he takes off running again, not knowing where he is headed.

INT. INSIDE THE MANHOLE AND IN THE SEWAGE TUNNEL – NIGHT

Luis is shaking like a leaf. Having just heard the soldier go by, he decides to go down the manhole ladder all the way to the bottom. At the foot of the ladder, he tries to orient himself by looking around. He can't see a thing because it's pitch-black, so he reaches into his pocket and pulls out a book of matches. He lights one up, but it dies rather quickly. He then reaches into his shirt pocket and pulls out his pen. From his suit pocket, he pulls a handkerchief and hooks it onto the pen, wrapping the handkerchief around until it's nice and tight. He lights up another match and then torches the handkerchief. The light barely illuminates the tunnel. Luis gets his bearings and heads down one of the tunnels. As Luis walks through the tunnel, he avoids rodents and garbage after every step. He passes one ladder heading up, then another. Finally, he stops at the third ladder. He goes up the ladder and slightly opens it to take a peek. As he surveys the area, he sees the coast is clear.

EXT. STREET LEVEL BY THE MANHOLE – NIGHT

Quickly, Luis climbs out, closes the manhole and walks briskly down the street.

EXT. AT A BUS STOP – NIGHT

Luis arrives and sits next to several people apparently waiting for the bus. He checks out the people around him and takes off his jacket to mix in with the crowd. Not a minute has passed when several people get up off the bench.

LUIS POV

The bus is a couple of blocks away picking up passengers.

BACK ON LUIS.

He breathes a sigh of relief. As he stands to get in the bus-line, he feels a presence behind him. Without warning, his knees buckle as the thrust of a large knife penetrates his lower back. The blade protrudes out the front of his shirt, twisting and turning as the killer moves it to guarantee maximum damage. Luis is dead. He just hasn't fallen yet. The killer pushes Luis forward as he pulls the knife out.

His lifeless body falls forward in front of the oncoming bus. The bus driver unable to stop runs over him, crushing what remains of this confused young man. The killer walks away as a multitude of people gather to witness what's happened.

DISSOLVE TO:

EXT. HOMESTEAD AIRFORCE BASE MAIN ENTRANCE – NIGHT

ON SCREEN "2:00 a.m., April 15th, 1961."

Pepe arrives in a taxi escorted by two men. They get out and approach the guard gate.

                    PEPE
          My code name is Thunder.

                    GUARD
          Wait here.

The guard makes a quick phone call then turns to Pepe.

                    GUARD
          Wait by the gate. They'll pick you up in
          a minute.

They walk over to the gate. Less than a minute has passed when an MP drives up in a jeep and picks them up. He gets in the front.

EXT. WITH THE JEEP – NIGHT

The Jeep drives through a section of the base where military preparations are in process. They arrive in front of a two-story building. The MP gets out.

                    MP
          Follow me please.

The MP escorts Pepe and the two men into the building.

INT. MILITARY BUILDING – NIGHT

Pepe follows the MP through the main entrance and down the hall. They reach a set of double doors. As they enter, he's surprised to see

Pablo in fatigues, sitting, waiting for him. There are three other military officers in the room.

PEPE
What in the hell are you doing here?

PABLO
Waiting for you. I'm your date tonight!

PEPE
You're CIA, aren't you?

Pablo nods affirmative. Pepe is a little upset.

PABLO
Pepe, please understand, we had to be
certain we could trust you.

PEPE
Maricon coño! (You son of a bitch!)

PABLO
Settle down. Let me introduce you.

Pablo stands up and introduces the officers present. Pepe shakes hands with each of them.

PABLO
This is Commander Johnson, Lieutenant
Smith, and Sergeant Carter.

Pepe turns to Pablo.

PEPE
I trust you, Pablo. Don't let me down.

PABLO

I haven't, have I?

(a beat)

Look, we don't have a minute to waste. I'll
brief you on our way there. Follow me.

COMMANDER JOHNSON

Good luck, men!

Pablo and the other two officers salute Commander Johnson. They
exit and head toward a helicopter pad adjacent to the building.

The four men get into an Air Force helicopter ready for takeoff.

INT. FLYING HELICOPTER SOMEWHERE OVER THE
CARIBBEAN SEA – NIGHT

PABLO

We are meeting a NAVY battle group just
off the southern coast of Isla de Pinos.

PEPE

A battle group?

Pepe's eyebrows go up.

PABLO

Don't ask any more questions. Soon
you'll know the details of the mission.

CUT TO:

EXT. ARRIVING ON TOP OF A US CARRIER AT SEA – NIGHT

The four men get out of the helicopter. A NAVY SEAL is waiting for them. He greets them and leads them below deck.

INT. US CARRIER – NIGHT

An officer welcomes the four men as they arrive on the main deck.

> LIEUTENANT SMITH
> Welcome aboard. You are right on schedule. Please follow me.

Lieutenant Smith leads them to the operations center, the heart of the ship. Captain Harper is waiting for them.

> CAPTAIN HARPER
> Gentlemen, welcome to Operation 90 Miles.

Pablo and the other two officers salute Captain Harper. Pepe follows them in.

> CAPTAIN HARPER
> We have a critical job to do, and we must meet our timetable.

> (a beat)

> Listen up! At exactly 0300 hours, we will rendezvous with the USS *Seawolf*. You will board her by 0315. Officer Clements on the *Seawolf* will provide you with the rest of the details upon boarding. Your gear is ready below, and Lieutenant Smith will show you where to pick it up.

Captain Harper looks at his wristwatch.

                    CAPTAIN HARPER
          Please synchronize your watches. The
          time is now 0214:40. Any questions?

No questions.

                    CAPTAIN HARPER
          Good luck, men!

EXT. THE SHACK IN CUBA – NIGHT

CUT IN THE SOUND OF ALICIA CRYING AND SOMETIMES
SCREAMING.

INT. THE LIVING ROOM: CAMERA PANS TO THE SLIGHTLY
AJAR DOOR OF THE BEDROOM – NIGHT

Alicia is now BLARING in pain. She's in bed, and we can barely see what's going on inside.

CAMERA SLOWLY ZOOMS IN, PEEKING THROUGH THE
CRACK OF THE BEDROOM DOOR.

Alicia is trying to give birth. Rosa is encouraging her to breathe and push harder. Oscar is motionless standing next to Rosa, concerned about the process in progress.

                    OSCAR
          What's happening, Rosa? Is everything
          okay?

Rosa is at the foot of the bed, trying to help Alicia.

ROSA

Hush up, Oscar. Everything is going
fine.

(a beat)

Keep pushing, honey, keep pushing.

Alicia is trying her heart out, but little progress is being made.

CLOSE ON ROSA.

ROSA

Oscar quick, get me more hot water and
clean towels.

Oscar hustles out of the bedroom to get what Rosa requested. Rosa closes and locks the bedroom door behind him.

CLOSE ON OSCAR.

Although Oscar is puzzled by the locking of the door, he continues as if nothing happened.

INT. ALICIA'S BEDROOM – A MONTAGE – NIGHT

Alicia pushes, fighting for her life and the life of her baby. Rosa is doing all she can.

DISSOLVE TO:

INT. OUTSIDE ALICIA'S BEDROOM – DAY

A few hours have passed. Oscar is back knocking on the bedroom door again. As he returns, he notices that an eerie silence has engrossed the house and that Alicia can no longer be heard crying or screaming. Oscar, carrying more towels and hot water, knocks again and again on the bedroom door.

> OSCAR
> Rosa, open the door. I have more hot
> water and clean towels.

Finally, Rosa unlocks and opens the door. She comes out carrying a baby wrapped in towels. Rosa's dress is drenched in blood and perspiration. Rosa stands like a zombie.

> ROSA
> Alicia had a girl.

> OSCAR
> A girl?

> ROSA
> Yes, a beautiful girl.

Oscar looking over Rosa's shoulder, immediately notices that something is terribly wrong.

> OSCAR
> Rosa…what's wrong with Alicia?

Rosa is nodding her head in despair.

> ROSA
> She's dead! She didn't make it.

OSCAR
How? How could it happen?

Rosa crosses the line. She's almost hysterical.

ROSA
I tried to stop the bleeding, But it was
too much. I couldn't save her.

Oscar can't believe it. So he enters Alicia's bedroom.

OSCAR'S POV

Alicia is lying still in blood-covered sheets.

Oscar can't bear the sight of Alicia's condition, so he turns right around and leaves the bedroom.

BACK ON ROSA.

Oscar enters the frame. He approaches Rosa and hugs her and the baby at the same time. Trying to be strong, he consoles them. Finally, he also breaks down, bawling uncontrollably.

CAMERA PULLS BACK AND FADES TO BLACK.

EXT. OFF THE COAST OF CUBA ON THE DECK OF A SUB – NIGHT

Pepe and Pablo walk over to the forward hatch followed by Lieutenant Smith. Suddenly, intense flashes of lightning light up the horizon. They are immediately followed by the sound of explosions. Apparently, some type of raid seems to be in process and can be heard in the background. Pepe and Pablo look at each other.

                    PABLO
It's the Bay of Pigs Invasion.

                    PEPE
The Americans?

                    PABLO
No, they call themselves freedom
fighters. They're a group of 1,400 men
trained by the CIA for this invasion.

Pepe nods knowingly.

                    PEPE
That's not enough. Fidel has Migs and
tens of thousands of troops.

                    PABLO
Don't worry, the Americans will provide
air support during the invasion and mop
up after the landing is finished.

Pepe clenches his fist, showing his exuberance.

                    PEPE
Yeesss!

                LIEUTENANT SMITH
Move it. We haven't got all day.

INT. SUBMARINE'S BRIEFING ROOM – NIGHT

Colonel Clements welcomes the team.

COLONEL CLEMENTS
Good morning! I'm Colonel Clements, welcome to the Sea Wolf. At exactly 0430 hours, we will be surfacing two miles off the coast of Cuba in an area called Playa Majana.

PEPE
I know it well.

COLONEL CLEMENTS
That's why you're here, Mr. Martinez.

(a beat)

Eight Marines plus you two men (pointing to Pablo and Pepe) will disembark and hit the beach by 0500 hours. Your primary mission is to determine what nuclear capabilities Castro has, if any. We have unconfirmed data indicating that Castro has built a nuclear missile launch site in San Cristobal. You will report back any confirmed sittings immediately and obtain pictures to substantiate your findings. Any questions?

LIEUTENANT SMITH
Sir, do you have the frequencies?

As Colonel Clements hands an envelope to Lieutenant Smith.

COLONEL CLEMENTS
You are to avoid all contact with the enemy.

                    PEPE
          Except for helping me remove my
          family, right?

Colonel Clements ignores Pepe's question.

                    COLONEL CLEMEMTS
          We will extract you from here at 0430
          hours Thursday. That's approximately
          seventy-two hours from now. Any more
          questions?

Pepe, ignored by Colonel Clements and concerned about his family, begins to ask a question when Pablo holds him back. Pablo gestures to silence Pepe.

                    PABLO
          Sshhhh. He knows.

No further questions are asked.

                    COLONEL CLEMENTS
          Happy hunting, gentlemen.

Colonel Clements leaves the room.

Pablo turns to Pepe.

                    PABLO
          You ready to go?

                    PEPE
          Nuclear missiles, huh?

PABLO

They're not confirmed. That's why we're here.

PEPE

That's why you're here. What about my family? When do we get them out?

PABLO

After we finish our mission.

PEPE

Great, just great!

Pepe is concerned and uneasy.

PABLO

Will you stop worrying? We have plenty of time.

DISSOLVE TO:

EXT. THE BAY OF PLAYA MAJANA – THE SUB HAS SURFACED – NIGHT

In the distance, you can see the coast of Cuba. Operation 90 Miles is on its way. Two rafts with five men in each of them leave the sub.

EXT. THE BEACHES OF MAJANA, CUBA

The rafts arrive undetected.

LIEUTENANT SMITH

Let's go, let's go, get the lead out!

The men bolt out of the rafts, pulling them up the beach next to sand dunes and rocks. They quickly bury the rafts and excess gear. They gather around Lieutenant Smith. He gives a hand signal to move out. The men move into the dense tropical jungle.

EXT. EARLY MORNING – ESTABLISHING SHOT OF A COUNTRY STORE IN CUBA

A rooster is heard in the background. Oscar walks out of the store with a bag of groceries. Suddenly, two trucks loaded with Cuban soldiers storm by. Oscar ducks behind a telephone booth. Two more army trucks speed by. One with supplies and the other hauling a howitzer cannon. A young man runs across the street right past Oscar. Oscar stops him.

> OSCAR
> What's all the commotion? What's going
> on?

The young man speaks frantically.

> YOUNG MAN
> Haven't you heard? The Americans in-
> vaded the Bay of Pigs!

The kid takes off running. Oscar can't believe his ears.

> OSCAR
> Coño! (Holy Shit!)

Oscar starts running, holding on to the grocery bag in one hand and balancing his stride with the other.

EXT. THE SHACK – DAY

Oscar storms in the front door.

INT. THE SHACK – DAY

Oscar kicks the door shut. All excited, he throws the groceries on the sofa.

> OSCAR
> Rosa, Rosita, I've got great news!

Rosa walks out from the bedroom.

> ROSA
> Calm down! The baby is sleeping.

> OSCAR
> Calm down? The American invasion is here!

> ROSA
> What are you saying?

> OSCAR
> Rosita, I'm not kidding. I just saw several trucks of soldiers and supplies heading toward the Bay of Pigs.

> ROSA
> The Bay of Pigs?

> OSCAR
> Yeah! That's where the Americans landed.

Rosa ecstatically.

                    ROSA
          Thank God!

                    OSCAR
          Yes! Our nightmare is over.

Rosa and Oscar hug each other. They jump around the room like two little kids.

The baby starts crying.

EXT. SOMEWHERE IN THE JUNGLES OF SOUTHERN CUBA – DAY

The SEAL team is making its way through the tropical forest and approaching the small town of San Cristobal. Pepe and Pablo bring up the rear. They're about to cross a main road when the sound of heavy vehicles stops their progress. The men freeze and blend into their surroundings.

POV OF THE MEN.

The vehicles include a half-track, a fuel tanker, a huge tractor hauling a surface-to-surface missile, and several personnel carriers. The personnel carriers are loaded with Soviet troops, and the tractor is hauling a portable missile launcher. The convoy passes.

BACK ON LIEUTENANT SMITH.

                    LIEUTENANT SMITH
          Holy shit! These assholes have tactical
          nukes.

SERGEANT CARTER

Yes, sir, that was an SS-19 sir. Did you notice the personnel carriers?

LIEUTENANT SMITH

Those weren't Cubans. They look more like Russians to me.

SERGEANT CARTER

10-4, sir. Those were Russian troops.

LIEUTENANT SMITH

You sure sergeant?

SERGEANT CARTER

Yes, sir, those were Soviet Special Forces.

Lieutenant Smith turns to Corporal Williams carrying the radio equipment.

LIEUTENANT SMITH

Corporal, radio back a code 6 to Mother Goose and use a 4-D scramble. Now!

The corporal gets right on it.

LIEUTENANT SMITH

I sure hope we're in time.

SERGEANT CARTER

Yes, sir, so do I.

Pablo turns to Pepe.

> PABLO
> We weren't counting on this.

> PEPE
> Hell, everyone knows Russian troops
> have been in Cuba for months.

> PABLO
> I'm talking about the nuclear missiles.

> LIEUTENANT SMITH
> Okay, cut the CHIT-CHAT! Move out.
> We'll stay out of sight until dark.

EXT. ESTABLISHING SHOT OF CIA HEADQUARTERS – DAY

INT. CIA HEADQUARTERS – DAY

A uniformed officer briskly walks down the hall with an envelope in his left hand. The camera follows close behind. The soldier walks through a set of double doors and into a conference room. Present is the top brass of the US military and the CHAIRMAN of the Joint Chiefs of Staff. A roundtable meeting is in full swing. The Cuban situation is being discussed.

INT. CIA HQ CONFERENCE ROOM – DAY

> AIR FORCE COLONEL EDWARDS
> The scheduled air support has been can-
> celled by President Kennedy.

> MARINES GENERAL INGLE
> The men on the beach don't stand
> a chance unless they get air support
> immediately.

The officer who brought the envelope hands it to the Joint Chiefs of Staff (JCS) Chairman. He reads it.

> JCS CHAIRMAN
> Gentlemen, We've just received new information from our team on the island. Intelligence indicates that there are at least one division of Soviet troops deployed near the beach. In addition, we have visual confirmation that mobile Soviet SS-19 nuclear missiles exist in Cuba.

The room goes silent.

> AIR FORCE COLONEL EDWARDS
> Did you say that visual confirmation was obtained?

> JCS CHAIRMAN
> Affirmative! That is precisely what I said.

> AIR FORCE COLONEL EDWARDS
> I recommend that we postpone military intervention until we can further assess the situation.

> MARINES GENERAL INGLE
> I agree. Furthermore, we must notify the president immediately.

The JCS chairman picks up the red phone sitting in front of him.

>   JCS CHAIRMAN
> This is a matter of national secu-
> rity. I need to speak to the president
> immediately.

EXT. THE CITY OF SAN CRISTOBAL – NIGHT

This is a small town southwest of Havana. Pablo, Pepe, and the rest of the SEAL team arrived in one piece and undetected. From the outskirts of the city, the lights of the air base are visible. The group settles in as Sergeant Carter scouts the base through his binoculars.

>   SERGEANT CARTER
> Sir, you better take a look at this.

Sergeant Carter hands the binoculars to Lieutenant Smith. Pablo and Pepe are next to Lieutenant Smith as he looks through the binoculars.

>   LIEUTENANT SMITH
> Sonnavabitch! Looks like they've got
> SAMs too.

>   SERGEANT CARTER
> Lieutenant, do you see those tarps cam-
> ouflaging something about a hundred
> yards east of the SAMs?

Lieutenant Smith, looking through the binoculars, pans to his right.

>   LIEUTENANT SMITH
> Yes, it looks like they're covering up
> some type of launcher. We need to find
> out what the hell is under those tarps.

SERGEANT CARTER

There's only one way to find out, sir.

He stops looking at the base and turns around.

LIEUTENANT SMITH

If those are long-range missiles, we're in deep shit.

(a beat)

Okay, we're going in. Sergeant Carter, take Pepe and Pablo and cover the high ground on the west side of the base. I want pictures of the entire facility.

SERGEANT CARTER

Yes, sir.

Lieutenant Smith turns around to the other men.

LIEUTENANT SMITH

Bob, Jerry, it's showtime! Let's find out what's under those tarps. Keep your eyes and ears open.

(a beat)

Men, if the shit hits the fan, we'll meet back by the main road immediately. Any questions?

(another beat)

Rock and roll!

EXT. OUTSKIRTS OF THE CITY – NIGHT

Lieutenant Smith and six of his men work their way through the woods and toward the base. Slowly and methodically, they penetrate the area, always staying in the shadows and away from the moonlight. Finally, they reach the perimeter of the base. The woods around the perimeter have been cut back, creating a thirty-yard killing field. Only three inches of grass grows in this killing field and searchlights periodically scan the area, probing for undesirables. Lieutenant Smith turns to one of his men.

> LIEUTENANT SMITH
> Okay, measure the frequency of the searchlights.

Bob times the searchlights.

> BOB
> They scan the area every two minutes.

LIEUTENANT SMITH points to first two men who will penetrate the base.

> LIEUTENANT SMITH
> You got two minutes. Ready? Go!

Just as the lights finish sweeping the area, two of the Navy SEALs run through the perimeter to the main fence. With a pair of wire cutters, they quickly cut their way through and hide behind some barracks. They signal back to Lieutenant Smith for the others to join them.

> LIEUTENANT SMITH
> Okay, Bob, Joe, your turn.

Bob and his partner follow identically the same path to the fence, only Joe trips and falls. The lights systematically scanning the area almost catch Joe in the open. Lieutenant Smith and the two remaining men take positions to secure their exit. The four men in the base work their way into the tarp. Bob and Joe go inside.

INT. INSIDE THE TARP – NIGHT

Several generators are running and plugged into a control panel. The panel has a TV screen with a geographical map of the USA A series of bright-red lights illuminate the cities of Miami, Washington D.C., and New York. Several amber lights flash on and off at the base of the panel.

BOB

Screw this!

JOE

I can't believe this shit.

The men are stunned. Several long-range nuclear missile launchers are loaded and seemingly ready to fire. Joe quickly pulls out his camera and snaps off shot after shot of the missiles, the launchers, and the panel.

EXT. OUTSIDE THE TARP – NIGHT

The two SEALs outside guarding the entrance to the tarp notice that several men are coming out of their barracks. A group of Soviet soldiers exit their quarters and head toward their tarp. The two SEALs outside alert Bob and Joe inside to get out. The Soviet soldiers enter the tarp. Bob and Joe manage to exit the tarp undetected by cutting a hole at the rear of the tent. Bob and Joe rejoin the other two SEALs and exit the base without being noticed.

EXT. THE OTHER SIDE OF THE BASE – NIGHT

CAMERA PANS TO PABLO, PEPE, AND SERGEANT CARTER.

They survey the area from the woods just outside the killing zone, their eyes and ears wide open.

>   SERGEANT CARTER
>   Let's get pictures of the Soviet troops.

Pablo pointing to a tall tree with an unobstructed view of the base.

>   PABLO
>   Sarge, you see that tree?

>   SERGEANT CARTER
>   Yeah.

>   PABLO
>   With the telephoto, I can get all the
>   pictures you want.

The sergeant hesitates a moment.

>   SERGEANT CARTER
>   You'll also be a sitting duck if anything
>   goes wrong.

>   PABLO
>   You got a better idea?

>   SERGEANT CARTER
>   All right, do it! I'll cover your left flank.
>   Pepe, cover the other side.

Pepe looks at Pablo, a bit concerned.

PEPE
I'm not so sure that's a good idea.

PABLO
Don't give me that bullshit. Use that
rifle if you have to.

SERGEANT CARTER
You've got ten minutes.

Pablo turns to Pepe.

PABLO
Let's go!

Pepe and Pablo head off in one direction as Sergeant Carter heads in
another.

CLOSE ON SERGEANT CARTER.

SERGEANT CARTER
God help 'em!

Sergeant Carter settles into a hollow log on the ground, setting himself up with a good line of fire.

EXT. BY A TALL PINE TREE – NIGHT

Pepe and Pablo arrive at the tree. Pablo pointing to several tall bushes.

PABLO
Set up over there. Cover my backside.

> PEPE
>
> Be careful.

> PABLO
>
> To warn me, just whistle like a sinsonte
> (a Cuban bird).

Pablo shows Pepe how to whistle. Pepe smiles and acknowledges by whistling back identically. Pablo satisfied, starts climbing the tree.

CLOSE ON PABLO.

Slowly and quietly, Pablo climbs his way up the tree to a spot where he has a bird's eye view of the entire base. Swiftly, he grabs his camera and focuses on the base. With the camera, he snaps picture after picture.

BACK ON PEPE.

Below, Pepe is wide-eyed and sweating bullets. As he settles between several bushes, he feels his own heart beating like a drum. Suddenly, Pepe hears a couple of Cuban soldiers talking and walking toward him. Pepe, nervous, tries to whistle, but nothing comes out. He tries again and again, but his lips are dry and he panics, so no sound comes out. He looks up at Pablo. Without thinking, he grabs a stone and throws it at Pablo.

CLOSE ON PABLO.

He reacts to the stone hitting him.

CLOSE ON THE STONE FALLING.

The stone bounces off several limbs before finally hitting the ground.

BACK ON PABLO.

Pablo has stopped taking pictures.

CLOSE ON THE TWO CUBAN SOLDIERS.

The sound of the falling stone has alerted the soldiers of someone else's presence in the jungle. They stop and draw their weapons. One signals to the other, "You go that way. I'll go this way."

BACK ON PEPE.

Using hand signals, Pepe alerts Pablo of two soldiers coming.

BACK ON PABLO.

He puts the camera away and pulls his knife out.

PABLO'S POV

He can see the two soldiers approaching Pepe from different directions but can't make a move yet. One of the Cuban soldiers walking toward Pepe passes right underneath him.

BACK ON PEPE.

Pepe hears the soldiers coming, but he plays possum.

CLOSE ON CUBAN SOLDIER 2.

Unknowingly flanking Pepe and approximately ten yards away, he starts poking the bushes with his bayonet.

BACK ON PEPE.

Realizing he's surrounded, he makes the first move. He attacks the soldier closer to him and struggles to take his rifle away. The soldier goes for his pistol, but Pepe knocks him down before he can pull it from his holster. They continue to wrestle.

BACK ON CUBAN SOLDIER 1.

He hears the struggle and hurries to help his buddy.

BACK ON PABLO.

Pablo grabs a vine and uses it to swing down from the top of the tree and on top of Soldier 1.

BACK ON PEPE.

Pepe gains control over the .45-caliber pistol and fires one round into the soldier. Without warning, more shots ring out, and pandemonium breaks out. Spotlights focus on Pepe from every direction, lighting up the evening sky. Bullets zing past him. A siren wails, adding to the chaos. Pepe panics and takes off, running toward Pablo.

BACK ON PABLO.

He has beaten the other soldier unconscious and is just getting up off the ground. Pepe runs into frame.

PEPE
I guess I messed up?

PABLO
Forget it, let's go.

They both run out of frame.

EXT. THE ENTRANCE TO THE BASE – NIGHT

A series of search teams are gathering by the main entrance of the base. Both Soviet and Cuban troops are mobilizing organizing search teams. All the search teams have K-9s. The search teams storm out of the base and in the direction of Pepe and Pablo.

BACK ON PABLO AND PEPE blazing a trail through the jungle, running faster than humanly possible.

EXT. WITH LIEUTENANT SMITH, BOB, JERRY, AND THE OTHER MEN IN THE JUNGLE – NIGHT

A searchlight finds Lieutenant Smith.

> LIEUTENANT SMITH
> What the hell? Move out!

The men take off, doing triple time for the main road. They run in full stride.

> LIEUTENANT SMITH
> Willie, did you see what started it?

> WILLIE
> All I heard were shots.

> (a beat)

Then all hell broke loose.

LIEUTENANT SMITH
Hurry and radio back code red.

WILLIE
What scramble code should we use, sir?

LIEUTENANT SMITH
Forget the code. Just do it!

Willie, running at full tilt, swings the radio around and transmits the message.

Bob and Joe arrive first at the main road. They're out of breath. You can vaguely hear the barking of dogs in the background. Then Sergeant Carter arrives.

JOE
Jesus Christ, Sarge! What happened?

SERGEANT CARTER
Pablo and Pepe must have tangled with
a patrol.

Lieutenant Smith arrives with Willie and the other men.

LIEUTENANT SMITH
Where are Pepe and Pablo?

SERGEANT CARTER
They should be here any minute.

The barking of the K-9s gets louder and closer.

> BOB
>
> Sir, if we don't leave right now, we'll all be dogmeat.

> LIEUTENANT SMITH
>
> Easy, Bob! We'll wait one minute, then we're out of here.

The men position themselves back-to-back, protecting each other's flanks.

BACK ON PABLO AND PEPE RUNNING FULL SPEED THROUGH THE JUNGLE.

As they run, Pablo speaks.

> PABLO
>
> Right now, I wish we were bussing tables.

> PEPE
>
> It sure was easier.
>
> (a beat)
>
> Aren't we going in the wrong direction?

> PABLO
>
> We've got to slow down them dogs... and buy some time. (He slows down for Pepe.) Hurry, c'mon!

BACK ON A SOVIET SEARCH TEAM.

Hot on pursuit, they cut the dogs loose. The K-9s take off like bolts of lightning. The soldiers chase them and plow through the jungle.

BACK ON PABLO AND PEPE.

Running through a gully and a stream. On the other side of the brook, they stop and double back toward the main road. Pablo turns around, checking on Pepe. Pepe seems to be keeping up.

BACK ON LIEUTENANT SMITH AND THE SEAL TEAM.

Lieutenant Smith looks at his watch.

> LIEUTENANT SMITH
> Come on, Pablito, don't let me down
> now.
>
> (several beats)
>
> Shit, we've waited enough. Let's go!

Just as they gear up to evacuate, Pablo comes storming in. Pepe is just a few feet behind. Both of them are gasping for air. Pablo is still holding on to the camera. He raises it.

> PABLO
> Got them!
>
> LIEUTENANT SMITH
> Good! Bob, head for the beach.

A Soviet-made helicopter flies, almost touching the treetops. Everyone hits the dirt except for Pepe, who didn't move a muscle. At the top of his lungs.

PEPE

Head for the beach? Where do you think you're going?

Pepe jams a round in the chamber of his rifle. Aiming at the Lieutenant Smith, he's apparently ready to shoot the first person that heads toward the beach. Everyone freezes.

PABLO

Are you crazy?

PEPE

No, but you are if you think I'm leaving my family behind.

LIEUTENANT SMITH

You're going to get us all killed.

Sergeant Carter starts making a move. Pepe reacts, speaking directly at Sergeant Carter.

PEPE

You want to be the first to die?

Sergeant Carter backs down. The K-9s are getting closer and closer.

LIEUTENANT SMITH

Look, Pepe, you might kill two or three of us, but I guarantee one of us will kill you.

Tensions escalate. Definitely a touch-and-go moment.

PABLO
Don't do it. This is suicide for both you
and your family.

PEPE
(desperately)

It's my only chance to get them out!

Suddenly, the helicopter flies by again, only this time, closer and with a blinding searchlight illuminating the area.

LIEUTENANT SMITH
Listen to me, Pepe. If you have a death
wish, that's fine. But I'm responsible
for these men, and I'm not going to get
them killed.

Several beats pass. Without notice, a K-9 arrives rushing the group and attacks Pablo. *Blam! Blam!* Pepe blows the dog's head clean off. The situation allows the Navy SEALs to point all their weapons directly at Pepe. To complicate things, its starts raining.

LIEUTENANT SMITH (CONT'D)
You go! Save your family. We're leaving.
Move out.

Pablo turns to Lieutenant Smith.

PABLO
I'll stay with him.

LIEUTENANT SMITH
You going AWOL with your buddy?

PABLO
What about his family?

LIEUTENANT SMITH
What about it? This is not a debate. It's
an order. Move out!

Pablo doesn't know what to do.

PEPE
You got no reason to stay. Go!

Lieutenant Smith, Pablo, and his men disappear into the jungle, all in the same direction. Pepe bolts in the opposite direction.

FADE TO BLACK.

FADE IN:

EXT. THE SHACK – DAY

Several chickens are roaming in front of the shack. The rain has stopped, and it's a steamy early morning.

INT. THE LIVING ROOM – DAY

Rosa is packing her personal belongings, as is Oscar, stuffing them into a duffel bag. She's anxious to leave the shack and return to her home in Havana. The baby is on the sofa, wrapped in a quilt. She finishes stuffing the bag.

ROSA
I wonder how the invasion is going?

OSCAR

It's unbelievable, isn't it?

Rosa walks over to the door of the bedroom and cracks it open.

ROSA'S POV

Alicia's body is lying on the bed, covered by a sheet.

ROSA

What do we do with Alicia?

Oscar turns around. He hesitates for a moment.

OSCAR

We need to….

KAABOOMM!

The back door to the shack flies open. Pepe storms in, pointing his gun at anything that moves. Oscar and Rosa can't believe their eyes. Rosa runs to Pepe. She hugs him and kisses him. Pepe reciprocates. Oscar is in shock.

PEPE

I missed you.

ROSA

I missed you too.

Pepe looks over Rosa's shoulder at Oscar. PEPE signals OSCAR to come closer. Pepe breaks away from Rosa to hug and thank Oscar. They bear hug each other.

                    PEPE
How can I thank you?

                    OSCAR
You would've done the same for me.

Rosa, Pepe, and Oscar get into a three-way hug. The crying of a baby breaks up the celebration. Pepe's eyes light up. A smile comes to his face.

                    PEPE
        Is that my—

                    ROSA
        Daughter.

The crying is coming from the sofa. Pepe approaches his newborn child, hovers over her in amazement.

                    ROSA
        Alicia named her Lucia.

                    PEPE
        Where's Alicia?

An eerie silence blankets the room. Rosa walks over to Pepe. She can't find the words with which to tell him. Pepe perceives trouble. At the risk of being redundant, he turns to Rosa.

                    PEPE
        Where is Alicia?

Rosa starts crying. She hugs Pepe. Pepe looks at Oscar.

> PEPE
> What's wrong? Where is she?

Oscar in despair.

> OSCAR
> She died giving birth.

Pepe is DEVASTATED. He erupts into a fit of rage. Defiant at God and all creation, Pepe explodes.

> PEPE
> Oh, God, how can you do this to me? Why? Why have you forsaken me? I've never asked for anything, God! Why her? Why did you abandon her? If you exist, how could you? How could you allow this to happen? TELL ME WHY?

Pepe breaks down crying, weeping hysterically.

> PEPE (CONT'D)
> Why me, God? Why Alicia? Why?

Pepe cries uncontrollably for Alicia. Oscar embraces Pepe, trying to console him. Rosa tries to calm and comfort Pepe as well. Pepe, in awful pain, looks at the baby.

> OSCAR
> Your daughter was born yesterday.

> PEPE
> Where is Alicia?

OSCAR
(with some hesitation)

She's in the bedroom.

Immediately, Pepe turns around and walks toward the closed bedroom door. He hesitates. Then gently, he opens it.

PEPE'S POV

Slowly, Alicia's body is revealed on the bed covered with a sheet.

INT. THE SHACK BEDROOM – DAY

Quietly, he walks up next to her. Carefully, he pulls the sheet down exposing Alicia's face. She is pale and lifeless. Pepe falls to his knees and breaks down again. The pain is heart-wrenching, too much to bear.

FADE TO BLACK.

FADE IN.

INT. THE SHACK LIVING ROOM – DAY

Oscar and Rosa are sitting on the sofa with the newborn baby on her lap. Pepe closes the door to the bedroom and enters the living room. His appearance tells the whole story.

ROSA
You want something to drink?

Pepe nods his head. Rosa gives the baby to Oscar and goes to fetch a glass of water. Oscar looks at Pepe's child.

OSCAR
Lucia is going to be a heartbreaker.

Pepe walks over to Oscar. Oscar gives the baby to Pepe. An interesting moment, a moment you never forget. Several beats pass.

Suddenly—*CRASH! CRASH!* Both the front door and the rear door to the shack burst open. Pablo barrels in the front door with his M-14 rifle locked and loaded. Sergeant Carter blows in the rear door, fanning his submachine gun. Everyone freezes. The baby is startled and starts crying.

PEPE
God almighty!

PABLO
You didn't think we'd leave you behind,
did you?

Lieutenant Smith comes in after Sergeant Carter. Bob and Joe come in behind Pablo.

Pepe stares at Lieutenant Smith.

LIEUTENANT SMITH
What the hell are you looking at?

Pepe cracks a smile as Oscar, Pablo, and the rest of the men crack up laughing.

OSCAR
You see, Rosita, I told you the Americans
had invaded us.

PEPE

Not so fast, Oscar. Not so fast.

OSCAR

What do you mean not so fast?

PEPE

Fourteen hundred Cubans invaded the Bay of Pigs, not Americans.

LIEUTENANT SMITH

And there's good chance the invasion will fail.

OSCAR

Why? What do you mean?

LIEUTENANT SMITH

All our support has been cut off indefinitely due to those pictures we took.

OSCAR

What are you talking about?

LIEUTENANT SMITH

I'm sorry! The rest is classified.

The baby's crying gets louder. Lieutenant Smith looks at his watch.

LIEUTENANT SMITH

We haven't got much time.

> PABLO
>
> Pepe, we pushed our rendezvous back forty-eight hours. Are you all ready to go?

Pepe nods.

> PEPE
>
> We're ready.

> OSCAR
>
> What about Alicia?

> PEPE
>
> She's coming with us.

> PABLO
>
> Where is she?

> PEPE
>
> She's in the bedroom.

Pablo and Pepe go in the bedroom. Oscar, Rosa, and the men prepare for departure.

INT. ALICIA'S BEDROOM – DAY

Pablo walks in and notices a covered body on the bed. He looks back at Pepe. Pablo perplexed, walks over to the body and lifts the sheet. Pepe is somewhat shaken.

> PEPE
>
> She didn't have to die.

Several beats pass.

> PABLO

Pepe, we can't take her.

> PEPE

I'm not leaving without her.

> PABLO

Lieutenant Smith will never allow it.
She will endanger the entire mission.

> PEPE

You're wasting time. She's going with us!

Pablo feels Pepe's pain and notices his look and determination. Several beats pass.

> PABLO

Okay, give me a hand.

Pablo starts wrapping Alicia's body tightly in more sheets. Pepe, glassy-eyed, helps Pablo in the process.

BACK IN THE LIVING ROOM OF THE SHACK.

Pablo and Pepe enter the living room. Pablo is carrying Alicia's body wrapped in sheets and blankets. Pepe carries the rifles and a backpack.

> PABLO

We're ready.

> LIEUTENANT SMITH

What the hell?

> PABLO

Alicia needs our help.

PEPE

Our deal was to bring my family home.

Lieutenant Smith, puzzled and confused, looks at Sergeant Carter. Sergeant Carter seemingly understands Pepe's request. He nods to Lieutenant Smith, communicating his desire to help Pepe. Lieutenant Smith honors the deal.

LIEUTENANT SMITH
(with pride)

Okay, move out!

One by one they leave the SHACK.

DISSOLVE TO:

PRESENT DAY.

INT. THE LIBRARY (The same place where the story began) – DAY

Lucia is crying. She's being consoled by Pepe. Juan is holding a picture of Alicia, and his eyes are glassy and watery. Rosa cracks the door open to the library and peeks inside.

ROSA

Is this a private party?

PEPE

No, Mama, please come in.

Rosa picks up on the mood.

> ROSA

I guess you finally told Lucia the whole
story.

> PEPE

Yes.

> LUCIA

It was time, Grandma.

Pepe is about to break down.

> PEPE

It still hurts like the first day. Sorry.

> ROSA

There's nothing to be sorry about.

You did all you could.

Pepe looks at Lucia. Without a word, we feel the love and affection for each other. Pepe takes Lucia's hand and sits next to her.

> PEPE

Lucy, your mother wanted you to always
be strong and independent like she was.

> LUCIA

But I am, Dad.

Several beats pass.

> PEPE
> She believed in America. Somehow, she
> knew that if you persevere, your dreams
> could come true here!

Lucia wipes the tears from her eyes.

> LUCIA
> I will, Papa, I'll make her proud.

The telephone rings. Rosa picks up the phone and answers it.

> ROSA
> Hello?

Rosa's eyes light up. A beautiful smile is on her face. We can vaguely hear the caller on the other side.

> THE BUTLER
> Should I let him in?

> ROSA
> Of course.

Rosa hangs up the telephone.

> PEPE
> Who was it?

> ROSA
> The butler. We just received a FedEx.

> PEPE
> Okay, enough of this. Let's get back to
> the party.

Within seconds, the doors to the library swing open. In comes Pablo
and Oscar. Their hands loaded with pastelitos and gifts. They set them
down at the desk.

> PABLO
> What's up, chump? Worked in any
> hotels lately?

> OSCAR
> Man, you're getting old. What happened
> to your waistline?

Pepe and Rosa rebound from their sadness. They welcome Pablo and
Oscar with open arms. Lucia and Juan do the same. Lucia starts opening a gift.

> PEPE
> Man, oh man, will you look at these two
> criminals?

Rosa and Pepe teasing Pablo and Oscar. They share a special affection,
a feeling of genuine friendship. As they all sit down, Pablo speaks.

> PABLO
> Well, what do you think?

> PEPE
> About what?

> OSCAR
> Dammit, Pepe, don't you read the
> papers?

> PEPE
>
> I've been so busy lately, I hardly have
> time to watch the news.

> PABLO
>
> Well, check this out.

Pablo unfolds a magazine he's brought with him and throws it on top of the coffee table.

POV OF MAGAZINE COVER.

It's a copy of a magazine. The cover has a picture of Fidel Castro. He looks tired, worn out. The headlines read "FIDEL CASTRO THE END OF AN ERA."

> PEPE
>
> Too little, too late for many people who
> lost their lives.

> PABLO
>
> True, Pepe, but it's not too late for us.

Pepe, Oscar, and Pablo rejoice in a moment of freedom and joy. They burst with pride and cheer.

> PEPE
>
> You've got that right.

THE END

CREDITS ROLL OVER THE VIDEO AND A CUBAN BOLERO.

ON SCREEN BEFORE CREDITS

After more than fifty years in exile, most Cuban Americans still share the same hope and dream that someday they too can return to their homeland, "a free Cuba."

FOOTNOTES

Pepe died of diabetes in 1997.

Pablo supposedly retired from the CIA in 1977. His whereabouts are unknown.

Oscar died of a heart attack in 1980.

Rosa died of cancer in 1995.

ABOUT THE AUTHOR

Jose L. Gonzalez was born in Havana, Cuba on September 15, 1952, the son of a middle-class family. On November 2nd 1960, his direct family immigrated to Miami, Florida. None of the members of the family spoke English, nor did they have any friends or family in the United States at that time.

The first few weeks were very difficult. After bouncing around for more than three months from hotel to hotel where Jose's father would do odd jobs to pay for food and shelter, the family finally settled into a studio apartment where the For Rent sign up front said, "No Negros, No Cubans & No Pets." Imagine that?

Yes, the family suffered many injustices along the way. However, Jose Luis always believed in GOD and had a clear understanding and appreciation for the most wonderful blessing of all, the opportunity to live the American Dream in the USA.

Except for Jose's mom (who always refused to learn to speak English), they all slowly picked up the English language either by going to school or by necessity. It is from this perspective that this book is written, from an immigrant's point of view, starting at the bottom and knowing that the only way they had to go was UP! Thank GOD for this opportunity.

Jose Luis is a graduate of Miami Senior High School where he was inducted into the Miami Senior High Hall of Fame in 2012. Jose also graduated from the University of Miami where he earned his Bachelor's Degree (Major in Accounting) playing college football. From 1975 to 1978, he made a living playing professional football. Finally, in August of 1978, Jose retired from professional football and walked away from the Philadelphia Eagles.

In September of 1978, Jose embarked on his Accounting career with Ernst & Ernst (now EY) and ultimately worked for Deloitte and Grant Thornton for more than a decade. Jose feels truly blessed to have worked for such great public accounting firms where he obtained invaluable experience in Business and Finance.

In 1984, Jose became a Certified Public Accountant and has successfully practiced at the C Level position with several private and public American companies. He was also the executive producer of a couple of feature films (one of which is Shadow Force with Dirk Benedict). Jose also wrote, produced, and directed The Last Semester (aka Beach High), a low budget film in 1999.

Now at the twilight of his life, Jose has embarked on his final endeavor. He has written five different screenplays. His first to be published is Ninety Miles, based on a true story that transpired during the Cuban Revolution and the Cuban Missiles Crisis of October 1962.

Today Jose is amazed at the current transformation that America is currently experiencing. He cannot understand how and why educated professors at high schools, colleges, and universities have become so twisted with evil socialistic ideologies. This is not the first time in history that a successful society transformed itself into a Woke Culture. Every time this transformation has proven to fail on multiple levels throughout world history. Jose asks a simple question. Is this ignorance or stupidity? Is it the result of their own personal failures? Or is it their ill intent, envy, and greed that has cultivated this disgraceful and mindless attitude towards this great country? What is happening today in America is so similar to what transpired in Russia, Cuba, Venezuela, and China, just to mention a few.

There is no question that foreign forces, both religious and political, have been working morning, noon, and night for more than four decades to destroy this great nation from within. But we who inherited this great country from the greatest generation ever must protect and defend it. This Great American Experiment must not perish, and we must all fight to preserve our great culture for future generations.

America is at its most difficult point in its entire history. We are at an inflection point where the American people have been lied to for decades and generations of corrupted politicians and media have damaged the fabric of our nation... Hopefully, America is NOT damaged beyond repair.

The American people must rise and meet this challenge head on if America is to survive.

PHOTO GALLERY

↑
READ
THIS!   Meeting
TO
Raise Money

MISSILE ERECTOR
CABLE
MISSILE SHELTER TENT
TRACKED PRIME MOVERS
OXIDIZER TANK TRAILERS
FUEL TANK TRAILERS

NINETY MILES_INTERVIEW

_NINETY MILES_INTERVIEW

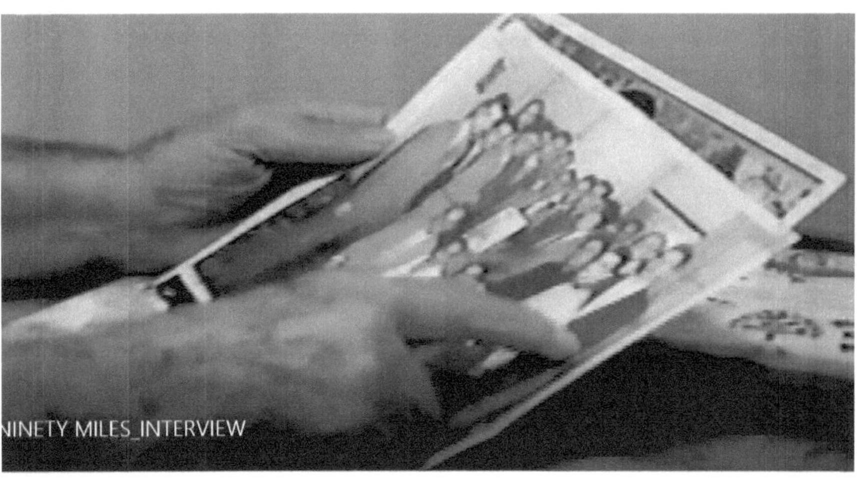
NINETY MILES_INTERVIEW

Marzo 19 de 1956

Estimado Ticayo:

La portadora me comunicó con verdadera esperanza la conversación que tuvo con usted y Pepín en su último viaje a Cuba. Me dijo que usted, según lo expresó, podía hacer mucho en el aspecto económico y que estaba dispuesto a hacer algún esfuerzo en ese sentido. No sabe usted cuan angustiosamente necesitamos ese esfuerzo suyo y lo vehementemente que se lo ruego, en la seguridad de que no será un esfuerzo inútil. Le doy las gracias a usted y a Pepín por el apoyo que que hicieron llegar a la Tesorería de nuestro Movimiento. Con las más firmes esperanzas en su gestión le envía un fuerte abrazo su amigo

Fidel

90 Millas 2.0

Los culpables del comunismo en las Americas

Jose L. Gonzalez

EXTERIOR (EXT.) DÍA

Una playa desierta, agua azul cristalina y arena más pura que el azúcar llenan el encuadre.

OLA TRAS OLA SE PRECIPITAN HACIA UNA PLAYA

CRÉDITOS comienzan.

MUSICA: SE INTRODUCE UN BOLERO CUBANO.

LA CÁMARA SE INCLINA HACIA ARRIBA Y VUELVE A UN GRAN ANGULAR DE LA COSTA

DISOLVER A: Un primer plano:

Trozos de una balsa flotan sin rumbo en el agua.

CORTE A:

VIDEO DE BALSEROS SUBIENDO A BORDO DE UN BARCO GUARDACOSTAS

Angulo más cerrado del personal del guardacosta mientras recogen a los muertos flotando cerca del barco.

Narración del comentarista en la televisión.

COMENTARISTA
Aproximadamente a las 5:00 AM de esta
mañana un guarda costa encontró los
restos de una balsa a la deriva cerca de la
milla 4 cerca de Cayo Hueso. 13 cubanos fueron recogidos hoy frente a la isla
de Dry Tortugas. Lamentablemente 2 de
los balseros al parecer mujeres jóvenes,
no lograron sobrevivir.

MÚSICA/El bolero y la imagen se disuelven a un cuadro negro y se DESVANECE en "MIAMI ACTUAL"

CORTE SE INTRODUCE MÚSICA DE SALSA:

CORTE A UN MONTAJE DE LA CIUDAD DE MIAMI, FLORIDA:

Una hermosa toma aérea de la ciudad de Miami. El cielo está despejado y el sol brilla en una cálida tarde de verano. Varias tomas de la ciudad reflejan el ritmo y el estilo de vida del sur de la Florida. La gente está de compras en Bayside con altísimos y modernos rascacielos al fondo... el horizonte sólo se ve acosado por gente guapa por todas partes. Dos mujeres seductoramente vestidas pasan y le sonríen a un joven apuesto. El joven les devuelve la sonrisa.

EXT. DÍA BAYSIDE ENTRADA PRINCIPAL

El valet se acerca en un Ferrari descapotable rojo fuego, "el carro más sexy que jamás hayas visto". El joven se sube y sale a toda velocidad.

EXT. DÍA EN UN REPARTO EXCLUSIVO CORAL GABLES FRENTE A UNA MAJESTUOSA RESIDENCIA

El mismo joven conduce y se abren las puertas de seguridad. El entra.

EXT. DÍA PUERTAS DE ENTRADA

Un sirviente le abre la puerta del carro al joven, que salta y se apresura a entrar en la casa.

FIN de CRÉDITOS

LA MÚSICA SE DESVANECE

INTERIOR (INT.). VESTIBULO DE DÍA

El joven entra . . . Se celebra una fiesta (Una Quinceañera)

Un hombre de mediana edad lo recibe en la puerta.

> PEPE
> ¿Qué paso mijo? ¿Por qué llegas tarde?
>
> (¿Qué ha pasado?)

> JUAN
> Nada PEPE... el tiempo se me fue volando.

> PEPE
> ¡Creo que estás en candela!

> JUAN
> Lo sé... Lo sé.

El joven sube corriendo las escaleras. . .

UN MONTAJE DE LA FIESTA

INT. BIBLIOTECA DE DÍA

Pepe está sentado en su silla fumando un puro cubano y bebiendo un whisky. Se está tomado un descanso y se ha marchado de la fiesta. En su regazo hay un viejo álbum de fotos. Lo abre y empieza a recordar. En la tercera página se detiene y se concentra en una foto 8x10.

SU PUNTO DE VISTA

Una foto de una hermosa y sofisticada joven posando para el fotógrafo.

VOLVER A PEPE

Está angustiado. Cuanto más se concentra en la imagen, más se acerca a las lágrimas.

> PEPE
> (Pensando)
>
> Daría mi mano derecha sólo para abraz-
> arte una vez más...

De repente, las puertas dobles de la biblioteca se abren y entra corriendo una hermosa joven. Es despampanante y asombrosamente parecida a la joven de la fotografía.

> LUCIA
> Papá... ¿Qué haces aquí?
>
> Te he estado buscando por todas partes.

Se acerca a él y se sienta en el reposabrazos de su silla.

PEPE
Sólo necesitaba un descanso.

Ella capta su estado de ánimo.

LUCIA
¿Qué estás mirando?

PEPE
Unas fotos antiguas.

LUCIA
Déjame ver.

Le entrega el álbum. Lucía ve la foto que está adorando.

LUCIA
¿Extrañas a mamá?

PEPE
Muchísimo.

Lucía no puede apartar los ojos de la foto.

LUCIA
Era tan hermosa.

PEPE
¡Igual que tú!

LUCIA
¿Qué edad tenía cuando. . .

Pepe interrumpe

PEPE

Demasiado joven.

Le quita el álbum a Lucía y lo guarda en una gaveta del escritorio.

Juan interrumpe. Juan de humor juguetón.

JUAN

¿Dónde está la festejada?

O debería decir solterona...

LUCIA

Gracioso... ¡Muy gracioso!

Juan, no tan perspicaz como Lucía, sigue bromeando.

JUAN

¿Por qué? ¿No te has enterado?

Brad Pitt está afuera buscándote.

LUCIA

Un comediante, qué original.

Por fin Juan se da cuenta.

JUAN

¿Qué pasa? ¿Por qué esas caras tristes?

Pepe mira a Juan... y luego a Lucía. Les tiende un abrazo a los dos.

Se abrazan. El calor y el amor mutuo llenan el momento.

PEPE

Siento haberte apartado de la fiesta.

Anímate y diviértete.

LUCIA

¿Perdón de Que? Ya es hora de confesar...

Lucía está decidida a conocer por fin toda la historia de cómo murió su madre.

LUCIA

Prometiste que cuando cumpliera 15 años me contarías todo.

PEPE

Y lo haré justo después de la fiesta.

LUCIA

¿La Fiesta? Dame un respiro...

PEPE

¿Y nuestros invitados?

LUCIA

Pueden esperar.

Un momento difícil para PEPE.

JUAN

Creo que ya es hora.

Juan coge una silla y se sienta junto a Pepe y Lucía. Lucía se sienta en el butacón frente a él. Se hace un silencio conmovedor. Pepe lucha contra las lágrimas.

PEPE

Tu madre era tan hermosa.

JUAN

¿Cómo murió?

PEPE

No debería haber ocurrido nunca.

Todo fue culpa mía.

Lucía coge la mano de Pepe y se la acaricia como diciendo: "No, no fue culpa tuya".

Pepe respira profundo, cruza el escritorio, abre una gaveta y saca varias fotos antiguas de un álbum. Mientras señala a una de las fotos

PEPE

Ella era mi razón de vivir.

CORTE A SU PERSPECTIVA DE LA FOTO

Alicia, la madre de Lucía, está con Pepe detrás de Fidel Castro y otros miembros del Partido Revolucionario Cubano.

NARRACION DE PEPE (CONTANDO LA HISTORIA)

Todo empezó en New Jersey, en Union City, alrededor de el año 1957. Tu madre y yo no estábamos casados, pero habíamos hablado de eso en varias ocasiones. Aquí (señalando una de las fotos) estábamos almorzando con Castro y varios miembros del Partido Revolucionario Cubano.

LA CÁMARA ENFOCADA EN LA FOTOGRAFÍA RETROCEDE EN EL TIEMPO

TODOS LOS QUE APARECEN EN LA FOTOGRAFÍA COBRAN VIDA

Un Fidel Castro muy joven está sentado en la cabecera de la mesa con varios colegas. Pepe está de pie justo detrás de Fidel con Alicia. El grupo habla y sigue adelante.

NARRACION DE PEPE
El hombre sentado a la derecha de Fidel era tu abuelo José Martínez. Roberto Martínez el hermano menor de tu abuelo, mi tío, era el que hacía la señal de la victoria. Y tu tío abuelo Luis, que murió cuando aún estaba en Cuba, es el hombre sentado a la izquierda de Fidel.

Mientras Fidel y el grupo de colegas se preparan para otra fotografía, Fidel detiene el proceso de toma de fotografías y cambia su plato por el plato de Ramón.

FIDEL
No quiero que la gente vea esta foto y
piense que soy un cerdo comiendo.

Flash, la cámara se dispara. El grupo reanuda la comida y Fidel recupera su plato. Alicia vuelve a la cocina.

CASTRO Y SUS COLEGAS IMPROVISAN DURANTE EL COMENTARIO DE PEPE

NARRACION DE PEPE
Era 1956 cuando empezamos a organizar la revolución cubana. A tu madre le encantaba la política. Siempre participaba en muchas actividades. Un grupo de nosotros se reunió en un hotel con Fidel para discutir la estrategia y la recaudación de fondos.

CONTINUACION NARRACION DE PEPE
Como saben, nuestro objetivo era noble... queríamos derrocar la dictadura de Batista. Era un criminal despiadado, corrupto y ladrón. Teníamos muchos seguidores gracias a tu madre. Ese año recibimos contribuciones de varias empresas estadounidenses, ciudadanos estadounidenses y muchas familias cubanas adineradas.

ENFOQUE A TONY ALVAREZ

NARRACION DE PEPE
Por ejemplo, Tony Álvarez, un ingeniero cuya familia poseía doce ingenios azucareros independientes al oeste de La Habana.

ENFOQUE A ERNESTO CARBONEL

NARRACION DE PEPE
Otro querido amigo, Ernesto Carbonell, propietario de la empresa de transporte de mercancías de La Habana.

ENFOQUE A RUBEN Y ENRIQUE GARCIA

NARRACION DE PEPE
Y sí, cómo olvidar a Rubén y Enrique García. Los propietarios de la siembra más grande de tabaco de Cuba.

ENFOQUE en RAMON MOREJON

NARRACION DE PEPE CONTINUACIÓN
En 1957 ya habíamos almacenado armas, municiones y otros suministros necesarios para la guerra contra Batista. Ramón Morejón, recién graduado en Ciencias Políticas de la Universidad de La Habana, era el encargado de llevar la cuenta de todos los progresos.

CERCA DE FIDEL CASTRO

NARRACION DE PEPE CONTINUACIÓN
(algo sarcástico)

Y por último, pero no por ello menos importante, nuestro intrépido líder Fidel Castro, también conocido como bola de churre, que nació en Biran, Cuba, el 13 de Agosto de 1926.

EL VÍDEO DE PEPE SE DESVANECE MIENTRAS LA CONVERSACIÓN EN LA MESA DEL COMEDOR REGRESA.

INT. DÍA LA CÁMARA RETROCEDE AL COMEDOR

El grupo se ríe de un chiste interpretado por PEPE.

JOSE
Señores, no quiero aguar la fiesta pero creo que la reunión debe comenzar. Enrique, Danos el informe de Tesorería.

FIDEL
Buena idea.

Silencio por favor...

ENFOQUE EN ENRIQUE CUANDO SE DIRIGE A ERNESTO

ENRIQUE
¿Trajiste los libros contables?

ERNESTO
Si, están en mi maletín.

Rubén coge su maletín y se lo da a Enrique.

LA CÁMARA ENFOCA UN MALETÍN DE CUERO EN EL QUE SE APRECIAN LAS INICIALES DE ERNESTO CARBONEL (EC).

ENFOQUE EN ENRIQUE Y ERNESTO

Enrique coloca el maletín encima de la mesa del comedor, lo abre y saca los documentos necesarios para su informe. Se aclara la garganta.

> ENRIQUE
> Muchas gracias por su atención.
>
> Les informo que a partir de Agosto 30, tenemos en depósitos exactamente $ 75,155.67 DOLARES.

El grupo lo celebra. Fidel da una calada a su puro cubano.

> ENRIQUE
> La semana pasada recibimos una grandísima donación de una compañía petrolera Norte Americana en Cienfuegos.

> FIDEL
> Menos mal que los gringos sirven para algo.

Fidel vuelve a encender su puro cubano.

> ROBERTO
> Al paso que vamos, la victoria será nuestra.

ENFOQUE EN FIDEL CASTRO

FIDEL

Me gusta que pienses así Roberto, pero
cuidado en quien confías.

ENFOQUE EN ROBERTO

ROBERTO

Solamente confío en nosotros.

VOLVER A FIDEL

FIDEL

Bien, muy bien...

Todos han terminado de comer. Pepe es el primero en recoger su plato
y dirigirse a la cocina. José le sigue de cerca.

INT. COCINA DE DÍA

Rosa está de pie delante del fregadero de la cocina enjuagando los
platos y vasos sucios. Alicia, joven y guapa, los seca mientras Rosa
se los entrega. Pepe descarga sus platos en el fregadero. José hace lo
mismo.

ROSA

¿Están listos para el postre?

PEPE

Creo que sí.

José saca un puro de su caja y lo enciende.

JOSE

La verdad es que la comida estuvo fabulosa.

José se acerca a Rosa y le da un beso en la mejilla. Rosa le devuelve el beso.

Pepe agarra suavemente a Alicia por la cintura. Ella le devuelve la mirada.

>ROSA
>
>Me alegro de que todos disfrutaran la comida.

>PEPE
>
>Los frijoles negros y el arroz estaban buenísimos.
>
>Jose riéndose de Pepe.

>JOSE
>
>Creo que te encanta la cocina de tu madre.
>
>Alicia viene al rescate.

>ALICIA
>
>Creo que a todo el mundo le encanta la cocina de Rosa.
>
>¿No dirías José?

La respuesta de José es con lenguaje corporal.

>ROSA
>
>En esta familia todos tienen buen apetito.

Roberto entra en la cocina

ROBERTO
¿Tienes otro de esos puros que le diste a
Fidel?

JOSE
Claro, aquí tienes.

José abre un armario de la cocina, saca una caja de puros, la abre y le
ofrece un puro a su hermano. Roberto se sirve varios puros. José se
acerca a la puerta del comedor y se asoma por la rendija para com-
probar que nadie más entra en la cocina. El grupo de la cocina siente
curiosidad por las acciones de José. José se vuelve hacia el grupo y dice
con cautela

JOSE
Escúchame rápido.

Hay que tener mucho cuidado y vigilar
lo que se dice.

Durante estas reuniones... Especialmente
cuando Fidel está presente.

ROBERTO
¿Por qué?

JOSE
Debemos ser prudentes.

No confío en todos los presentes.

ROBERTO
Si te refieres a Fidel, te equivocas, es un
amigo sincero y digno de confianza.

JOSE

Roberto, Mi experiencia me dice que incluso los amigos se vuelven unos contra otros.

ROBERTO

¿Estás paranoico o simplemente loco?

JOSE

No, estoy siendo prudente.

Me lo advirtió la semana pasada un viejo compañero militar.

Mi amigo descubrió que se celebran reuniones a las que ninguno de nosotros somos invitado. ¿Por qué?

Roberto está enfadado. Luis entra en la cocina. Cuando Roberto sale de la cocina, se vuelve hacia Luis.

ROBERTO

Tu padre ha perdido el contacto con la realidad.

No sé qué le pasa.

Roberto sale apurado disgustado y molesto con José.

LUIS

¿Qué pasa, papá?

JOSE

Nada hijo, nada.

Hablaremos más tarde.

Rosa reconoce que es necesario cambiar de tema.

ROSA

Todo el mundo... fuera de la cocina.

Ahora... ¡Vamos!

El postre está casi listo. Saldrá enseguida.

CÁMARA PANEA A ALICIA Y PEPE

Alicia abre el horno y saca un plato hondo de arroz con leche. El olor rompe la tensión en la cocina.

PEPE

MMM Huele delicioso!

Pepe prepara la encimera donde Alicia coloca el plato caliente. José y Roberto salen de la cocina.

ENFOQUE EN PEPE Y ALICIA

PEPE

¿Cuándo vuelves a La Habana?

ALICIA

Me voy el sábado por la mañana.

PEPE

Bien, entonces cenemos mañana.

ALICIA

¿Me recoges a las ocho?

PEPE

¡Claro que sí!

Pepe le da un beso en la mejilla a Alicia y sale de la cocina.

INT. SALA DE DÍA

El grupo se ha trasladado del comedor a la sala.

PEPE lentamente regresa a la sala.

> ENRIQUE
> Anticipamos que para finales de mes, tendremos más de $ 100,000. DOLARES.

> FIDEL
> No está mal.

> (silencio)

> Antes de que se me olvide, Quiero que Ernesto y Ruben vuelvan a Cuba la próxima semana.

> ERNESTO
> ¿Por qué, qué pasa?

> FIDEL
> Necesito que recojas unos documentos de nuestros amigos jugadores en La Habana.

> JOSE
> ¿Qué documentos? ¿Te refieres al soborno de la mafia ¿no?

> FIDEL
> Así es.

> JOSE

Fidel, esto podría ser un problema para nosotros por qué . . . .

Fidel interrumpe.

> FIDEL

No me importa de quién sea el dinero. "Dinero es dinero".

Lo necesitamos para la revolución.

> JOSE

Si aceptamos dinero de la mafia no seremos diferente a Batista.

Fidel se levanta. Está furioso. Mira directamente a José.

> FIDEL

Dejemos algo perfectamente claro aquí y ahora.

Nadie, pero nadie, tiene derecho a cuestionar mi juicio.

Se detiene antes de explotar.

> FIDEL

Por favor, no me malinterpreten.

No olvidemos nunca por qué estamos todos aquí.

> (una pausa)

Debemos permanecer unidos.

Un silencio inquietante llena la habitación.

FIDEL

¿Entienden?

Fidel se vira hacia Rubén y Ernesto.

FIDEL

Necesito su cooperación y apoyo.

¿Lo tengo?

RUBEN

Sí.

ERNESTO

Saldremos para La Habana mañana.

EXT. DÍA LA CIUDAD DE LA HABANA

Las calles del centro de La Habana lucen prósperas. Carros, camiones y autobuses circulan en todas direcciones. Los "billeteros" venden billetes de lotería en cada esquina. Las calles están abarrotadas de gente.

Un Ford Fairlane de 1956 se detiene en un semáforo en rojo. Cuando la cámara se acerca al conductor, vemos a Ernesto en el asiento del conductor.

Ernesto fuma nerviosamente. El semáforo se pone en verde.

LA CÁMARA SIGUE AL CARRO CUANDO GIRA A LA DERECHA EN LA ESQUINA

El carro se detiene. Ernesto sale del carro con su maletín de cuero. Alimenta el parquímetro y mira a su alrededor orientándose por la numeración de los edificios. Sube los escalones de un edificio y se dirige directamente a su puerta principal.

Ernesto llama a la puerta con un inusual golpe secuencial. La mirilla de la puerta se abre. Detrás de la puerta se ve el ojo de una persona. Pasan unos segundos. Una anciana desbloquea la puerta y la abre desde adentro. Entra en el vestíbulo, oscuro y húmedo. La anciana cierra la puerta tras él. Rubén entra en el vestíbulo desde una habitación contigua. Se saludan.

INT. DÍA CAMINANDO POR EL PASILLO

> RUBEN
> Me alegra ver que lo has conseguido.

> ERNESTO
> Fue fácil... quizás demasiado fácil.

> RUBEN
> No te preocupes, Fidel lo tiene todo
> bajo control.

> ERNESTO
> Sí, pero tratar con la mafia me da
> escalofríos.

> RUBEN
> Vamos, acabemos con esto.

INT. OFICINA DE DÍA

Rubén conduce a Ernesto por el pasillo hasta un despacho. Ernesto cierra la puerta tras de sí y deja a la anciana fuera. Ernesto deja el maletín encima de una mesa de conferencias. Rubén saca las llaves de una caja fuerte situada justo detrás del escritorio.

>   RUBEN
> Veamos lo que esos mafiosos piensan de
> Fidel.

Ernesto abre el maletín.

>   ERNESTO
> ¡Mierda!

>   RUBEN
> ¡Coño!

Se les ilumina la cara.

EL PUNTO DE VISTA DE ERNESTO Y RUBEN

El maletín está lleno de dinero (billetes de cien dólares). Se quedan sin habla.

>   RUBEN
> Supongo que Fidel tenía razón.

>   ERNESTO
> ¡Batista es historia!

Rubén cierra el maletín.

>   RUBEN
> Ok, ¿tienes las instrucciones de Fidel?

Sacando dos sobres de su bolsillo.

ERNESTO

Aquí están.

Abren los sobres, leen las instrucciones y, con un mechero, encienden ambos juegos de instrucciones. Mientras las instrucciones arden.

ERNESTO

Debo irme inmediatamente.

RUBEN

Tengo varias cosas que hacer antes de poder volver a New Jersey.

ERNESTO

Ten cuidado, no te arriesgues.

Si no tienes noticias mías antes de las nueve de esta noche, te tienes que ir sin mí.

(una pausa)

Hasta luego.

Ernesto cierra el maletín, coge las llaves de Rubén y sale. Rubén le acompaña hasta la puerta principal. La anciana espera en una silla junto a la puerta.

EXT. DÍA FRENTE DEL EDIFICIO

Ernesto sale rápidamente del edificio y se dirige al carro con su maletín. Abre la puerta del carro, deja el maletín en el asiento del pasajero atrás y sube.

PUNTO DE VISTA DE RUBEN A TRAVÉS DE LA MIRILLA.

Ernesto arranca el carro y se va. Rubén cierra la mirilla.

EXT. DÍA FRENTE DEL EDIFICIO DOS CARROS DETRÁS DEL VEHÍCULO DE ERNESTO

Un carro sin matrícula con tres hombres en su interior observa cómo se aleja Ernesto. Arrancan el carro y empiezan a seguir a Ernesto.

EXT. DIA CALLES DEL CENTRO DE LA HABANA

El tráfico está congestionado y el carro de Ernesto está atascado en un tranque de automóviles. Varios carros tocan sus fotutos para que el tráfico circule más deprisa. Ernesto no se ha dado cuenta de que lo siguen. El carro sin matrícula se detiene justo detrás del carro de Ernesto.

EXT. DÍA EN EL INTERIOR DEL CARRO DE ERNESTO

Está incómodo e inquieto. Le molesta algo sin saber qué.

EXT. DÍA EN EL CARRO QUE SIGUE A ERNESTO

Los tres hombres observan todos los movimientos de Ernesto. Uno de los tres hombres sale del carro y se dirige hacia Ernesto por el lado del pasajero.

EN LA PARTE TRASERA DEL CARRO DE ERNESTO

El tráfico en el carril contiguo al de Ernesto se relaja temporalmente. El carro con los otros dos hombres se detiene junto a Ernesto. Están tan cerca del carro de Ernesto que ningún ser humano puede caminar entre los carros. Ernesto se da cuenta de lo cerca que están. Tiene contacto visual con los dos hombres. Un escalofrío recorre sobre la espalda de Ernesto. Presiente que algo va muy mal, Ernesto busca su revólver debajo del asiento del carro. El tráfico sigue sin moverse en ninguno de los dos carriles. Ernesto empieza a sudar. Su frente lo demuestra. Ernesto sostiene su revólver de calibre 38 sobre su regazo. El conductor adyacente a Ernesto abre su puerta y a propósito golpea el carro de Ernesto, abollando y rayando ambos vehículos. El hombre empieza a gritar obscenidades a Ernesto. Ernesto para su carro y carga el gatillo de su arma. De repente, suenan varios disparos. Desde muy cerca, el hombre a pie ha disparado a Ernesto a través de la ventanilla del carro. La sangre salpica el interior del carro. Ernesto cae hacia delante contra el claxon del carro. El asesino termina de romper la ventanilla del carro, mete la mano y se roba el maletín de Ernesto. Con el claxon sonando, el tráfico se detiene. El hombre del maletín regresa a toda prisa a su carro y sube. Con el chirrido de los neumáticos, se ponen delante del tráfico y dan media vuelta, derribando un puesto de fruta y casi atropellando a varios peatones. El carro arranca en dirección contraria.

VUELTA A LA FACHADA DEL EDIFICIO DONDE RUBEN SE ENCONTRO CON ERNESTO

El carro con los tres hombres se detiene.

INT. DÍA OFICINA TRASERA

Rubén está sentado en el escritorio dando instrucciones a la anciana. Alguien llama a la puerta principal con el mismo golpe que Ernesto había dado antes.

RUBEN

¿Qué demonios?

Rubén, desconfiado por la llamada a la puerta principal, busca en la gaveta de su escritorio y saca una pistola de calibre 45.

INT. PASILLO Y VESTÍBULO

Rubén sale de la oficina y camina por el pasillo con la anciana siguiéndole de cerca. Rubén abre la mirilla. Ve a un hombre que no reconoce apuntándole directamente a la cabeza con una pistola. Rubén se asusta y cierra la mirilla. Cuando se da la vuelta, la anciana le clava un gran cuchillo de carnicero en el estómago. La anciana sonríe cínicamente mientras se lo clava aún más profundo.

> ANCIANA
>
> ¡Por hijo Puta!
>
> Maricón....

Rubén suelta la 45 y cae de rodillas. La anciana abre la puerta.

Los hombres que siguieron y mataron a Ernesto están en la puerta. Ella les invita a pasar.

> EL ASESINO
>
> Buen trabajo, abuelita.

ENFOQUE A RUBÉN

Rubén sigue vivo. Sangra profusamente mientras intenta contener sus tripas.

DE NUEVO EN EL VESTÍBULO CON LA ANCIANA

La anciana entrega su trofeo a los tres hombres.

ANCIANA
Aquí lo tienes. Es todo tuyo.

El asesino levanta la pistola apuntando a la cabeza de Rubén. Está a punto de apretar el gatillo cuando vuelve a apuntar a la anciana.

EL ASESINO
¡Por traidora!

El asesino dispara dos veces a la anciana. Cae muerta al suelo. El asesino apunta ahora a Rubén.

EL ASESINO
¡Come mierda!

¡Ahora es tu turno Maricón!

¡BLAMM! ¡BLAMM! ERNESTO Y RUBEN SON HISTORIA

INT. NOCHE HABITACIÓN DE HOTEL EN NUEVA YORK

Fidel Castro con una vista de Manhattan a sus espaldas está sentado

fumando un puro y bebiendo un coñac. Suena el teléfono.

Fidel responde.

FIDEL
¿Hola?

NARRACION LA VOZ DE UN HOMBRE

UN HOMBRE
Picadillo.

FIDEL

¿Con huevos o con arroz?

UN HOMBRE

Con los dos.

FIDEL

¡Muy bien!

Fidel cuelga el teléfono y da una calada a su puro.

CORTE A INT. NOCHE EMBAJADA SOVIÉTICA, CUBA, LA HABANA.

Una mano cuelga el teléfono. La cámara se desplaza hacia arriba para mostrar al Che Guevara junto a dos diplomáticos soviéticos.

CHE GUEVARA

Todo va por buen camino.

(una pausa)

Hablemos del envío de armas.

Corte de sonido:

Una batalla en proceso.

DISOLVER A

ESCENAS DE CASTRO EN LA SIERRA MAESTRA LUCHANDO CONTRA SOLDADOS DE BATISTA

DISOLVER A

EN PANTALLA " Enero 1ro, 1959 "

Fidel Castro encima de un tanque Sherman mientras llega triunfante a la ciudad de La Habana. La celebración está en pleno apogeo y miles de cubanos bailan, ondean la bandera cubana y besan a los soldados que llegan con Fidel.

CERCA DE FIDEL Y VARIOS MIEMBROS DEL EJERCITO LIBERTADOR

Fidel lleva un gran crucifijo

SOLDADO
¿Desde cuándo llevas un crucifijo?

FIDEL
Sólo tenemos una oportunidad para la primera impresión... Así que debemos tener mucho cuidado cómo nos presentamos.

Es un pueblo muy religioso.

Fidel saluda a la multitud.

CORTE A IMÁGENES DE LA HUIDA DE BATISTA DE CUBA.

Cuando la cámara retrocede, nos damos cuenta de que estas imágenes se están viendo por televisión en la casa de José y Pepe en Union City, New Jersey el mismo salón donde se celebraron las reuniones para organizar la revolución. Sentados alrededor del televisor están Pepe, Alicia, José, Luis, Roberto, Tony, Ramón y Enrique. Mientras el grupo ve el noticiero...

PEPE

Creo que hemos cometido un gran error.

ROBERTO

Dale una oportunidad a Fidel.

JOSE

Una oportunidad, ¿una oportunidad de hacer qué?

¿Quieres que nos mate de la misma manera que mató a Ernesto y a Rubén?

Roberto disgustado.

ROBERTO

¡Mentira y lo sabes!

No tenemos pruebas de que Fidel lo hiciera.

¡Fueron hombres de Batistas!

Muy sarcástico.

JOSE

Entonces explica por qué Castro nunca intentó cazar a los bastardos que mataron a nuestros colegas y robaron el dinero. Explícamelo .... una pausa, Al fin y al cabo, "dinero es dinero".

LUIS

Mira, todos tenemos nuestras dudas y con razón, pero la realidad es que Fidel Castro es nuestro nuevo líder.

¿Qué demonios quieres hacer? ¿Matar al bastardo?

Enrique salta.

ENRIQUE

Creo que Fidel es sucio como el pecado y No confío en ese hijo de puta.

Pienso averiguar quién mató a Ernesto y a Rubén.

TONY

Caballeros, por favor, cálmense.

No olviden que somos responsables de lo que ha pasado.

(una pausa)

Vamos a esperar 6 meses a ver qué pasa.

CORTE A: INT. DÍA PALACIO PRESIDENCIAL EN LA HABANA, CUBA

Los soldados de Castro están limpiando el palacio, deshaciéndose de personas y cosas.

DESVANECE A NEGRO

EN PANTALLA " SEIS MESES DESPUÉS "

EXT. DIA EN LA FABRICA DE TABACOS

INT. DÍA OFICINA DE ENRIQUE EN LA FÁBRICA DE TABACOS

Enrique está en su escritorio. Una foto de él con su compañero fallecido "Rubén", juntos sentados en sus oficinas. Enrique mira la foto recordando. Suena el teléfono.

ENRIQUE

¿Hola?

RAMÓN

¡Soy yo!

ENRIQUE

¿Qué pasa?

RAMÓN

¡Ya lo tengo!

ENRIQUE

¿Qué tienes?

RAMÓN

Tengo pruebas de que la policía secreta
de Castro es responsable del asesinato de
Ernesto y Rubén.

ENRIQUE

No digas ni una palabra más.

No confío en estos teléfonos.

(una pausa)

Nos vemos en El Encanto para almorzar.

ENRIQUE

No puedo. Tengo una reunión con otros productores de tabaco en el Palacio Presidencial en unos minutos.

(una pausa)

Te veré para cenar esta noche a las 9:00 PM en el Tropicana.

RAMÓN

Esta bien, pero ten cuidado.

He oído rumores de que podríamos ser los próximos.

ENRIQUE

¡Nos vemos esta noche!

Enrique cuelga el teléfono, coge su abrigo y sale del despacho.

EXT. DÍA TOMA DE ESTABLECIMIENTO DEL PALACIO PRESIDENCIAL

INT. DÍA EL PALACIO PRESIDENCIAL

Enrique camina por el pasillo en camino a su reunión. Justo afuera de la sala de reuniones, se le acerca un guardia de seguridad.

GUARDIA DE SEGURIDAD

¿Sr. García?

ENRIQUE

Sí.

GUARDIA DE SEGURIDAD
Fidel Castro me ha pedido que le escolte
a su oficina inmediatamente.

ENRIQUE
¿Para qué?

GUARDIA DE SEGURIDAD
No lo sé. Sólo obedezco órdenes, señor.

Enrique es conducido al despacho de Fidel. Cuando se acercan a las puertas dobles del despacho privado de Fidel, el Che Guevara con su guardaespaldas personal sale del despacho de Castro. Enrique se da cuenta de que "El Che" lleva el maletín de Ernesto.

VISTA DEL MALETÍN

Es idéntico. El maletín tiene las iniciales EC de Ernesto.

VUELTA A ENRIQUE A CÁMARA LENTA

Enrique reconoce el maletín. Las iniciales le hacen una profunda herida en el alma. Indignado, Enrique ataca al Che y lo inmoviliza contra la pared. En una fracción de segundo, tanto la escolta de Enrique como los guardaespaldas de "El Che" lo sujetan. Castro oye la conmoción fuera de su despacho y sale a toda prisa. El Che Guevara saca su pistola y está a punto de volarle los sesos a Enrique cuando Castro interviene.

FIDEL
¿Qué demonios está pasando aquí?

CHE GUEVARA
Este imbécil se volvió loco.

Voy a matar a este hijo de puta.

FIDEL
¡Aguanta! ¡Un momento!

(una pausa)

Coño... Enrique, ¿cuál es tu problema?

¿Qué te pasa?

Enrique echando espuma por la boca.

ENRIQUE
A la mierda contigo y el Che.

Tu mataste a Ernesto.

FIDEL
¿De qué estás hablando?

Enrique señala el maletín y lucha por liberarse.

ENRIQUE
¡Ese es el maletín de Ernesto!

Fidel se da cuenta que Enrique lo ha descubierto. Hace una señal a los guardaespaldas para que lleven a Enrique a su oficina.

Los guardaespaldas arrastran a Enrique hasta el despacho de Fidel. Las puertas se cierran.

INT. DÍA DESPACHO DE FIDEL

Fidel sin dudarlo a sangre fría.

FIDEL
Mata a este hijo de puta.

ENRIQUE

¡Bastardo cobarde!

¡Pagarás por esto!

Tú…

¡BLAMM! ¡BLAMM! ¡BLAMM!

El Che enfunda su pistola.

CHE GUEVARA

Deberíamos eliminar el resto de tus amigos lo antes posible.

FIDEL

No tan rápido… Tenemos que ser cuidadoso cómo nos deshacemos de ellos.

No podemos permitirnos más errores.

(una pausa)

Tira su cuerpo sobre las líneas de ferrocarril.

CHE GUEVARA

¿Por qué allí?

FIDEL

Sólo haz lo que te digo…

El guardaespaldas y el escolta recogen el cuerpo de Enrique y se lo llevan.

EXT. DÍA PLANO GENERAL DE LA CASA DE JOSE

INT. DÍA CASA DE JOSE EN LA HABANA, CUBA

Encima de la mesita del salón hay un periódico.

LA CÁMARA SE ACERCA A LOS TITULARES

"Asesinan a tiros al presidente de la empresa Tabacos Cubanos".

La cámara retrocede para mostrar a José, Pepe, Roberto, Tony, Ramón y Luis. Sentados alrededor de la mesa dé la sala.

PEPE
Primero Ernesto y Rubén.

Ahora Enrique.

¿Cuál de nosotros es el siguiente?

LUIS
Paciencia, paciencia. Hay todavía muchos anticastristas tratando de debilitar la revolución.

JOSE
¿Estás ciego? ¿O simplemente eres estúpido?

Batista no tuvo nada que ver con esto.

ROBERTO
Estoy de acuerdo... ¿Qué motivo tendría Batista?

Está viviendo en lujo con todo lo que robó.

LUIS

¿Desde cuándo Batista necesita un motivo para matar a alguien?

JOSE

Déjense de tonterías. ¿Quieren? Ustedes no quieren creer en este artículo ¿verdad?

José se levanta y empieza a pasearse por la habitación.

JOSE

Hay dos cosas claras.

Uno, Enrique, Ernesto y Ramón fueron asesinados por el mismo elemento que nos ha eliminado de la revolución.

Dos, Fidel lo ha cambiado todo. Tenemos que averiguar quien está apoyando todos sus movimientos.

PEPE

Me informaron que el proyecto de la Refinería Shell a sido cancelado.

TONY

He oído que varias empresas norte americanas han visto sus bienes confiscados.

PEPE

Bueno, si no son los estadounidenses o nosotros, entonces ¿quién está apoyando a este animal?

RAMÓN

Lo que realmente me preocupa es lo que está pasando en el gobierno. Están prohibiendo a todos los profesionales salir del país.

TONY

¿Estás seguro?

JOSE

Sí, es cierto. Varios amigos han tenido que falsificar sus pasaportes para poder salir.

PEPE

Tenemos que hacer algo.

LUIS

¿Y si Castro se entera?

PEPE

Entonces tomamos otras medidas.

LUIS

Seguro que no estás pensando en ...

Interrupción

ROBERTO

Caballeros, creo que estamos exagerando. Tal vez Fidel intenta estabilizar las cosas y controlar el gobierno.

JOSE
¡Estabilizar nada! No se estabiliza un país nacionalizando los bancos, la industria petrolera y quién sabe…qué más. ¿Y reunirse con él? (una pausa) Ernesto se reunió con Fidel y mira lo que le pasó.

La discusión se acalora y los ánimos se caldean. Discretamente Pepe intenta cambiar de tema.

PEPE
Cálmate… ¿Quizás deberíamos tomarnos un tiempo libre?

TONY
Sí, Varadero es bonito en esta época del año.

Tenemos que alejarnos de La Habana.

Tanto Luis como José siguen peleando como locos.

PEPE
Buena idea. Tómense un tiempo libre.

Papá y yo arreglaremos las cosas con Fidel.

José mira a Pepe y lee entre líneas.

DESVANECE A NEGRO

EN LA PANTALLA "1960"

DESVANECE A:

EXT. NOCHE CASA DE ALICIA EN LA HABANA

Pepe y Alicia llegan de una cena. Se detienen en la puerta principal.

ALICIA

¿Quieres una taza de café?

PEPE

Sí, claro.

Alicia abre la puerta y entran en la casa.

INT. NOCHE SALA DE ALICIA

ALICIA

Ponte cómodo.

Lo tendré listo en un minuto.

Alicia se dirige a la cocina, pero ellos siguen hablando entre sí. Pepe se sienta en el sofá.

PEPE

¿Has podido conseguir tu visa?

ALICIA

No. Siguen diciéndome que el mes que viene.

PEPE

Lo sé, me han estado diciendo lo mismo durante más de un año.

ALICIA

Ten paciencia; conseguiremos las nuestras.

PEPE

No lo creo. No tienen intenciones de
dejar marchar a nuestras familias.

Alicia sale de la cocina con una bandeja y dos tazas de café.

ALICIA

¿Has venido a hablar de tu visa?

PEPE

Lo siento cariño, no quería arruinar
nuestra noche.

Sabes que eres mi pasaporte al cielo.

Alicia pone la bandeja en la mesita. Se sienta en el sofá a su lado.

Pepe se olvida de que el café está ahí. Su atención se concentra en Alicia.

ALICIA

¿No querías café?

PEPE

No tanto como te quiero a ti.

La cara de Pepe está a centímetros de la de Alicia. Se cierne sobre ella
explorándola, anticipando su contacto. Suavemente, Pepe la acaricia.
Sostiene a Alicia más cerca de él hasta ese momento mágico en el que
los labios se tocan y pierden todo sentido de la realidad. Comienza el
amor apasionado. Pepe la desnuda. Primero la blusa, luego el vestido.
Alicia desabrocha la camisa de Pepe y luego se zambulle en sus pantalones bajándoles la cremallera alcanzando su…

SE DISUELVEN A NEGRO

EN LA PANTALLA "1961"

CUBA EXT. NOCHE PLAYA VARADERO

Es un cielo iluminado por la luna y apenas podemos ver la silueta de Pepe con otros tres hombres que se apresuran a poner ramas, arena y maleza encima de una balsa y lo que parecen ser provisiones para un viaje.

CERCA DE PEPE, LUIS, TONY Y RAMON

De repente, a lo largo de la playa y no muy lejos de la orilla, oyen el ruido de una patrullera. Se quedan inmóviles. Los hombres ven un foco que ilumina las playas con una intensidad cegadora. Al mismo tiempo, pero desde la dirección opuesta, se oye una patrulla a pie de soldados cubanos. Parecen caminar directamente hacia ellos.

PEPE

¡Piérdanse!

Los hombres se dispersan. El jefe de la patrulla a pie ve la patrullera y camina hacia la orilla.

JEFE DE PATRULLA

Capitán, No he visto nada, no he visto
rastro de los hombres.

(una pausa)

Parece que la información que nos dio el
G-2 no servía.

La policía secreta está fallando.

Mientras los soldados se toman un respiro

LA CÁMARA SE DESPLAZA PARA REVELAR DÓNDE SE ESCONDE CADA HOMBRE

Tony está totalmente enterrado en la arena, con la nariz apenas visible en la superficie. Él está a menos de cinco metros de uno de los soldados.

Ramón está en el agua agarrándose con toda su fuerza a una enorme roca. Intenta evitar que las olas y la corriente lo arrastren mar adentro y lo expongan a los patrulleros cubanos.

Pepe se ha subido a un cocotero y tiene una vista panorámica de toda la situación.

Luis se ha escondido en la hierba alta junto a las dunas de arena. Está inmóvil.

LA CAMARA SE DESPLAZA POR LA ESPALDA DE LUIS

Varios cangrejos con enormes tenazas se arrastran por sus muslos y trasero.

ENFOQUE A PRIMER PLANO DE LUIS

Le gotea sudor frío por la frente.

CAPITÁN
Busquen bien por toda esta zona.

Esos gusanos tienen que estar por aquí.

JEFE DE PATRULLA
Si Capitán.

La lancha acelera y reanuda la búsqueda mientras la patrulla a pie se dirige en dirección opuesta. Cuando no hay moros en la costa, Pepe se desliza por el cocotero. Rápidamente inspecciona la zona y susurra

PEPE

Tony...Ramon...Luis ¿Dónde demonios están?

De la arena, justo delante de él, aparece Tony dándole un susto de muerte.

PEPE

Cabrón, no me asustes así.

Tony se ríe.

Ramón se acerca, visiblemente adolorido. Un primer plano de él revela múltiples heridas en el pecho y el abdomen debido a los golpes que recibió contra las rocas. Pepe se quita la camiseta y la utiliza para ayudar a Ramón a detener el sangramiento.

TONY

¿Estás bien?

RAMÓN

Viviré.

TONY

¿Dónde demonios está Luis?

PEPE

No lo sé.

TONY
Luis deja de jugar ¿dónde estás?

Tenuemente desde detrás de las dunas de arena.

LUIS
Estoy aquí…

¡Ayúdenme!

Tony y Pepe corren hacia las dunas donde encuentran a Luis cubierto de cangrejos listos para hacer de Luis una cena.

TONY
¡Mierda!

PEPE
Luis, no te muevas… ni un músculo.

LUIS
Sí, claro. Para ti es fácil decirlo.

Pepe se vuelve hacia Tony.

PEPE
Rápido, consígueme varias hojas de coco.

TONY
¡Ya voy!

Tony corre hacia la rama caída de un cocotero. Arranca varias hojas y vuelve corriendo hacia Pepe… se las entrega.

PEPE

Como dije antes, No muevas ni un músculo.

LUIS

Claro, sólo consigue quitarme estos Cangrejos de arriba.

Con la habilidad de un cirujano, Pepe coge una de las hojas y la pasa entre las tenazas de un cangrejo. El cangrejo tenazmente muerde con su tenaza y se aferra a la hoja. Pepe levanta el cangrejo del trasero de Luis y lo arroja al agua. Pepe repite el proceso hasta que todos los cangrejos están fuera de su espalda excepto uno. El último cangrejo se ha agarrado al trasero de Luis y no lo suelta. Pepe consigue que este cangrejo se agarre a una hoja con su otra tenaza, pero el cangrejo se niega a soltar el culo de Luis. Finalmente, Tony utiliza su fosforera para encender fuego bajo la tenaza que sujeta a Luis. El cangrejo lo suelta y Pepe también lo tira al agua.

Luis se levanta quitándose la arena y el sudor. Se palpa el trasero.

LUIS

¡Gracias, mi hermano!

PEPE

¿Gracias por qué?

LUIS

Gracias por salvarme literalmente el culo.

Comparten una buena carcajada.

PEPE

Está bien muchachos, escúchenme.

Nos reunimos aquí el próximo martes a medianoche.

Quien llegue tarde se queda atrás... Si perdemos los vientos y corrientes previstos, todos seremos cebo para peces.

LUIS

¿De verdad crees que lo lograremos?

PEPE

¡Puedes apostarte el culo que lo haremos!

Si tienes dudas sobre ir, ¡no vengas!'

TONY

Dijiste que cada uno de nosotros podría traer una persona. ¿Verdad?

PEPE

Bien, pero asegúrate de traer a alguien que pueda cuidar de sí mismo.

RAMÓN

Pepe, ¿cuándo podremos avisar nuestro viaje a nuestras familias?

PEPE

30 minutos antes de nuestra salida.

Antes sería peligroso y demasiado arriesgado.

Un helicóptero de la guardia costera cubana pasa a muy baja altura asustándolos a todos ellos.

PEPE

Bien, salgamos de aquí.

LUIS

Recuerda la palabra clave.

LANCHA... Esta clave confirmará nuestro viaje 24 horas antes de la salida.

Mientras se adentran en el bosque, hablan de la fiesta de aniversario de esta noche. Fidel Castro celebra la fiesta del aniversario de la Revolución Cubana en el Palacio Presidencial.

LUIS

¿Vas a ir a la fiesta de Fidel esta noche?

TONY

No, yo no. No puedo soportar la cara de ese hijo de puta.

PEPE

Luis y yo estaremos allí.

Creo que la policía secreta tiene sus ojos puestos en nosotros, así es que iremos para hacer presencia.

RAMÓN

¡Nos vemos allí!

Los hombres se dispersan en la oscuridad de la noche.

DISOLVER A NEGRO

EXT. NOCHE EN EL PALACIO PRESIDENCIAL DE FIDEL CASTRO

Una toma del Palacio Presidencial.

Toda la zona está fuertemente vigilada y acordonada por militares. Los soldados van vestidos de etiqueta o con uniforme de combate. Todos llevan como mínimo un arma lateral. Llegan varias limusinas de aspecto extranjero. Las limusinas llevan banderas de diferentes países extranjeros (la Unión Soviética, Corea del Norte, Vietnam del Norte y China, etc.). Los invitados van vestidos a la última. En pocas palabras, se trata de algo más que otro evento de etiqueta.

INT. NOCHE EL PALACIO PRESIDENCIAL

Mientras seguimos a algunos de los invitados al interior, observamos que absolutamente todos son detenidos por soldados justo en la entrada principal para verificar su invitación, sus credenciales y un registro de armas. Encima de ellos hay una enorme pancarta colgada en la entrada principal. En la pancarta se lee "Bienvenidos a la Fiesta Aniversario de la Revolución Cubana". La cámara continúa siguiendo a los invitados después de que hayan sido fiscalizados. Fotos de Fidel Castro están estratégicamente situadas por todo el salón de baile del palacio.

Mientras la cámara sigue a los invitados, una multitud de personas, todas impecablemente vestidas, disfrutan de champán y aperitivos en el interior. Una suave música clásica suena en un piano de cola negro situado al fondo del salón de baile. A medida que la cámara sigue, enfoca a una dama increíblemente hermosa. Nos damos cuenta de que un hombre alto, de espaldas a la cámara, está hablando con esta bella mujer. Cuando la cámara se desplaza alrededor de ellos, revelamos su identidad, Alicia y Pepe.

CERCA DE PEPE Y ALICIA

                    PEPE
Estás absolutamente impresionante.

                   ALICIA
Estás enamorado.

                    PEPE
Sí, estoy enamorado de ti.

                   ALICIA
Me siento un poco mareada.

                    PEPE
¿Por qué? ¿Estás enferma?

                   ALICIA
No, no enferma, sólo mareada.

Estoy segura de que todo desaparecerá
pronto.

Alicia lo mantiene a raya; la salva un camarero que les ofrece champán
de su bandeja llena de copas.

                    PEPE
Si continúas sintiéndote mal, tienes que
ir al médico.

                   ALICIA
A su debido tiempo Pepe... todo a su
debido tiempo.

Pepe sonríe sin darse cuenta y bebe un sorbo de su copa de champán.

PEPE

¿Le damos la noticia a la familia?

ALICIA

¿Qué noticia?

PEPE

Sobre nuestro compromiso, por supuesto.

Alicia se sorprende al ver que PEPE no se ha percatado.

ALICIA

Por supuesto, anunciemos nuestra unión.

PEPE

Buena ayuda eres tú.

(bromeando)

Hagámoslo antes de que cambie de opinión.

Alicia sonríe de oreja a oreja complacida por la inocencia y la decisión de Pepe.

Pepe, de manera muy caballerosa escolta a Alicia hacia el fondo del salón de baile.

INT. SALÓN DE BAILE NOCTURNO JUNTO AL PIANO DE COLA NEGRO

Un grupo de tres parejas muy sofisticadas y distinguidas están junto al piano de cola, bebiendo champán y hablando de la actualidad.

De manera condescendiente.

> ROBERTO
>
> Bueno, ¿qué piensas de la revolución
> ahora?

> JOSE
>
> Mi querido hermanito... No quiero dis-
> cutir este tema ni aquí ni ahora.

> ROBERTO
>
> ¿Por qué? ¿Has cambiado de opinión?

> JOSE
>
> No, hay damas presentes.

Roberto se calienta rápidamente. Rosa interviene sin dudarlo.

> ROSA
>
> ¿Es política todo lo que saben hablar?
>
> No puedo creer que sean tan opuestos.
>
> (una pausa)
>
> Ahora compórtense y dejen de discutir
> sobre esta maldita revolución.

Un oficial cubano mulato se acerca al grupo. Se dirige a José.

> OFICIAL
>
> ¿Es usted el Sr. José Martínez?

> JOSE
>
> Lo soy.

OFICIAL
Tengo órdenes de ponerte bajo arresto.

Por favor, date la vuelta.

El Oficial saca las esposas de su cinturón. La tensión inunda el ambiente.

Todo el mundo está a punto de estallar. Roberto se agarra los huevos con su mano izquierda y desafiantemente dice,

ROBERTO
¡Arresta esto!

El oficial cubano (Oscar) comienza a reír incontrolablemente mientras José lo abraza.

JOSE
Ha pasado mucho tiempo.

OSCAR (EL OFICIAL)
Sí, mucho tiempo...

ROBERTO
¿Dónde demonios has estado?

OSCAR
En Angola.

Oscar abraza a Ramón y finalmente a Luis.

JOSE
¿Angola? ¿Para qué?

OSCAR

Como asesor militar.

José mira a Roberto como diciéndole "te lo dije". Sigue hablando con Oscar.

JOSE

¿Por qué gastamos dinero y enviamos soldados a Angola cuando necesitamos toda la ayuda posible aquí en Cuba?

¿Puede explicármelo?

ROBERTO

No puede. No es su trabajo explicar la estrategia o las decisiones de Castro.

Pepe y Alicia se acercan. Pepe acompaña a Alicia directamente al lado de su madre (Rosa). Rompen la tensión que se está creando entre Roberto y José.

PEPE

Hola a todos.

Oscar se acerca a Pepe y lo saluda con un abrazo.

OSCAR

Hace años que no te veo.

Mírate, ya eres un hombre.

PEPE

Gracias por el voto de confianza.

Ahora todos, por favor escuchen.

(una pausa)

Odio romper esta reunión pero tengo
una noticia muy importante que hacer.

El grupo se acomoda y presta toda su atención a Pepe y Alicia.

PEPE
Alicia y yo estamos comprometidos.

Nos casamos el 2 de noviembre.

Pepe saca de su chaleco un precioso anillo de diamantes y lo coloca en
el dedo anular de Alicia sorprendiendo a todos, incluyendo a Alicia.

ALICIA
Es precioso.

ROSA
¡Estoy tan feliz!

Rosa se gira hacia Alicia y le da un beso y un abrazo, luego se gira
hacia PEPE y le da un abrazo maternal.

ROSA
¡Enhorabuena, hijo!

Espero que ambos sean muy felices.

ALICIA
Estoy segura de que todos estaremos
felices...

De repente, empieza a sonar el himno nacional cubano. Alicia es in-
terrumpida y no se le permite terminar su comentario.

INT. NOCHE EN LA ENTRADA PRINCIPAL DEL SALÓN DE BAILE

La multitud empieza a aplaudir y un séquito de soldados en uniforme de faena abre paso entre la multitud al invitado de honor "Fidel Castro". Unos pasos por detrás le siguen el Che Guevara, Raúl Castro y otros dignatarios. Mientras sigue sonando el himno, los invitados se unen al canto del himno nacional cubano.

INT. CABECERA DEL SALÓN DE BAILE NOCTURNO

Fidel y los dignatarios se sitúan junto a sus asientos en la mesa principal. Todos saludan a la bandera cubana al final del himno y ocupan sus asientos asignados.

INT. NOCHE JOSE Y PEPE EN LA FIESTA

José se vuelve hacia su hijo y le susurra.

> JOSE
> ¿Estás seguro de que esto es lo que quieres?

> PEPE
> La quiero mucho papá...
>
> No quisieras que fuera de ninguna otra manera.

> JOSE
> Bien hijo, pero dime algo;
>
> ¿Es con ella donde has estado pasando la mayor parte de tus noches?

> PEPE
> No papá, en absoluto.

> JOSE
> Entonces, ¿dónde has estado?

Un tono serio se apodera de la conversación.

> PEPE
> ¿Podemos hablar de esto más tarde?

> JOSE
> Bien, asegúrate de venir en algún momento mañana a nuestra casa.
>
> Quiero saber qué te traes entre manos.

CORTE A:

EXT. DÍA ESTADIO DE BÉISBOL

Se está jugando un partido. Una pelota de béisbol es bateada por encima de la cerca para un home run.

El público se enloquece. La cámara se desplaza para mostrar a Pepe, Tony y Luis disfrutando el partido.

CERCA DE PEPE, TONY Y LUIS

> PEPE
> Las cosas se están poniendo bastante pegajosas.

> LUIS
> ¿De qué estás hablando?

PEPE

Papá quiere saber qué pasa.

Sabe algo.

LUIS

¿Deberíamos irnos el martes?

PEPE

Si el tiempo lo permite.

El público se pone en pie. Varios aficionados abuchean la decisión del árbitro. Pepe mira a su alrededor buscando a Ramón.

PEPE

¿Dónde diablos está Ramón?

TONY

No lo sé. Yo estaba preguntándome lo mismo.

LUIS

No es costumbre de él llegar tarde.

(una pausa)

Seguro que está bien... Iré a verlo esta noche y lo pongo al día.

CORTE A:

INT. DÍA UNA CÁMARA DE TORTURA

Ramón está desnudo de la cintura para arriba y atado a una silla. Está siendo interrogado por varios soldados. Se le ven los puntos en el pecho y el abdomen de las palizas que se dio contra los percebes y las rocas en la playa. El padre y la madre de Ramón también han sido detenidos y están atados a postes de madera como animales salvajes listos para ser sacrificados justo delante de Ramón. El soldado que fuma un cigarrillo saca una navaja de 20 cm de su bota y se acerca a Ramón. Primero apaga el cigarrillo sobre las heridas de percebes y los puntos de Ramón. Ramón grita del dolor. Luego coge la cuchilla y empieza a abrir los puntos de Ramon, uno a uno. Cuando los puntos se abren, Ramón hace una mueca de dolor.

SOLDADO

Ramoncito, mi querido muchacho...
Dime cómo conseguiste esos cortes hor-
ribles. ¿Qué estabas haciendo?

El soldado abre otro punto... esta vez intentando infligir más dolor.

SOLDADO

¿Qué te traes entre manos?

Ramón escupe en la cara del soldado. El soldado levanta su cuchillo hacia la garganta de Ramón casi cortándosela.

SOLDADO

Te voy a dar una lección cabrón.

Algo que aprendí hace mucho tiempo.

El soldado se acerca al padre de Ramón y empieza a descuartizarlo. Agarra una oreja y se la corta limpiamente. El padre de Ramón grita de dolor. El soldado continúa y corta la otra oreja. La escena es desgarradora. Ramón grita a pleno pulmón suplicando al soldado que pare. El soldado se vuelve hacia Ramón.

SOLDADO

No ignoremos a Mamacita.

Hace una señal a otro de los soldados para que empiece a hacer lo suyo. El otro soldado se acerca a Mamacita y le arranca la ropa. Mamacita desnuda grita pidiendo clemencia. El soldado se baja los pantalones, y sodomiza a la madre de Ramon. Reina el caos.

Ramón gritando a todo pulmón tratando de liberarse suplica.

RAMÓN

¡Paren! ¡Paren! ¡Por favor, deténganse!

Les diré cualquier cosa que quieran saber, pero por favor paren.

El soldado reconoce la súplica de Ramón y se da la vuelta. Agarra a Ramón por el pelo y le tira la cabeza hacia atrás.

SOLDADO

Cabroncito, si me mientes, me vas a rogar que te mate.

¿Comprendes?

RAMÓN

Si, si lo entiendo, pero por favor déjelos ir.

El soldado acerca una silla para escuchar la confesión de Ramón.

DISOLVERSE A

INT. CASA DE JOSE, EL DORMITORIO

Rosa desempolva una foto familiar reciente. En ella aparecen José, Luis, Pepe y Rosa. Rosa deja la foto y sigue quitando el polvo del resto de los muebles. Inesperadamente encuentra una gaveta parcialmente abierta. Una prenda impide que la gaveta se cierre correctamente. Cuando Rosa abre la gaveta para volver a meter la prenda, encuentra una carpeta negra. La coge y la abre. Lee lo que está adentro.

CERCA DE ROSA

La expresión de Rosa es de horror e incredulidad. Llama inmediatamente a José.

ROSA

José, José, ven a ver esto.

JOSE

¿De qué se trata?

ROSA

José por favor. ¡Ven aquí!

A Rosa le tiembla la voz. Está temblando de miedo. José se acerca a Rosa. Le quita la carpeta a Rosa y la examina. Una mirada más atenta de José provoca una reacción similar.

JOSE

No lo puedo creer.

¿Dónde has encontrado esto?

ROSA

En la gaveta de Luis.

JOSE

¡Jesucristo!

¿Cómo es posible?

Empieza a pasearse sujetando la carpeta con una mano y rascándose la cabeza con la otra. Se detiene, vuelve a empezar y se detiene.

JOSE

Yo me encargo de esto.

Ni una palabra a nadie.

ROSA

¿Qué vamos a hacer?

JOSE

Aún no lo sé. Necesito tiempo para pensar.

CORTE A:

INT. NOCHE PALACIO PRESIDENCIAL, DESPACHO DE CASTRO

Fidel está fumando un puro y frente a su escritorio hay dos oficiales soviéticos. También está presente un traductor. El diálogo entre Castro y los oficiales soviéticos es en ruso.

EL TRADUCTOR DE FIDEL

¿Cuándo debemos esperar la entrega?

El traductor traduce

OFICIAL SOVIÉTICO N.º 1

Quince misiles con 30 cabezales llegarán
en aproximadamente 45 días.

¿Estarán listas las bases?

El traductor traduce

FIDEL

¡Claro que sí!

Un oficial cubano, ayudante de Castro, llama a la puerta e interrumpe la reunión. Se acerca a Castro y le susurra un mensaje relativo a una nota que lleva consigo.

FIDEL

No me molestes con esos detalles.

Dile a Raúl que se ocupe de este asunto inmediatamente.

CORTE A:

INT. NOCHE EN LOS APOSENTOS DE RAUL CASTRO

El aposento esta bellamente decorado con lo mejor que el dinero puede comprar.

Desde la entrada se ven dos cuerpos haciendo el amor apasionadamente en el dormitorio. Los sonidos de lujuria y placer llenan el ambiente. A medida que la cámara se acerca lentamente, podemos ver el trasero de Raúl Castro que está sodomizando sádicamente a su compañero sexual, un joven negro.

Tocan a la puerta.

RAÚL

¡Jesucristo!

Los golpes se hacen más fuertes.

RAÚL

Ya voy coño, Ya voy. Ya voy, maldita sea,
ya voy.

Se pone rápidamente los pantalones y abre la puerta.

MENSAJERO

Perdóneme ... Fidel ordenó que le informe de este asunto inmediatamente.

El mensajero le entrega la nota a Raúl. Raúl la lee, se vuelve hacia su
amante en la cama.

RAÚL

¡Piérdete!

Se vuelve hacia el mensajero.

RAÚL

Me vestiré.

Nos iremos inmediatamente.

VOLVER A:

INT. NOCHE DESPACHO DE FIDEL

Los dos oficiales soviéticos se marchan. El ayudante de Castro les da
una caja de puros cubanos a cada uno.

FIDEL

Diles a estos malditos rusos que los
americanos son más cobardes que ellos.

El traductor mira a Fidel consternado. Fidel se ríe de la reacción del traductor y con una sonrisa cínica dice.

FIDEL

Diles lo que quieras.

Sólo sácalos de aquí.

El traductor hace su propia traducción y acompaña a los oficiales soviéticos fuera del despacho de Castro. Al abrirse las puertas dobles, Raúl entra seguido de cerca por el mensajero.

RAÚL

Fidel, esto es un asunto muy delicado.

¿Cómo quieres que lo maneje?

Raúl tiene la nota en la mano señalando un párrafo especifico. Fidel cierra las puertas de su despacho.

FIDEL

Manéjalo de la misma manera que todos
los demás....

(una pausa)

Espera, espera un minuto. Déjame tener
el placer de llegar al fondo de esto.

Tráeme a Roberto. Y sí, no olvides traer
a su hermano. ¿cómo se llama él?

Castro chasquea los dedos intentando recordar el nombre del hermano de Roberto.

RAÚL

¡José!

FIDEL

Ese mismo. Tráemelos a los dos.

EXT. DÍA CASA DE JOSE

Rosa está en la cocina cuando alguien toca a la puerta.

ROSA

Ya voy. Ya voy.

Cuando Rosa abre la puerta, cinco soldados se abren paso a empujones y entran en la casa sin identificarse ni pedir permiso.

ROSA

¿Qué pasa? ¿Qué es esto?

¿Qué es lo que quieren?

El sargento que permanece junto a la puerta principal se dirige a Rosa.

SARGENTO

¿Dónde está José Martínez?

Se oye a los otros soldados destrozando la casa. Rosa tiene miedo.

ROSA

No está aquí.

Creo que fue a la bodega.

La humildad de Rosa se convierte en ira.

ROSA

¡Para y lárgate de mi casa ahora mismo!

¡Dije que no está aquí!

Los soldados ignoran a ROSA. José, siempre conocido por su gran sincronización, entra por la puerta principal con bolsas de víveres en cada mano.

JOSE

¿Qué está pasando aquí?

¿Qué creen que están haciendo?

El sargento agarra inmediatamente a José. Las bolsas de la compra caen al suelo.

SARGENTO

Fidel te ha convocado.

JOSE

¿Por qué? ¿Por qué razón?

Sin dar explicaciones, los soldados obligan a José a subir a la camioneta que le espera. Rosa está horrorizada. Se llevan a José mientras Rosa se queda estupefacta en la puerta principal.

Cuando la camioneta se aleja, llega Pepe y ve a su madre vencida y llorando.

PEPE

¿Qué pasa, mamá?

¿Qué ha pasado?

Rosa llorando incontrolablemente.

ROSA

Acaban de llevarse a tu padre.

PEPE

¿A dónde?

ROSA

Soldados, acaban de llevarse a tu padre.
Dios mío. Algo está mal. Algo esta terriblemente mal.

A Pepe le pasan por la mente los peores pensamientos. El intenta controlar sus emociones y consuela a su madre con valentía y aplomo.

PEPE

No te preocupes, lo encontraré.

Averiguaré adónde se lo han llevado.

Todo irá bien, ya lo verás.

FUNDIDO A NEGRO

DESVANECE A:

INT. OFICINAS DE ROBERTO EN EL CENTRO DE LA HABANA

En estos despachos se nota que Roberto es abogado y un profesional
en regla. Mientras está sentado en su escritorio revisando un expedi-
ente, un grupo de soldados invaden las oficinas y rodean a Roberto en
su escritorio.

SOLDADO

¿Roberto Martínez?

ROBERTO
Lo soy,

SOLDADO
Tenemos órdenes de arrestarlo por crímenes contra la revolución.

Un latido mientras se asienta la noticia.

SOLDADO
Vámonos.

Roberto se dirige a su secretaria al salir.

ROBERTO
No te preocupes, estaré bien. Avísale a PEPE ahora.

Los soldados empujan a Roberto fuera de su despacho y lo meten en el ascensor. Roberto está confuso y desconcertado.

EXT. DÍA PLANO GENERAL DEL PALACIO PRESIDENCIAL

Una camioneta se detiene en una de las entradas laterales. Los soldados sacan a José de la camioneta y lo introducen en el Palacio. En unos segundos vemos llegar otra camioneta. Roberto es sacado de esta camioneta y escoltado también por soldados al interior del Palacio.

LA CÁMARA RETROCEDE PARA REVELAR EL PUNTO DE VISTA DE OSCAR

Oscar, el oficial mulato del partido revolucionario, ha observado todo el proceso. Está preocupado. Decide seguir a Roberto y José y entra al Palacio.

INT. DÍA PALACIO PRESIDENCIAL

Oscar sigue a los escoltas por el pasillo y se dirige directamente al despacho de Fidel. Las puertas dobles del despacho de Castro se abren de golpe. Entran Roberto y José escoltados por los soldados. A pocos metros de las puertas dobles abiertas está Oscar evaluando la situación.

INT. DÍA OFICINA de CASTRO ENTRADA/VESTÍBULO

Castro da la bienvenida a José y Roberto.

FIDEL

Bienvenidos Colegas de la revolución.

Raúl Castro, sentado en el sofá, se levanta. Todos entran en el despacho de Fidel.

ROBERTO

¿Por qué nos traes con tanta prisa?

¿Qué es tan urgente?

Las puertas dobles del despacho se cierran de golpe.

EL PUNTO DE VISTA DE OSCAR SE CORTA

INT. DÍA FUERA DEL DESPACHO DE CASTRO

Tras pensar unos segundos, Óscar decide quedarse y averiguar qué está pasando. Entra en las oficinas administrativas que hay justo enfrente y empieza a hablar con varios trabajadores. Cada vez que puede, echa un vistazo a las oficinas de Fidel esperando que ocurra algo.

EXT. TARDE CASA DE ALICIA

Pepe llega a casa de Alicia. Sale del carro, se acerca a la puerta y llama. No hay respuesta. Vuelve a llamar, esta vez con más fuerza. Finalmente, Alicia abre la puerta.

ALICIA

¿Qué haces aquí?

PEPE

Tenemos problemas... Fidel acaba de recoger a mi padre y a Roberto.

ALICIA

¿Por qué?

PEPE

Papá me advirtió sobre esto. Me dijo que si Castro lo recogía, que me llevara a mamá y que nos desapareciéramos. Quizás irnos a los EE.UU.

Papa enfatizo que no lo esperemos ni pusiéramos a nadie en peligro para tratar de salvarlo.

ALICIA

Entra, pasa.

INT. TARDE SALA DE ALICIA

Pepe entra en casa y se sienta en el sofá. Alicia se sienta a su lado.

ALICIA

¿Qué vas a hacer?

PEPE
Mamá dice que no se irá sin papá.

Pepe está nervioso y le gotea el sudor por la frente.

ALICIA
No crees que Castro es...

Pepe pone su dedo índice sobre los labios de Alicia haciéndola callar momentáneamente.

PEPE
Sé lo que vas a decir.

Por favor, no lo hagas.

PEPE
¿Confías en mí?

ALICIA
Por supuesto... ¿qué clase de preguntas son ésas?

¡Te confío mi vida!

Pepe se levanta y empieza a pasear por la habitación. Se da cuenta de que hay ropa de bebé encima de la mesa del comedor.

PEPE
¿Para quién es eso?

Alicia vacila brevemente. No puede mantener el contacto visual con PEPE

ALICIA
Es para una amiga. Va a tener un bebé.

PEPE

¿La conozco?

ALICIA

No lo creo...

(cambiando el tema)

ALICIA CONTINÚA

Por favor, Pepe. ¡Detén esto!

Dime qué está pasando.

PEPE

Bien, escúchame con atención. Luis, Ramón, Tony y yo estamos robando un barco y nos vamos para Miami mañana.

ALICIA

¿Estás loco?

PEPE

Escúchame.

(una pausa)

Mírame, Castro ya mató a Ernesto, Rubén, y quién sabe cuántas otras personas. Mi padre sabía que estaba en la obtener visas para toda la familia.

ALICIA

¡Estás loco!

PEPE

El hecho es que mi padre ya pudiese estar muerto y me dejó instrucciones específicas de que debo seguir.

ALICIA

¿Vas a dejar atrás a tu padre?

PEPE

Claro que no, desde Miami puedo conseguir esas visas a través de España o México y sacarlo.

ALICIA

¡Si alguien se entera nos fusilarán a todos!

Pepe alcanza a Alicia, la toma en sus brazos

PEPE

Quiero que vengas conmigo.

Un momento de silencio. Alicia está desolada. Lucha por tomar una decisión. Internamente quiere ir, pero se da cuenta de que no puede arriesgar la vida de su hijo nonato. Está embarazada de PEPE. Resiste la tentación de revelar algo y finalmente encuentra las palabras para responder.

ALICIA

No puedo...

¡No puedo!

Mejor dicho... ¡No lo haré!

Pepe estrecha a Alicia contra él.

PEPE
¿Por qué no? ¿Por qué no?

Alicia se separa; está a punto de echarse a llorar.

ALICIA
¿Cómo puedes ser tan egoísta?

No puedes esperar que las cosas ocurran
exactamente como tu quiere.

PEPE
¿A qué te refieres?

ALICIA
¡Definitivamente no voy a ir!

Alicia se esfuerza por ocultar sus sentimientos más íntimos. Se hace
pasar por alguien que no es. Pepe se sorprende de su reacción.

PEPE
Pero pensé que tu ...

Alicia se da la vuelta interrumpe a Pepe

ALICIA
Quiero que te vayas.

No quiero discutir más este asunto.

PEPE
Pero cómo puede ser...

Alicia vuelve a interrumpir. Camina hacia la puerta principal, la abre

ALICIA
¡Quiero que te vayas ahora mismo!

Pepe, totalmente incrédulo, camina hacia ella. Alicia le indica la salida. Pepe frustrado y enfadado se marcha dando un portazo al salir.

CORTE A

EL PALACIO PRESIDENCIAL, FRENTE AL DESPACHO DE FIDEL

Se abren las puertas del despacho de Fidel y salen José y Roberto escoltados por varios soldados. Oscar oye el alboroto y se da la vuelta.

PUNTO DE VISTA DE OSCAR (PDV)

José y Roberto han sido esposados y escoltados a toda prisa por el pasillo.

VOLVER A OSCAR

Oscar se da cuenta de lo que está a punto de ocurrir. El terror empieza a correr por sus venas.

DE VUELTA AL PDV DE OSCAR

Uno de los soldados que escolta a los prisioneros saca su pistola. Giran al final del pasillo y entran en una habitación. Oscar sigue cautelosamente a los prisioneros desde lejos. La puerta se cierra de golpe.

VOLVER A OSCAR

Totalmente angustiado, Óscar busca la manera de detener lo que teme que pueda ocurrir. Antes de que pueda organizar un pensamiento, suenan 2 disparos. A Oscar se le doblan las rodillas, se le revuelve el estómago... le cuesta respirar. Suenan otros dos disparos. Oscar mira a su alrededor para ver si alguien reacciona al sonido de los disparos. Para su sorpresa, todo el mundo sigue como si nada.

INT. DIA PASILLO DEL PALACIO

Oscar retrocede fuera de la habitación y se dirige a la salida más cercana.

PALACIO DÍA EXT. ENTRADA LATERAL

Al salir del palacio, Oscar se detiene. Busca una cabina telefónica. Encuentra una y entra.

INT. CABINA TELEFÓNICA DE DÍA

Oscar está hiperventilando. Mete una moneda en el teléfono público y empieza a marcar. Se equivoca. Cuelga y vuelve a empezar. Finalmente hace la llamada.

> NARRACION ROSA
> Hola.

> OSCAR
> ¿Rosa?

> NARRACION ROSA
> ¡Si!

Rosa capta el tono de voz urgente de Óscar.

NARRACION ROSA

Si Oscar, ¿Qué pasa?

OSCAR

Ocurrió algo terrible.

INT. DÍA ROSA EN EL TELÉFONO EN SU SALA

Los ojos de Rosa se abren de par en par, su peor temor se hace realidad. Tiene miedo de respirar fuerte o de hacer ruido.

OSCAR

¡Han MATADO a Jose y Roberto!

Rosa entra en shock, empieza a temblar. Ni una palabra sale de su boca.

VOLVER A OSCAR

OSCAR

¿Estás ahí?

¿Has oído lo que he dicho?

Rosa no puede hablar.... Oscar puede oír su respiración, el comienzo de su crisis.

OSCAR

Rosa, sé que puedes oírme.

Escucha y haz exactamente lo que te digo.

Coge a Pepe y vete a mi casa inmediatamente.

Rosa cuelga el teléfono. Oscar maldice frustrado y cuelga también. Se da la vuelta para salir de la cabina y un soldado espera de pie. Oscar se sobresalta. Abre la puerta de la cabina, saluda con la cabeza al soldado y se va. El soldado entra en la cabina para hacer una llamada.

EXT. DÍA LA ENTRADA AL APARTAMENTO DE TONY

Pepe llega a casa de Tony. Justo cuando Pepe se dispone a tocar a la puerta, Tony la abre.

> TONY
> Escuché que recogieron a tu padre y tío,
> y ahora te están buscando.

> PEPE
> Mierda, esos malditos bastardos están en
> un alboroto.
>
> Las cosas están peor de lo que pensaba.

Pepe entra en el apartamento de Tony.

> TONY
> También he oído que Ramón está
> muerto.

> PEPE
> ¿Cómo?

> TONY
> ¡El rumor es que Ramón y su familia
> están todos muertos!
>
> Hace días que no se les ve.

                    PEPE
No podemos esperar hasta mañana.

Creo que deberíamos irnos esta noche.

                    TONY
¿Y el tiempo?

                    PEPE
El tiempo no importará si estamos
muertos, ¿verdad?

                    (una pausa)

No podemos esperar más... ¿Dónde está
Luis?

Tony agarra el brazo de Pepe.

                    TONY
Pepe... siéntate.

Tenemos que hablar.

                    PEPE
¿Sentarse? ¿Cuál es tu problema?

                    TONY
Siéntate, por favor.

Pepe se sienta de mala gana. Tony se toma su tiempo.

                    PEPE
Sácalo hombre. ¿Qué demonios es esto?

TONY

La misma persona que delató a tu padre delató a Ramón, Ernesto, ya sabes... a todo nuestro grupo.

PEPE

Sí, y me gustaría poner mis manos en el hijo de puta que lo hizo.

TONY

Es Luis. . .

PEPE

¿Qué estás diciendo?

TONY

Es un chivato, un fidelista. Trabaja para la policía secreta, para el G2.

Pepe en negación.

PEPE

¿Mi hermano? ¡Estás loco!

La noticia empieza a calar.

TONY

Él es responsable de todo lo que ha pasado.

PEPE

¡Mentira!   ¡ESTÁS   HABLANDO MIERDA!

Pepe indignado, le sale vapor por las orejas. Tony con mucho cuidado.

> **TONY**
> Por eso casi nos atrapan en la playa...
> ¿recuerdas?
>
> Nos había delatado.

Pepe se abalanza sobre Tony agarrándolo por la chaqueta.

> **PEPE**
> ¡Estás loco! ... ¿Quién es el cabrón que
> te está diciendo esta mierda?

Tony empuja a Pepe exigiendo respeto.

> **TONY**
> ¡Quítame las malditas manos de encima!

Pepe suelta.

> **TONY**
> Escúchame.
>
> (una pausa)
>
> Somos amigos desde hace mucho
> tiempo.
>
> ¿Eso significa algo para ti?

Pepe en busca de respuestas.

> **TONY**
> Ven conmigo. Te lo voy a demostrar.

Tony lleva a Pepe a su dormitorio.

INT. DÍA DORMITORIO DE TONY

Tony saca de debajo de una silla un gran sobre de papel manila. Se lo entrega a Pepe. Pepe lo abre. Dentro está la carpeta con negativos y fotos que Jose y Rosa habían encontrado en la gaveta de Luis. Saca varias fotos. Sorprendido por lo que ve, se sienta en el borde de la cama. Por la expresión de su cara, está tratando de ordenar sus pensamientos. Intenta controlar sus emociones.

> PEPE
> ¿Cómo es posible? ¿Cómo pudo delatarnos?

Tony se sienta junto a Pepe,

> TONY
> Pepe, no podemos cambiar lo que ha pasado.
>
> (una pausa)
>
> Deberíamos intentar irnos lo antes posible.
>
> Si no, estaremos muertos por la mañana.

Pepe se levanta, su frustración y mal genio empiezan a aparecer.

> PEPE
> Mi propia sangre...
>
> ¿Por qué lo haría?

Pepe se dirige hacia la puerta. Tony lo agarra y lo empuja contra la pared.

TONY

¡Pepe, espabila!

Maldita sea, no me abandones ahora.

Tony sacude a Pepe como un muñeco de trapo.

TONY

¡Olvídate de Luis! Te necesito; tu madre te necesita, Alicia te necesita.

Varias pausas . . .

TONY

Si no tenemos cuidado, no estaremos aquí para deshacernos de esta pesadilla.

Finalmente, Pepe recupera su compostura. Tony lo suelta lentamente.

PEPE

Está bien, tienes razón.

(una pausa)

Dame papel y lápiz.

TONY

¿Para qué?

PEPE

Tengo que dejarle instrucciones a mamá y a Alicia.

Tony le da papel y lápiz. Pepe empieza a escribir.

PEPE
¡Nos iremos esta noche!

EXT. TOMA NOCTURNA DE LA CASA DE JOSE Y ROSA

INT. NOCHE EN EL CARRO DE OSCAR

Oscar se dirige a la casa. Al llegar, se da cuenta de que un carro sin matrícula vigila el lugar.

PDV DE OSCAR

Dos miembros de la policía secreta sentados en un carro frente a la casa.

DE VUELTA EN EL CARRO DE OSCAR

Decide no detenerse y pasa junto a la casa y dobla la esquina. Al girar, ve a un policía uniformado en el callejón.

PDV DE OSCAR

Un agente de la policía fuma un cigarrillo apoyado a un poste telefónico.

Una vez más, Oscar sigue conduciendo calle arriba y finalmente detiene su carro a media manzana del policía que está en el callejón.

EL PUNTO DE VISTA DE OSCAR DESDE SU ESPEJO RETROVISOR

La parte trasera de la casa de Rosa y el policía en el callejón.

EXT. NOCHE CARRO DE OSCAR

Después de observar la situación durante un minuto desde su carro, Oscar sale de él y se acerca al policía que está en el callejón.

EXT. NOCHE EN EL CALLEJÓN

El policía sigue fumando y apoyado al poste telefónico.

> OSCAR
>
> Buenas Noches.

El policía no reconoce ni saluda a Óscar. Oscar sigue caminando hacia el policía y se repite a sí mismo.

> OSCAR
>
> ¡Buenas Noches compañero!

El policía se vuelve reconoce el uniforme de Oscar y saluda.

> POLICÍA
>
> Buenas noches, señor.

> OSCAR
>
> Descanse, descanse. ¿Tienes un cigarrillo?

> POLICÍA
>
> Sí, señor.

Cuando el policía coge sus cigarrillos, Oscar lo agarra y lo empuja con una fuerza tremenda contra el poste telefónico, clavándole uno de los estribos en la espalda. El policía entra en estado de shock. Su cuerpo tiembla como sí un millón de voltios de electricidad fluyeran por su cuerpo. Una expresión de horror en su rostro. Su pecho está empapado de sangre y la punta del estribo sobresale de su uniforme. Finalmente, el policía muere. Oscar lo arranca del poste telefónico y lo esconde detrás de un muro.

EXT. NOCHE PARTE TRASERA DE LA CASA

Óscar cruza corriendo el callejón y entra en casa de Rosa por la puerta trasera.

INT. NOCHE EN EL INTERIOR DE LA CASA

Suavemente.

OSCAR

Rosa, Rosa.

Óscar oye llorar a alguien en casa. Sigue el rastro del sonido. Mientras busca a Rosa, evita todas las luces y ventanas por las que pasa. Con frecuencia, mira el carro que está aparcado enfrente para asegurarse de que nadie le ha visto o se dirige hacia la casa. Oscar entra en el dormitorio. Rosa está llorando en la cama.

OSCAR

Dios mío Rosa...

Oscar se acerca a ella con cuidado.

OSCAR

Por favor Rosa . . . Por favor, deja de llorar.

Rosa tiene el aspecto esperado, acaba de perder a su marido.

Oscar la consuela, la abraza y le suplica.

OSCAR

Tienes que ser fuerte Rosita.

ROSA

¿Para qué? Para que ese hijo de puta nos
pueda matar a nosotros también?

OSCAR

No pienses así Rosita. Piensa en PEPE,
Alicia,...

Rosa no responde. A Oscar parece que se le acaban las palabras. Ahora
el tiempo es oro.

OSCAR

Vamos, ven conmigo.

ROSA

No, ¿por qué?

OSCAR

No es seguro para ti aquí.

ROSA

¿Seguro? ¡Ja! Nadie está a salvo en esta
isla olvidada por Dios.

OSCAR

¿Dónde está Pepe?

Rosa se vuelve loca. En un ataque de ira, empieza a tirar cosas y a
gritar obscenidades sobre Fidel Castro. Oscar intenta contenerla, lo

que resulta casi imposible. Temiendo ser oído por la policía secreta, Oscar abofetea a Rosa. Ella rompe a llorar de nuevo y entre lágrimas.

ROSA

¿Crees que también tienen a Pepe?

OSCAR

No! Si lo tuvieran, la policía secreta no estuviera estacionada afuera.

Rosa mira largamente a Oscar...

OSCAR

Echa un vistazo...

Oscar baja las luces y abre lentamente una persiana.

PDV DE OSCAR Y ROSA DESDE LA CASA

NARRACION OSCAR

¿Ves ese carro blanco al otro lado de la calle?

NARRACION ROSA

Sí.

NARRACION OSCAR

Son ellos.

VOLVER A OSCAR Y ROSA

ROSA

¿Qué hacemos ahora?

OSCAR

Tengo que sacarte de aquí.

Mi carro está atrás... vamos a buscar a Pepe.

EXT. NOCHE CASA DE ALICIA

Pepe está en la puerta principal. Saca dos sobres blancos de su chaqueta.

Pepe toca a la puerta.

INT. NOCHE VESTÍBULO DE ALICIA

Alicia abre la puerta, pero no hay nadie. Mira a su alrededor y ve dos sobres pegados a la puerta. Alicia coge los sobres.

EL PUNTO DE VISTA DE ALICIA SOBRE LOS SOBRES

Un sobre dice Querida Alicia el otro dice Queridos mamá y papá, con amor Pepe.

Alicia abre el sobre dirigido a ella.

NARRACION DE PEPE

Mi querida Alicia:

Me cuesta entender por qué no quisiste venir conmigo. Sé que me quieres tanto como yo a ti. Por ahora acepto tu decisión, pero quiero que sepas que volveré por ti cuando estés lista para acompañarme. Me pondré en contacto contigo en cuanto llegue a Miami. Te echaré de menos y pensaré en ti todos los días. Por favor, prepárate para partir pronto. Con todo mi amor y devoción.

Pepe

Alicia rompe a llorar desconsoladamente.

INT. NOCHE CARRO DE PEPE

Pepe y Tony van por una calle residencial.

> PEPE
>
> ¿Cuánto falta?

> TONY
>
> Pocas cuadras.
>
> (una pausa)
>
> Este tipo era el guardaespaldas personal de mi padre y está en gran forma.
>
> Pablo probablemente pueda remar hasta Miami.

> PEPE
>
> Claro, pero ¿se puede confiar en él?

> TONY
>
> Tranquilo Pepe; es como un hermano para mí.
>
> Conozco toda su vida.

> PEPE
>
> ¿De dónde es?

> TONY
>
> Nació en New York educado en Annapolis y sus padres eran de Pinar del Río.

PEPE
¿Te he oído decir que eran?

TONY
Sí, lo fueron. Fueron asesinados el pasado año en un accidente muy inusual en Santiago.

(una pausa)

... dobla izquierda aquí.

Pepe gira el volante.

TONY
Pablo debe estar esperando en la esquina.

Al doblar la esquina, un hombre alto y fuerte les espera con una pequeña bolsa de lona. Pepe detiene el carro.

EXT NOCHE EN EL CARRO DE PEPE

TONY
¡Entra!

INT NOCHE EN EL CARRO DE PEPE

PABLO
Hola Tony.

TONY
Este es Pepe.

PABLO

Mucho gusto Pepe.

PEPE

¿Hablas bien el inglés?

PABLO

Si, fui a escuelas americanas.

TONY

Yo también, pero mi acento es horrible.

Pablo y Pepe se dan la mano. El apretón de Pablo es como una prensa de banco. Pablo es ENORME. Apenas cabe en el carro. Este tipo usa la talla "G" de Gorila. Pepe se da la vuelta, sonríe a Tony, arranca el carro y se marchan.

INT CARRO DE PEPE CONDUCIENDO

TONY

Pablo te acuerdas del plan ¿no?

PABLO

¡Claro que sí!

PEPE

¿Qué hay en la bolsa de lona?

PABLO

¡Salvavidas!

Pepe mira a Pablo un poco raro.

TONY

¡Tranquilícense! Los conozco a los dos.

No confían del uno al otro, pero sé que
los dos confían en mí... Recuerden eso.

PEPE

¡Muy bien, muy bien!

(una pausa)

Si algo sale mal esta noche y nos separa-
mos, recuerden que nos encontraremos
en la Embajada de España en 48 horas.

PABLO

Estoy preparado.

Mientras PEPE sigue conduciendo, un tono serio se apodera de la
conversación.

TONY

¡Que Dios nos ayude!

EXT. TOMA NOCTURNA DE LA SELVA TROPICAL

El carro entra en cuadro.

Pepe reduce la velocidad del vehículo y apaga las luces. Entra en un
camino de grava. El vehículo se detiene.

INT NOCHE EL CARRO DE PEPE

PEPE

Estamos aquí... ¡Vamos!

Los hombres salen del carro.

EXT. NOCHE SIGUIENDO A TONY, PABLO Y PEPE EN LA PLAYA

Juntos, empiezan a caminar por la selva tropical y pasan junto a unas altas palmeras. El suelo se convierte en arena y reconocemos que se trata de la misma playa en la que los muchachos estuvieron a punto de ser capturados por las patrullas de playa. Está oscuro, y sólo la luz de la luna ilumina la playa. Pepe conduce a Pablo y Tony a través de la oscuridad, cada vez más cerca del lugar donde está enterrada la balsa. De repente, oímos el chirrido de un fusil automático. Pepe se queda paralizado y se gira lentamente hacia el sonido.

EL PUNTO DE VISTA DE PEPE

MIRANDO EL CAÑÓN DE UN NERVIOSO AK-47

SOLDADO
¡De rodillas gusano! Traidor.

EXT. NOCHE EN PABLO Y TONY DETRÁS DE PEPE

Tony y Pablo se congelan detrás de Pepe. Apenas pueden ver la punta de un fusil apuntando directamente a la cabeza de Pepe. El soldado está inquieto y nervioso. Es evidente que el soldado no ha visto a Pablo ni a Tony.

EXT. NOCHE SOLDADO / PATRULLA DE PLAYA

El soldado es un joven de unos veinte años. Ni Pablo ni Tony son visibles desde su posición.

SOLDADO
¿Eres sordo?

Dije de rodillas hijo de puta.

VOLVER SOBRE PABLO Y TONY

Pablo parece relajarse. Empieza a caminar hacia la luz.

DE VUELTA A PEPE CON EL SOLDADO

Pablo se acerca por detrás de Pepe. El joven soldado se ve asombrado cuando ve a Pablo. El soldado suelta el gatillo y empieza a bajar su arma.

SOLDADO
¿Qué demonios haces aquí?

PEPE
¿Ustedes se conocen?

PABLO
Sí, supongo que se podría decir eso.

¡Es mi hermano!

Pepe respira mejor. Tony sale de atrás de los arbustos.

TONY
¡Hola Augie!

Me pareció reconocer tu voz.

AUGIE/SOLDADO
¿Qué es lo que pasa?

Augie se echa el fusil al hombro para abrazar a su hermano Pablo.

EXT NOCHE PABLO, AUGIE, TONY Y PEPE

PABLO

Mira, no podía decirte nada.

Juré guardar el secreto.

Además, no quería poner en peligro tu vida o nuestra huida.

AUGIE

¿Mi vida?, … ¿tu escapada?

(varias pausas)

Ah, ya veo. Ustedes son los tipos que estamos buscando.

PEPE

Mierda.

PABLO

¿Sabes de nuestra fuga?

AUGIE

Yo y cualquier otro patrullero de esta playa.

Hemos tenido tu balsa vigilada durante semanas.

Pablo se vuelve hacia Pepe y Tony. Tony un poco preocupado.

TONY

No te preocupes, tuvimos un pequeño problema con el hermano de Pepe.

PABLO

¡¡Yo diría!!...

PEPE

Ya está solucionado.

PABLO

Eso espero.

AUGIE

¿Por qué te vas? Pensé...

Pablo interrumpe.

PABLO

No importa lo que pienses.

No me quedaré aquí para luchar por estos comunistas.

AUGIE

Pero..

PABLO

Sin peros, sólo escucha.

Pablo agarra a su hermano por los hombros para enderezarlo.

PABLO

No me gusta lo que está pasando aquí.

No es lo que se prometió.

PABLO CONTINUA
Ahora matan a más gente que durante la revolución. Y mírate, ¿dónde está tu libertad, tu futuro? No gracias, quiero control sobre mi vida.

De fondo se oye el motor de una patrullera.

ENFOQUE EN AUGIE

AUGIE
Escóndete, rápido.

Un foco ilumina a Augie. La intensidad de la luz es cegadora. Sobre un megáfono.

CAPITÁN DEL BARCO
¿Quién va allí?

DEL PUNTO DE VISTA DE AUGIE

Mirando directamente a una luz cegadora.

AUGIE
Soy yo, señor... Soldado Serra.

NARRACION CAPITÁN
¿Por qué no estás en tu posta?

AUGIE
Me pareció oír un ruido por aquí, así que decidí investigarlo, señor.

NARRACION CAPITÁN
¿Y qué encontraste?

AUGIE

Nada, señor.

NARRACION CAPITÁN

Soldado Serra, si vuelves a dejar tu posta sin avisar por la radio, estarás sirviendo el resto de tu gira militar en Siberia. ¿HE SIDO CLARO?

AUGIE

¡Sí, Señor!

NARRACION CAPITÁN

¡Adelante!

El barco continua su patrulla. El foco deja a Augie mientras que el gira y se seca el sudor de su frente. Augie susurra a Pablo.

AUGIE

¡Fuera de aquí!

Pablo susurra

PABLO

Volveré por ti.

Tony Pablo y Pepe se retiran a la selva. Se reagrupan junto al carro.

EXT. NOCHE EN EL CARRO DE PEPE

TONY

¿Qué hacemos ahora?

Sin barco, sin provisiones, sin nada.

PEPE
¡Estoy pensando! ¡Estoy pensando!

PABLO
Sé dónde podemos robarnos un barco.

PEPE
¿En el Puerto de Mariel?

PABLO
¡Exacto!

TONY
¿Y qué esperamos?

PEPE
Vámonos.

Se amontonan en el carro.

EXT. NOCHE CASA DE ALICIA

Oscar y Rosa tocan a la puerta de Alicia. Rosa lleva un chal en la cabeza que le oculta la cara. Alicia mira por la ventana lateral antes de abrir la puerta. (La puerta se abre).

ALICIA
Entra Rosa. ¡Entra!

Entran rápidamente en la casa

INT. NOCHE SALA DE ALICIA

OSCAR
¿Dónde está Pepe?

ALICIA

No lo sé. Se fue de aquí hace horas.

ROSA

¿Adónde ha ido?

Alicia duda. (varias pausas) Coge el sobre que le ha dejado Pepe.

ALICIA

Pepe me pidió que te diera esto.

Alicia le entrega la carta a Rosa. Rosa la abre. La lee. A Rosa se le salen las lágrimas. Le entrega la carta a Oscar. Alicia consuela a Rosa mientras Oscar lee la carta.

OSCAR

Es lo mejor que puede hacer.

ALICIA

Me pidió que fuera con él.

ENFOQUE EN ROSA Y ALICIA

Rosa sollozando

ROSA

¿Lo hizo?

ALICIA

Sí, pero no pude.

ROSA

¿No pudiste o no quisiste?

Sabes cuánto te quiere.

ALICIA

No podíamos arriesgarnos.

(varias pausas)

Y sí, ¡nosotros también le queremos!

A Rosa se le iluminan los ojos.

ROSA

¿Nosotros? Estas ...

Alicia asiente con la cabeza.

ALICIA

¡Embarazada!

La expresión de Rosa cambia al instante. Oscar se queda boquiabierto.

ALICIA

Por favor, no te enfades conmigo.

No podía decírselo. No se hubiera ido.

Fidel lo hubiera cogido y matado por seguro.

Alicia llorando.

ALICIA

Oh Dios, ¿por qué no se lo dije?

Rosa abraza a Alicia. El tierno contacto de una madre la reconforta.

EXT. NOCHE EL PUERTO DE MARIEL

LA CÁMARA SE DESPLAZA HASTA UN CARTEL "BIENVENIDOS AL PUERTO DE MARIEL"

CÁMARA SE DESPLAZA HACIA PEPE

Pepe, Pablo y Tony están tirados en el suelo escondidos detrás de los árboles justo sobre una cresta que domina la entrada del puerto.

SU PUNTO DE VISTA

El puerto y la marina lleno de todo tipo de embarcaciones.

LA CÁMARA SE DESPLAZA A LA DERECHA

Hay una patrullera atracada cerca de la entrada principal. Dos soldados bien armados patrullan a pie por los muelles. Otro soldado está sentado en la caseta de vigilancia de la entrada del puerto.

DE VUELTA A LA CRESTA CON PEPE, TONY Y PABLO

PEPE

Bien Pablo, ¿qué hacemos ahora?

Pablo saca una botella de whisky de su bolsa de viaje. Bebe un trago enorme y luego se rocía el cuello, los brazos y la camisa. Cuando los guardias no están mirando, se levanta y empieza a caminar hacia la caseta como si estuviera borracho. Tony susurra.

TONY

No te olvides de tambalearte.

ENFOQUE EN PABLO

Pablo se pone a cantar como si estuviera borracho. Eructa y se tambalea casi cayéndose.

> PABLO
> ¡Mulata! Que nalgas tienes, Que rico
> cuerpo tú tienes.

El soldado sentado en el puesto de guardia oye la conmoción y se levanta. Se quita la arena del trasero y camina cautelosamente hacia Pablo.

EXT. NOCHE EN LA CASETA DE VIGILANCIA

> GUARDIA #1
> Oye Niche. ¿Cuál es tu problema?

Pablo en una actuación increíble continúa y se acerca cada vez más al guardia.

> GUARDIA #1
> ¡Alto ahí!

> VOLVER A PABLO

Pablo se detiene tras tambalearse varias veces.

> PABLO
> Estoy celebrando mi cumpleaños.

Guardia #1

Bien, pero no aquí.

Vete a casa a dormir la mona.

PABLO CONTINUA

Justo después de que termine lo que
queda de esto.

Pablo señala la botella media vacía.

PABLO

¿Quieres tomar algo?

EXT. NOCHE EN LA CASETA

GUARDIA #1

No, no estando de guardia.

El guardia mira a su alrededor para ver dónde están los demás guardias.

GUARDIA #1

Vamos, sal de aquí antes que me causes
un problema.

Pablo persistente pero cuidadoso.

PABLO

Si te tomas una copita conmigo Prometo
que me iré en silencio.

GUARDIA #1

¿Un trago?

Pablo levanta el dedo índice indicando uno.

PABLO

Palabra de honor.

EXT. NOCHE PABLO Y EL GUARDIA JUNTOS

El guardia vuelve a mirar a su alrededor y, con el rifle al hombro, se acerca a Pablo. Tony y Pepe observan todos los movimientos de Pablo. Pablo le entrega la botella al guardia. El guardia levanta la botella para beber un trago, pero antes de que empiece a tragar, Pablo le mete el resto de la botella en la garganta y lo mata al instante. El guardia cae muerto al suelo. Rápidamente, Pablo arrastra el cuerpo adentro de la caseta. Hace una señal a Pepe y Tony para que bajen. Pepe y Tony corren hacia la caseta. Tony, el último en entrar, cierra la puerta tras de sí.

INT CASETA DE VIGILANCIA NOCTURNA

> TONY
>
> ¿Y ahora qué?

> PEPE
>
> Mira a ver si encuentras las llaves de el
> barco cañonero.

Tony se da la vuelta y empieza a buscar las llaves en un llavero colgado en la parte trasera de la puerta. Pepe vigila por si hay problemas. Pablo está canibalizando armas y municiones del guardia muerto y le da la pistola a Pepe.

> PABLO
>
> Toma esto.
>
> Me llevaré el rifle.

Pepe se vira hacia Tony.

> PEPE
>
> ¡Date prisa!

Pepe sigue vigilando de cerca a los otros guardias que caminan por el muelle. Tony revisa las llaves tan rápido como puede. ¡Por fin!

TONY
¡Las tengo! ¿Y ahora qué?

PABLO
Dame las llaves.

(una pausa)

Corramos hacia el barco.

PEPE
Espera ... ¿Y los guardias qué?

PABLO
Que se jodan, los rociaré con AK unas
cuantas veces.

De repente, se oye el ruido de varios camiones que se acercan por la carretera. Todos se viran para ver lo que viene.

PEPE
Mierda, ahora nunca lo lograremos.

PABLO
Es ahora o nunca.

(una pausa)

Ustedes diríjanse hacia el barco.

Yo los cubriré.

El momento de la verdad...

Pablo carga una bala en la recámara y Pepe también.

PABLO

¿Preparado?

A la una.

A las dos.

¡Y a las TRREEESSSS!

Pablo, Tony y Pepe salen corriendo de la caseta y disparan contra los guardias del muelle. Pablo alcanza a uno de ellos. El guardia cae al agua con el dedo aún firme en el gatillo desatando una ira de balas por toda la creación. El segundo guardia corre a refugiarse. Pablo se detiene para refugiarse detrás de varias cajas grandes. Tony se esconde detrás de una maquina elevadora mientras las balas repiquetean a su alrededor. Pepe ya está en la lancha, arrancando el motor. El motor gira una vez, dos veces, y finalmente arranca. ¡VAAArrrooommmm!

A pleno pulmón.

PEPE

Vamos... Vámonos.

Pablo a unos quince metros del barco, corriendo a toda velocidad, zigzagueando y esquivando disparos salta y al fin llega al barco en un pedazo.

Los vehículos que avanzan por la carretera se detienen en la puerta principal. Los soldados salen por detrás y se apresuran a cubrirse. Los soldados dirigen su fuego hacia el barco.

Pablo suelta los amarres del barco y se coloca detrás de una ametralladora de calibre 30 en la proa del barco. Inmediatamente el la gira y empieza a disparar. El estruendo de la ametralladora lanza una ráfaga tras otra contra los soldados junto al camión. Varios soldados son heridos. De repente, ¡¡¡KKAAABOOOMMMM!!! Uno de los camiones explota por el aire como si fueran fuegos artificiales en un cuatro de julio. Pablo sigue disparándole al guardia del muelle, inmovilizándolo.

Tony está muriéndose de miedo. Siente una brisa helada que le recorre por la espalda. Es como si la muerte hubiera venido por él. Finalmente, reúne el valor suficiente para correr hacia el barco.

ENFOQUE EN TONY A CÁMARA LENTA:

Tony corre tan rápido como le es humanamente posible. Toda su vida pasa ante sus ojos. El barco se ha alejado unos tres metros del muelle. Pablo y Pepe le animan. A medida que se acerca, salta hacia el barco con toda su fuerza. De repente, una sensación de quemazón le desgarra los huesos de la espalda.

Una bala le atraviesa la parte baja de la espalda y le hace un agujero en la parte delantera del pecho. Una segunda bala (la asesina) penetra en el centro de su espalda para no volver a ser vista. Tony cae sobre la cubierta del barco sin vida, rebotando como un muñeco de goma.

Pepe revoluciona los motores y acelera la lancha a toda velocidad dejando atrás el muelle. Pablo sigue disparando ráfagas tras ráfagas de calibre 30 contra el muelle, matando a más soldados y destruyendo varias lanchas en el proceso.

La lancha patrullera desaparece en la noche.

FUNDIDO A NEGRO

EXT. TOMA NOCTURNA DE LA CASA DE ALICIA

INT. NOCHE SALA DE ALICIA

CAMARA EN OSCAR

> OSCAR
> No te preocupes, esconderé a Rosa donde nadie la encontrará.
>
> (una pausa)
>
> ¿Y tú? ¿Qué vas a hacer?

> ALICIA
> Estaré bien, nadie piensa en mí como una amenaza.

Suena el teléfono. Alicia contesta.

> ALICIA
> ¡Hola!

> NARRACION LUIS
> Hola, soy Luis.

> ALICIA
> ¡Luis! ¿Qué pasa? ¿Cómo te va?

Alicia sorprendida se vira hacia Rosa y Oscar. Rosa reacciona como si hubiera visto un fantasma. Inmediatamente, coge papel y lápiz y empieza a escribir frenéticamente algo para Alicia.

> NARRACION LUIS
> A mí me va bien. ¿Y a ti?

ALICIA

Estoy bien.

Rosa termina de escribir la nota y se la enseña a Alicia.

EL PUNTO DE VISTA DE ALICIA SOBRE LA NOTA DE ROSA

¡No le digas dónde está Pepe!

¡No le digas que estamos aquí!

¡No te fíes de él!

NARRACION LUIS

¿Has visto a Pepe o a mamá?

Alicia desconcertada por la nota de Rosa. Decide colaborar con Rosa.

ALICIA

No, no he visto a ninguno de los dos.

Pero si ves a Pepe, dile que necesito
hablar con él.

NARRACION LUIS

¿Puedo ayudarte en algo?

ALICIA

No, es sólo un asunto personal. Pepe me
debe una explicación.

NARRACION LUIS

Suena como si estuviera en problemas.
(una pausa)

Le diré que te llame en cuanto lo vea.

ALICIA

Gracias.

NARRACION LUIS

Luego hablamos.

ALICIA

¡Adiós!

Alicia cuelga el teléfono. Rosa respira aliviada.

ROSA

Siéntate Alicia. Tú también Oscar.

Tengo que dar algunas explicaciones.

Rosa prepara a Alicia y Oscar para la mala noticia.

ROSA

Tengo noticias terribles y no sé por dónde empezar.

ALICIA

¿A qué te refieres?

OSCAR

¿Se trata de Luis?

Rosa buscando las palabras adecuadas y con los ojos llorosos.

ROSA

¡Luis trabaja para la policía secreta! Es un traidor.

Las emociones interrumpen las palabras de Rosa. Oscar indignado interrumpe.

                              OSCAR

        ¡Lo sabía!

        Sabía que no se podía confiar en él.

                              ROSA

        Estoy muy avergonzada.

                              ALICIA

        No te avergüences.

        No es culpa tuya.

Alicia se arrodilla delante de Rosa. Oscar se da cuenta de que necesita mantener la cabeza clara.

                              OSCAR

        Alicia tiene razón. No te culpes.

        Nos ocuparemos de eso.

                              ROSA

        ¿Cómo?

Oscar se acerca y se sienta al otro lado de Rosa. La abraza.

                              OSCAR

        No te preocupes. Lo tengo todo previsto.

Oscar se vira hacia Alicia

OSCAR

Sabes, Luis está vigilándote. Estás tomando un gran riesgo quedándote aquí. Tu tienes que venir con nosotros.

ALICIA

¿Adónde van?

OSCAR

Con el tiempo lo sabrás.

Lo importante es que tenemos que hacer un acto de desaparición.

Alicia asienta con la cabeza.

EXT. DÍA EN ALGÚN LUGAR EN EL MEDIO DEL CARIBE

Es temprano por la mañana. El sol se asoma por el horizonte. Cuando la cámara se desplaza hacia abajo, vemos la patrullera a la deriva, sin combustible, con Pablo, Pepe y Tony dentro. Pablo está desplomado sobre los mandos del timón, durmiendo de puro agotamiento. Pepe también duerme. Tiene la cabeza de Tony acunada en su regazo intentando consolarlo. Tony está pálido, blanco, sin vida. Tiene los ojos abiertos, las pupilas dilatadas y congeladas. Su pecho está empapado de sangre.

La humedad y el calor han empezado a descomponer el cuerpo de Tony. Un olor repugnante emana de Tony. Varios tiburones grandes se agitan alrededor del barco. Sus aletas dorsales son visibles de vez en cuando. La conmoción en el agua despierta a Pablo.

El levanta la cabeza, se da la vuelta y contempla la desgarradora escena de Pepe abrazado a Tony. Se acerca a ellos y cierra suavemente los ojos de Tony. Pepe se despierta. Mira a Tony. Al darse cuenta del dolor, empieza a llorar descontroladamente.

> PABLO
> Vamos Pepe, mantente fuerte.
>
> Tenemos un largo camino que recorrer compañero.

Pablo abraza simultáneamente a Tony y a Pepe. Las lágrimas no se pueden negar.

VARIAS PAUSAS

> PABLO
> Vamos, levántate. Ayúdame con Tony.

> PEPE
> ¿Qué vas a hacer?

> PABLO
> Su cuerpo se está descomponiendo rápidamente Tenemos que deshacernos de él.

> PEPE
> ¿Quieres decir tirarlo por la borda?

> PABLO
> No tenemos otra opción.

Pepe se levanta. Juntos levantan a Tony y lo colocan en el travesaño del barco. Tony está tieso como una tabla. Pepe y Pablo rezan el Padrenuestro. Los tiburones se agitan como si supieran lo que va a pasar.

Empiezan la oración EL PADRE NUESTRO

VARIAS TOMAS AÉREAS DEL BARCO EN EL MAR

> NARRACION PABLO y PEPE JUNTOS
> Porque tuyo es el reino el poder y
> la gloria, por los siglos de los siglos,
> AMEN.

Pablo y Pepe tiran el cuerpo de Tony al mar. Inmediatamente, los tiburones entran en frenesí mientras devoran los restos de Tony. Pepe no puede soportar el sonido y el tormento de lo que está ocurriendo. Se tapa los oídos y cierra los ojos en señal de agonía y desesperación.

LA EXCENA TERMINA. DEVANESE A NEGRO

INT. DÍA CASA DE OSCAR

Es temprano. Los gallos entonan su habitual canción matutina. Rosa está despierta sorbiendo una taza de café y sentada en un sillón junto a una mesita. Oscar entra con varias bolsas de comestibles.

> OSCAR
> Buenos días.

> ROSA
> Te levantaste temprano esta mañana.

> OSCAR
> Lo sé, tuve que ir a la tienda temprano
> porque si llego más tarde, no hay nada
> que comprar.

OSCAR CONTINUA

Además, no quiero que me vean comprando tantas cosas... La gente no es estúpida.

(una pausa)

¿Has visto el periódico de hoy?

ROSA

Sí, ya lo leí.

OSCAR

Parece que se escaparon.

Rosa se levanta y camina hacia el mostrador donde Oscar puso las bolsas de la compra y se dispone a guardar los comestibles.

ROSA

¿Cómo vamos a sobrevivir con esto?

(una pausa)

¡Necesitamos leche, huevos, pan!

Alicia entra en escena. Se le nota que está embarazada.

OSCAR

Usé todos los cupones de comida que tenía.

ROSA

Por favor, esta chica está embarazada de 3 meses. Necesita una nutrición adecuada.

OSCAR
Tal vez pueda gorronear algo en la base.

ROSA
Ve ahora, antes de que esas estanterías
también estén vacías.

Rosa mira a Óscar con ojos que se comunican telepáticamente.

OSCAR
Está bien, está bien, me voy.

Oscar se vuelve a poner la chaqueta y sale por la puerta.

DE NUEVO EN EL BARCO A LA DERIVA EN EL MAR

El sol brilla. Debe de haber más de 100 grados y no hay ni una nube en el cielo. El océano este liso como un espejo reflejando cada rayo de luz. El barco está a cierta distancia, todavía a la deriva. No hay viento, ni corriente, nada .... sólo un calor increíble.

EN PANTALLA "3 DÍAS DESPUÉS"

La cámara se acerca al barco. Pablo está tumbado sobre el travesaño del barco, con un brazo colgando por encima de la borda casi tocando el agua. No se oye ni un sonido. El silencio y la quietud dan miedo. La aleta dorsal de un tiburón rompe el agua. Las ondas se propagan por la parte trasera del barco, donde cuelga el brazo de Pablo, que está casi en el agua.

La cámara empieza a retroceder cuando

CORTE A

INT. DÍA UN HELICÓPTERO GUARDACOSTA EN VUELO

El piloto y el copiloto hablan del partido de fútbol americano de anoche.

> PILOTO
>
> Compadre, todavía no me puedo creer
> lo de los Jets.
>
> Anoche se lucieron.

> CO-PILOTO
>
> Creo que ganaron ese juego de milagro.

> PILOTO
>
> El equipo de los Packers no le ganan ni a su abuela.

El radar del helicóptero empieza a pitar.

> PILOTO
>
> ¿Por qué suena el radar?

> CO-PILOTO
>
> Aparece un barco a las 2 noreste, señor.

> PILOTO
>
> Reconfirma.

> (una pausa)

> CO-PILOTO
>
> Sí señor, tenemos un barco.

> PILOTO
>
> Transmítelo a la base.

El piloto gira el helicóptero.

PILOTO
Vamos a echarle un vistazo.

EXT. DÍA EN EL HELICÓPTERO DE GUARDACOSTA

El copiloto empieza a transmitir por via electrónica al Guarda costa lo que está ocurriendo. El helicóptero hace un giro de cuarenta y cinco grados y se sumerge hacia el horizonte.

DE VUELTA AL INTERIOR DEL BARCO

Pepe está totalmente deshidratado. Está tumbado y medio inconsciente en el suelo del barco. Pablo está apenas despierto todavía en el mismo lugar. Se oye débilmente el sonido de un helicóptero. Pablo se da cuenta de lo que oye y lucha por incorporarse. Se pone en pie. Busca en el cielo el sonido del helicóptero, pero no ve nada. Se acerca a su bolsa de lona. De la bolsa saca una bandera estadounidense. Coge la bandera y la engancha en el mástil del barco, pero al revés. Con su última descarga de adrenalina, sube la bandera por el mástil.

Pablo susurra

PABLO
Por favor, Dios. Que así sea.

¡Por favor, Por favor!

Pepe se despierta.

DE VUELTA AL INTERIOR DEL HELICÓPTERO

PILOTO

Santa madre de Dios... eso es una patrullera cubana.

CO-PILOTO

Sí, ¿pero ves lo que yo veo?

PILOTO

¡Claro que sí!

Punto de vista DE LA TRIPULACIÓN EN EL HELICÓPTERO

La patrullera exhibe la bandera Norte Americana al revés. Pepe le
llama y hace señas al helicóptero. El helicóptero sobrevuela la lancha
patrullera.

DE VUELTA AL INTERIOR DEL HELICÓPTERO

PILOTO

Esto es nuevo para mí.

CO-PILOTO

¿Y que si es una trampa?

(una pausa)

Quién sabe... quizá estén probando otro
de sus trucos.

Mientras el copiloto revisa el barco desde el helicóptero.

PILOTO

No lo creo. La tripulación no lleva uniforme y parecen más muertos que vivos.

CO-PILOTO
Sólo veo dos hombres a bordo.

PILOTO
Afirmativo. ¡Esto es increíble!

CO-PILOTO
Un signo de desesperación.

PILOTO
El precio de la libertad.

El copiloto asiente.

PILOTO
¡Vamos a recogerlos!

Baja el gancho.

CORTE A VARIAS TOMAS DEL RESCATE DE PEPE Y PABLO

EXT. DIA EL HELICOPTERO VUELA EN EL HORIZONTE CON PEPE Y PABLO A BORDO

DESVANECE A

EXT. TOMA DE LA OFICINA DE INMIGRACION EN MIAMI

INT. OFICINA DE INMIGRACIÓN

Los empleados de inmigración trabajan por todas partes procesando a los refugiados. Pepe y Pablo son escoltados a un tanque de retención (una celda grande). Llevan ropa naranja de inmigración.

INT. OFICINA DE CRISTAL JUNTO AL Tanque de retención de los no procesados.

AGENTE SANDERS
¿Están esos dos listos para el interrogatorio?

ASISTENTE JACK
Sí, señor.

Jack se vuelve hacia otro agente de la sala.

AGENTE SANDERS
¿Estás listo para ser malo otra vez?

AGENTE BOB
¡Listo y dispuesto!

AGENTE SANDERS
Bien. Traigan al primero.

Un ayudante se acerca al tanque de retención. Saca a Pepe. El agente conduce a Pepe a un despacho de cristal donde le piden que se siente en un extremo de la mesa. Dentro están los agentes aparentemente listos para interrogar a Pepe. Bob, vestido con el típico traje de poliéster, se sienta frente a Pepe.

AGENTE SANDERS
Bien, Sr. Martínez, empecemos por el principio. ¿Habla inglés?

Habla con dificultad debido en parte a sus labios agrietados.

PEPE

Sí, asistí a una escuela americana en La
Habana.

AGENTE SANDERS

Bien, entonces vayamos al grano.

¿Cómo conseguiste esa cañonera
cubana?

PEPE

Nos la robamos del Puerto de Mariel.

AGENTE BOB

¡Mentira! Estás mintiendo.

No esperarás que nos creamos esa
mierda, ¿verdad?

PEPE

Señor, no sé quién es usted y, franca-
mente, no me importa. Pero cuando me
hable, asegúrese de hacerlo con respeto,
de la misma manera que yo le hablo a
usted.

El agente Bob, furioso, salta de su silla y se acerca a Pepe. Está a
punto de explotar a centímetros de PEPE cuando interviene el agente
Sanders.

AGENTE SANDERS

Tranquilo Bob, tranquilo... dale a este
señor la oportunidad de explicarse.

Bob retrocede.

AGENTE SANDERS
Por favor, Sr. Martínez, necesitamos
una explicación detallada para nuestros
archivos. Usted necesita cooperar con
nosotros.

Pepe, frío como una lechuga, dirige su respuesta a Sanders.

PEPE
Lo estoy haciendo. Le estoy diciendo la
verdad. Mire, déjeme explicarle.

(varias pausas)

Pepe se acomoda en su silla.

PEPE
Tres de nosotros robamos la lancha del
Puerto Mariel.

(una pausa)

Pero uno de nosotros no sobrevivió.

(otra pausa)

Pueden confirmar lo que digo ex-
aminando las manchas de sangre en la
lancha.

CORTE A

INT. DÍA EN EL TANQUE DE RETENCION EN INMIGRACIÓN

Pablo está sentado en un banco mientras otros cuatro detenidos son
escoltados al interior del tanque. Llevan los mismos uniformes que

Pablo y Pepe tienen puesto. Un agente de inmigración cierra la celda detrás de ellos.

DETENIDO 1

¿Tienes un cigarrillo?

PABLO

No, no fumo.

DETENIDO 1

¿Eres cubano?

PABLO

Sí, soy de Guantánamo.

DETENIDO 2

De ahí vengo.

Los cuatro cubanos se presentan, se hacen amigos de Pablo. Pablo señala a Pepe en el despacho de cristal.

PABLO

Mi compañero y yo robamos una cañonera en Mariel.

Uno de los detenidos reconoce a Pepe.

DETENIDO 3

Conozco a ese tipo. ¿No era su padre ¿José Martínez?

PABLO

¡No era, es!

> DETENIDO 4
>
> No, "era". El tiempo correcto es "era".

> PABLO
>
> ¿A qué te refieres? ¿Qué quieres decir?

> DETENIDO 4
>
> ¿No lo sabías? ... Castro mato a su padre
> y a su tío.

El rumor era que estaban conspirando para derrocar a Castro.

> PABLO
>
> ¿Seguro?

> DETENIDO 4
>
> Por supuesto que estoy seguro, me
> deshice de sus cuerpos junto con varios
> otros detrás de EL CASTILLO del
> MORRO.
>
> Están en el fondo de la bahía.

Pablo se queda frio. Le pasan por la cabeza todo tipo de pensamientos.

INT. DÍA EN CASA DE JOSE Y ROSA

Luis está en la casa con varios soldados. Están poniendo la casa patas arriba en busca de pistas.

> LUIS
>
> Sigue buscando, seguro que encontrare-
> mos algo.

Mientras los soldados continúan su búsqueda, Luis se acerca al piano. Encima del piano hay fotos de la familia. Una de las fotos fue tomada recientemente en la Fiesta del Aniversario Revolucionario, donde José, Ramón y Óscar están todos juntos. Luis coge la foto.

LUIS PUNTO DE VISTA (PDV)DE LA FOTO

Los tres hombres disfrutando el momento.

ENFOQUE EN LUIS

El reflexiona y piensa en Oscar. Su intuición se apodera de él.

LUIS
Sargento, si encuentras algo, llámame a
la comisaría inmediatamente.

SARGENTO

¡Sí, señor!

Luis sale volando de la casa con el portarretratos bajo el brazo.

EXT. DÍA ENTRADA PRINCIPAL A LAS OFICINAS DE INMIGRACIÓN DE MIAMI

Pepe y Pablo salen vestidos con ropa civil. Empiezan a bajar las escaleras.

PEPE

¡Por fin lo hicimos!

Al pie de la escalera, Pepe respira profundo y se vuelve hacia Pablo.

PEPE

Gracias, Pablo.

Nunca lo hubiera logrado sin ti.

PABLO

Ni lo menciones.

PEPE

Hacemos un buen equipo.

PABLO

Creo que sí.

PEPE

¿Tienes dónde quedarte?

PABLO

No.

PEPE

¿Por qué no nos quedamos juntos?

PABLO

Bien, pero nada de cosas raras.

Comparten una carcajada.

PEPE

¿Tomamos el autobús?

PABLO

¿Sabes adónde vas?

PEPE

No. ¿Qué Importa?

Pablo suelta otra carcajada.

PABLO

Tony me advirtió sobre ti.

PEPE

Hemos llegado hasta aquí, ¿no?

PABLO

Voy a tener que hablar con Alicia cuando regresemos.

Se pasan los brazos por los hombros. Pepe apenas alcanza los hombros de Pablo. Mientras caminan hacia la parada del autobús, Pepe y Pablo bromean el uno con el otro.

PEPE

Escucha, uno de los agentes de allí me dijo que podemos conseguir trabajo en la playa tal vez como ayudantes de camareros.

PABLO

Nunca lograrás ser ayudante de camarero.

PEPE

¿De qué estás hablando?

Yo fui el jefe de camareros en el Tropicana.

Hipócritamente.

PABLO

Claro que sí.

Esto tengo que verlo yo.

PEPE

Miami Beach, ¡allá vamos!

EXT. PALACIO PRESIDENCIAL EN LA HABANA TOMA DE DIA

INT. OFICINA DE OSCAR DÍA

Oscar está sentado detrás de su escritorio. Tocan a la puerta.

OSCAR

¡Adelante!

Luis entra en el despacho seguido de cerca por dos diputados. Los dos diputados empiezan a acercarse al escritorio. Oscar corre instintivamente. Coge un abrecartas y se lo clava al diputado que tiene más cerca. Empuja al segundo diputado contra Luis y los derriba a los dos. Como un gato, salta por la ventana, atraviesa el cristal y cae en la calle.

Luis desenfunda su pistola y se precipita hacia la ventana.

LUIS PDV

OSCAR CORRE POR LA CALLE

> LUIS
> Atrapen a ese hijo de puta.
>
> Lo quiero vivo.

Otro policía militar sale volando tras Oscar saltando por la ventana hacia la calle, al igual que Óscar. Comienza la persecución por las calles de La Habana.

EXT. DÍA POR LAS CALLES DE LA HABANA

Un montaje de escenas de persecución por las calles de La Habana.

Los peatones son atropellados por Oscar, que corre a toda velocidad. Los carros se detienen súbitamente para evitar atropellar al policía militar. De repente, el policía militar se detiene y desenfunda su arma.

> POLICIA MILITAR
> ¡Alto! ¡O disparo!

La gente se dispersa cuando el policía militar dispara un tiro de advertencia al aire. Oscar ni siquiera mira hacia atrás. Oscar, como un corredor de Olimpiadas, sigue corriendo calle abajo.

PDV DE POLICIA MILITAR

No hay ningún rastro de Oscar. Oscar lo perdió.

VOLVER al POLICIA MILITAR

POLICIA MILITAR
¡Mierda!

EXT. NOCHE ENTRADA TRASERA DE UN HOTEL DE MIAMI BEACH

Pablo y Pepe salen del trabajo. Sus delantales están sucios y grasientos.

El sudor les ha empapado las axilas y la mitad de la espalda.

Pepe se seca el sudor de la frente.

PEPE
Vaya, fue un día infernal.

PABLO
Pan comido.

Imagínate cortando caña de azúcar en Cuba.

PEPE
Supongo que tienes razón.

(pausa)

Me pregunto cómo estarán mamá y papá.

Pablo no responde. Su rostro palidece. ¿Imagínate, un rostro pálido en ese mulato? Pepe es perspectivo, capta las vibraciones.

> PEPE
> ¿Qué pasa Pablo?
>
> ¿De qué se trata?

Pablo no responde.

> PEPE
> ¿Te sientes mal? ¿Necesitas una aspirina
> o algo?

Pablo sigue sin responder.

> PEPE
> Mira, sea lo que sea el problema, seguro
> que podemos solucionarlo.
>
> (varias pausas)

Silencio de Pablo

> PEPE CONTINUADO
> Vamos, háblame.

Pablo busca las palabras para darle la noticia a Pepe. Sin expresión ninguna

> PABLO
> ¡Tu padre está muerto!

Pepe no entiende el significado de lo que acaba de decir Pablo.

Pasan varios segundos.

PEPE

¿Qué has dicho?

Severamente

PABLO

Tu padre y tu tío están muertos.

A Pepe se le doblan las rodillas y se le hace un nudo en la garganta.

PEPE

¿Cómo?

PABLO

Castro los fusiló a los dos por traición.

Al fin Pepe entiende los hechos. Le duele el alma. Se le hinchan los ojos y empiezan a caerle lágrimas por la cara.

PEPE

¿Cuándo te enteraste?

PABLO

En cuanto llegamos a la oficina de Inmigración.

Pepe mira a Pablo con desesperación y luego con rabia.

PEPE

¿Con quién?

PABLO

¿Te acuerdas de aquellos hombres que conocimos en el tanque de detención?

PEPE

Si. ¿Cómo puedes estar seguro? ¿Por qué
confías en ellos?

PABLO

Vieron los cuerpos.

Ellos fueron los que arrojaron los cuerpos en puerto de La Habana.

Pepe conteniendo el dolor. Un momento desgarrador.

PEPE

¿Por qué? ¡Todo lo que hicimos fue
ayudar a ese hijo de puta!

Pablo abraza a Pepe intentando consolarlo. Pepe sollozando.

PEPE

Tony, mi tío, mi padre…

Cristo. Tanta gente ha muerto…

Pablo interrumpe.

PABLO

No es fácil Pepe. Sé cómo te sientes.

(pausa)

Yo también perdí a mis padres de forma
similar.

PEPE

¿Y mi madre?

PABLO
No se dijo nada.

PEPE
¿Estás seguro? Dime la verdad.

PABLO
No Pepe lo juro, no se dijo nada.

(una pausa)

Vamos, vamos para casa.

Pepe y Pablo se ayudan a caminar por el callejón detrás del hotel y se dirigen a casa.

EXT. DÍA PLANO GENERAL DE LA CASA DE OSCAR

Oscar llega en carro. Sale rápidamente del carro y entra en la casa.

INT. DÍA SALA DE OSCAR

Rosa está sentada escribiendo una carta. Oscar entra por la puerta principal sin aliento y asustado. Se asoma a la ventana para ver si lo han seguido. Empieza a cerrar todas las persianas venecianas que encuentra abiertas. Rosa le mira preguntándose qué le pasa. Alicia ya mostrando una enorme barriga sale de la cocina. A Oscar le falta el aire.

OSCAR
¡Ellos saben!

ROSA
¿Quién sabe?

OSCAR

Luis... Castro... ¡todos!

(recupera el aliento)

Luis y un par de diputados vinieron a arrestarme en mi oficina.

ROSA

¿Por qué?

OSCAR

¿Quién sabe por qué? ¿Por las mismas razones que se llevaron a José?

(una pausa)

Creo que perdí al Policía que me seguía; pero no puedo estar seguro.

ALICIA

¿Y ahora qué?

Oscar sigue tratando de recuperar su aliento.

OSCAR

Tenemos que irnos enseguida.

Conozco un lugar donde podemos escondernos.

ALICIA

¿Dónde?

OSCAR

Una pequeña choza cerca del Puerto de
Mariel.

ROSA

¿Y su bebé?

ALICIA

Soy fuerte, lo lograré.

Rosa se vira hacia Oscar. Le entrega un sobre. Es una carta de Pepe.

OSCAR

¿Cómo lo has conseguido?

ROSA

Deja de preocuparte.

Mi hermana trabaja en las oficinas del
Correo.

Me lo pasó de contrabando esta mañana.

Alicia resplandeciente.

ALICIA

Sabía que escribiría.

Encontrará la manera de sacarnos.

OSCAR

No puedes responder.

ROSA

¿Por qué?

OSCAR

Es el primer lugar que vigilarán.

Nos seguirán la pista.

ROSA

Mi hermana nos ayudará. Ellos nunca verán o sabrán de ninguna carta.

OSCAR

No. Eso está fuera de discusión.

ROSA

Vamos Oscar, no seas irrazonable.

Pepe necesita saber dónde estamos.

OSCAR

Si esa carta llega a las manos equivocadas....

ALICIA

Te dejaré leer las cartas antes de enviarlas por correo.

Oscar murmura para sí mismo.

ROSA

¿Qué has dicho?

OSCAR

Nada.

Oscar se vira hacia Alicia dando su consentimiento.

OSCAR
Está bien, pero veo cada carta y cada
línea.

Alicia besa a Oscar en la mejilla.

OSCAR
Ahora vámonos de aquí.

EXT. DIA EN EL HOTEL DE MIAMI BEACH DONDE TRABAJAN PEPE Y PABLO

INT. DÍA UN SALÓN DE BAILE PRIVADO - ENTRETENIMIENTO EN PROCESO

En el centro de la sala hay una mesa de póquer. Cinco hombres y una mujer están sentados alrededor de la mesa. Se está jugando una partida de grandes apuestas. Pepe sirve bebidas a los comensales. Pablo sirve entremeses calientes y manjares que complacerían el paladar de un rey. Uno de los invitados que se sienta en la mesa de póquer está siendo rudo y maleducado. Está fumando un puro. Mientras el humo se escapa de su aliento, habla de su vida y de sus logros.

SR. THOMPSON
Sí, solía tener varios negocios en La
Habana. Tenía una gran relación con
Batista hasta que el pobre bastardo fue
expulsado.

Hace una pausa para dar una calada a su puro. El crupier reparte una nueva mano de cartas.

SR. THOMPSON

Ahora las cosas son diferentes. Ya no es el paraíso que fue antes. Ahora La Habana solo sirve para putas mediocres y buenos puros.

CRUPIER NARRACION

¿Cuántos?

SR. THOMPSON

Dame dos.

Mientras el humo del puro sale de la boca del Sr. Thompson.

SR. THOMPSON

Es una pena... Ese maldito país solía ser mi patio de recreo favorito.

Pepe, que ya ha oído bastante, está a punto de perder la tabla. Las estupideces que salen de la boca de este hombre son para enojar hasta la Madre Teresa. Cuando se acerca a la mesa, la señora Fischman se da cuenta de las intenciones de Pepe. Se acerca al brazo de Pepe y lo detiene.

Sra. FISCHMAN

No vale la pena, hijo.

Pepe y la Sra. Fischman mantienen contacto visual. No hace falta decir nada más.

Sra. FISCHMAN

Por favor, tráeme un Vodka con Tónica.

Pepe reanuda su trabajo.

PEPE
Sí, señora...

El crupier se vuelve de nuevo hacia el Sr. Thompson.

CRUPIER
Usted decide, Sr. Thompson.

SR. THOMPSON
Estoy fuera.

El Sr. Thompson abandona sus cartas sobre la mesa. Pepe se dirige a la barra. Pablo está de pie junto a la barra doblando unas servilletas.

PEPE
¿Oíste lo que dijo ese imbécil?

PABLO
¿Quién? ¿El viejo salvaje?

PEPE
Sí.

PABLO
¿Y a ti que te importa?

¡CALIENTE!

PEPE
Putas y buenos puros... ¿eh?

PABLO
Tranquilo Pepe. Si escuchas las estupideces, Te volverás loco.

PEPE

Lo arreglaré.

Pepe se vira hacia el camarero.

PEPE

Dame dos Vodka con Tónica.

Pepe se tranquiliza un poco y pone las dos bebidas en su bandeja. Las lleva hacia la mesa de póquer. Pablo observa todos sus movimientos.

Pepe sirve una de las bebidas a la Sra. Fischman.

PEPE

Aquí tienes, señora.

SRA. FISCHMAN

Muchas Gracias.

PEPE camina por detrás del Sr. Thompson.

PEPE

¿Puedo ofrecerle algo de beber, señor?

SR. THOMPSON

Sí, tráeme uno de esos Cuba Libres.

Pepe, frío como una lechuga, inclina la bandeja y deja caer casualmente el otro Vodka sobre el Sr. Thompson. El Sr. Thompson se levanta de su asiento.

SR. THOMPSON

¡Jesucristo, hombre! Serás idiota????....

Pepe coge su bandeja y golpea al Sr. Thompson en la cabeza y luego en los huevos. El Sr. Thompson se agacha. Se desata el pandemónium.

El crupier aprieta un botón de alarma en el lateral de la mesa. El Sr. Thompson le tira un golpe a Pepe, fallando, pero haciendo que dos cartas escondidas en su manga salgan volando y caigan al suelo. Todos se fijan en las cartas. El Sr. Thompson se queda paralizado, entre enfadado y avergonzado. El silencio cubre la sala como una manta. Pepe recoge una de las cartas. (varias pausas)

> ### SRA. FISCHMAN
> Creo que es usted en quien no se puede confiar, Sr. Thompson. ¡Le debe a todos aquí una disculpa y ni mencionar sus ganancias!

El Sr. Thompson se queda sin palabras. Dos guardias de seguridad irrumpen en la sala. El crupier señala al Sr. Thompson. Los dos guardias agarran al Sr. Thompson y lo escoltan hacia fuera.

> ### SEGURIDAD #1
> Vamos imbécil.

El jefe de camareros hace una señal a PEPE llamándolo. La Sra. Fischman (la única que queda sentada en la mesa de póquer) se levanta y se acerca a Pepe.

> ### SRA. FISCHMAN
> Ahoranecesitarás un nuevo trabajo.

Pepe avergonzado no dice una palabra.

> ### SRA. FISCHMAN
> Ven a verme mañana por la tarde a las 2:00 PM.
>
> Puede que tenga algo para ti. Aquí está mi tarjeta.

La Sra. Fischman le da a Pepe su tarjeta y sale despreocupadamente del cuadro.

EXT. PLANO GENERAL NOCTURNO DEL ESCONDITE DE OSCAR / UNA CHOZA EN MEDIO DE LA NADA

Rosa, Alicia y Oscar caminan hacia la puerta principal.

INT. NOCHE LA CHOZA

Entran. Alicia, cada día más grande, apenas puede andar y se dirige directamente al sofá. Se quita los zapatos y empieza a abanicarse con una revista de la mesita.

ALICIA
Pensé que nunca lo lograríamos.

OSCAR
Deberíamos estar a salvo aquí por un tiempo.

Alicia sintiendo su vientre

ALICIA
No sé si podré aguantar mucho más.

Este bebé es enorme o he estado embarazada más tiempo de lo que pensaba.

ROSA
Está bien cariño, trajimos todo lo que necesitamos por si el bebé se adelanta.

OSCAR

Escuchen, señoras. Aquí están las reglas
que seguiremos.

Oscar recupera el aliento mientras se descarga una mochila de la
espalda.

OSCAR

Todo el mundo se queda en casa durante
el día.

Nadie sale de esta choza sin mi permiso.

Ni siquiera a la oficina de correos.
¿Entendido?

ALICIA

Por favor Oscar, no estamos en el
Ejército.

OSCAR

Debemos tener cuidado. Estoy seguro
de que en todos los carteles de la isla
somos "Los Más Buscados"

Rosa intentando aligerar el momento, le da un saludo militar a Oscar.

ROSA

Sí, señor.

Alicia se ríe.

OSCAR

Muy graciosas... Es bueno ver que todavía tienen sentido del humor.

Rosa inspeccionando la Choza.

ROSA

¿Qué días viene la criada?

A Óscar no le hace gracia el humor de Rosa.

ALICIA

Relájate Oscar, no te preocupes tanto.

El grupo se acomoda.

EXT. NOCHE UN VIEJO EDIFICIO DE APARTAMENTOS EN MIAMI

Pepe y Pablo entran por la puerta principal.

INT. NOCHE EN EL INTERIOR DEL EDIFICIO DE APARTAMENTOS

Pepe y Pablo están sudados y cansados. Empiezan a subir las escaleras cuando, de repente, Pepe se detiene.

PEPE

Revisaré el correo.

Pepe da la vuelta y baja a los buzones. Pablo sigue subiendo las escaleras.

PABLO

¿Por qué? Todo lo que recibimos son cuentas por pagar.

Pepe abre el buzón y, efectivamente, caen un montón de facturas. Entre ellas hay una carta de Cuba. Pepe contentísimo y ansioso empieza a abrir la carta mientras sube las escaleras. Pepe tropezando.

PEPE

Pablo, recibimos una carta de Alicia.

INT. NOCHE APARTAMENTO DE PEPE Y PABLO

Pablo mirando a un refrigerador vacío. Pepe entra y se sienta en una mesa con un par de sillas disparejas. Pepe empieza a leer la carta.

NARRACION PEPE

Mi querido Pepe,

CAMBIAR A

NARRACION ALICIA

Te extraño muchísimo y espero que estés bien cuando recibas esta carta. Estoy segura de que las noticias sobre tu padre y Roberto llegaron a Miami. Lamento no estar a tu lado especialmente en este momento de dolor. Desearía poder consolarte y reconfortarte en este momento tan triste.

He estado viviendo con tu madre y Oscar casi desde que te fuiste. No tuvimos elección, ya que el gobierno nos ha estado persiguiendo por razones obvias. Hace poco, nos mudamos a un lugar en el que tú solías jugar cuando eras niño. Oscar me dijo que te dijera que estamos en la vieja casa donde te caíste del techo y te abriste la barbilla.

Espero que puedas sacarnos pronto. Todos te echamos mucho de menos. No te preocupes por nosotros; Oscar está haciendo un gran trabajo manteniéndonos a salvo. Los cuatro estamos bien y sanos, aunque a veces nos cuesta conseguir lo esencial. Te quiero y estoy deseando que llegue el día en que pueda volver a tenerte en mis brazos.

Por siempre tu amada esposa, Alicia

LA NARRACION DE ALICIA TERMINA

ENFOQUE EN PEPE

Hace una pausa pensando.

PEPE

¿Nosotros cuatro?

ENFOQUE EN PABLO

Pablo levanta las cejas.

ENFOQUE A PEPE

Relee las dos últimas líneas. De repente, cae en la cuenta.

NARRACION PABLO

Felicidades mi hermano...

vas a ser padre.

Pepe no lo puede creer. Le falta el aire y sin palabras

PEPE

¡Voy a ser padre!

PABLO

Sí, lo sé, ¡es maravilloso!

PEPE

No lo puedo creer, ¡Voy a ser padre!

PABLO

Lo sé, ya lo dijiste.

Pepe se da cuenta de repente de por qué Alicia se negó a venir con él en el barco. El deja de celebrar el acontecimiento.

PEPE

Alicia estaba embarazada....

Por eso se negó a venir conmigo.

(pausa)

Ahora todo tiene sentido.

PABLO

¡Felicidades!

Pepe se acerca a Pablo y le da un fuerte abrazo. La palabra exuberante se queda corta.

PEPE

Pablo. ¡Voy a ser padre!

PABLO

¡Sí Pepe!

PEPE
Tenemos que conseguir las visas lo antes
posible. Tenemos que sacarlos de Cuba.

PABLO
No te preocupes. La embajada dijo que estarán listas en unas pocas
semanas.

INT. DÍA DESPACHO DE FIDEL CASTRO

Un limpiabotas lustra las botas de Fidel. Las puertas de su despacho
están abiertas y dos diputados acompañan a Luis. Luis tiene una
mirada preocupada.

LUIS
¿Quería verme, señor?

FIDEL
Sí, entra, siéntate conmigo un minuto.

Fidel hace una señal al limpiabotas para que se marche y le lanza una
moneda. Luis sigue de pie junto a la puerta.

FIDEL
¡Siéntate! ¡Siéntate!

Luis se sienta cautelosamente frente a Fidel.

FIDEL
¿Sabes por qué estás aquí?

LUIS
Sí, señor.

FIDEL

Dime por qué.

LUIS

Porque no he encontrado a Oscar, Alicia
o Rosa.

Fidel reconoce la declaración de Luis tratándolo con condescendencia.

FIDEL

Bien... me alegro que me entiendas
claramente.

(una pausa)

¿Cuándo debo esperarlos aquí?

LUIS

Al final de esta semana, señor.

Fidel, decepcionado con la respuesta, se acerca a Luis. Muy cerca de la
cara de Luis, Fidel exhala el humo del su puro directamente afectando
la respiración de Luis y susurra.

FIDEL

Sólo tienes 48 horas para encontrarlos.

¿Me explico bien?

Luis reconoce. El sudor cae por la frente de Luis. Fidel retrocede.

FIDEL

Ahora lárgate de aquí antes que cambie
de opinión.

Luis se levanta y sale a toda prisa por la puerta sin decir una palabra.

EXT. PUENTE DIURNO "STAR ISLAND" EN MIAMI BEACH

Hace un día precioso. El sol brilla en una tarde calurosa y húmeda. Pepe se baja del Metrobús y cruza el puente. Finalmente, llega a la puerta de guardia. Empapado en sudor.

> PEPE
>
> Disculpe.

El guardia abre la ventana de cristal de su puesto climatizado.

> GUARDIA
>
> ¿Puedo ayudarlo?

> PEPE
>
> Vengo a ver a la Sra. Fischman.

> GUARDIA
>
> ¿Le está esperando?

> PEPE
>
> Sí, tengo cita con ella a las 2:00PM.

Pepe saca la tarjeta de la Sra. Fischman del bolsillo de su camisa y se la enseña al guardia.

> GUARDIA
>
> ¿Cómo te llamas?

> PEPE
>
> Pepe Martínez.

El guardia consulta una lista de nombres en su portapapeles.

GUARDIA

Sí, aquí estas...

(una pausa)

Puedes entrar.

PEPE

Gracias.

Las rejas eléctricas se abren y Pepe entra.

EXT. DÍA EN LA MANSIÓN DE LA SRA. FISCHMAN

¡Qué lugar! Una casa increíble al lado del mar. Pepe se acerca a las puertas de bronce. Se da cuenta de que una cámara de vigilancia sigue todos sus movimientos. Pepe pulsa un botón. Le responde el mayordomo.

MAYORDOMO

¿Puedo ayudarle?

Un poco impaciente.

PEPE

Soy Pepe Martínez, vine a ver a la Sra. Fischman. Ella esta esperándome.

MAYORDOMO

Pase, por favor.

Las puertas se abren electrónicamente. Pepe atraviesa las puertas y se dirige a la entrada, donde el mayordomo lo espera.

MAYORDOMO

Sígame.

MANSIÓN DE LA SRA. FISCHMAN

Pepe sigue al mayordomo al interior de esta increíble mansión. Juntos recorren las habitaciones más bellamente decoradas y repletas de obras de arte de valor incalculable. Llegan a la parte trasera de la casa, que da a una enorme piscina con terraza frente a la bahía de Biscayne. La Sra. Fischman está sentada bajo una sombrilla tomando té.

SRA. FISCHMAN

Me alegro de que hayas podido venir.

PEPE

Gracias por invitarme.

SRA. FISCHMAN

¿Sam (el mayordomo) traerle algo de beber?

PEPE

Un vaso de agua fría estaría bien.

Pepe mira abrumado por la belleza de su entorno.

SRA. FISCHMAN

¿Seguro que no podemos ofrecerte algo más?

PEPE

No, gracias.

Sam agradece y se va a buscar el agua. Pepe se sienta frente a la Sra. Fischman.

PEPE
Tienes una casa preciosa.

SRA. FISCHMAN
Gracias, pero vamos a prescindir de todas las formalidades.

(una pausa)

A Pepe le sorprende su franqueza.

SRA. FISCHMAN
Tengo un trabajo para ti.

Es un trabajo peligroso, pero paga muy bien.

PEPE
Te escucho.

La señora Fischman fuma un cigarrillo

SRA. FISCHMAN
Sé todo sobre tu familia en Cuba.

(una pausa)

Cómo asesinaron a tu padre y la desaparición de algunos de tus amigos. También sé que tú y tu prometida están esperando un hijo.

Pepe está estupefacto, no tiene ni idea de cómo ella sabe toda esta información.

PEPE
¿Cómo?

La Sra. Fischman interrumpe

SRA. FISCHMAN
Creo que soy yo la que tiene que hacer
las preguntas.

Pepe retrocede y escucha.

SRA. FISCHMAN
Digamos que trabajo para el gobierno de
EE.UU. y que tenemos intereses vitales
en Cuba.

La Sra. Fischman toma un sorbo de su té.

SRA. FISCHMAN
Si completa con éxito lo que le pedimos, garantizaremos el salvo-
conducto para que su madre y su prometida salgan de Cuba. (pausa)
Además, a usted le pagaremos $50,000 dólares.

Los ojos de Pepe se iluminan, no puede creer lo que oye.

SRA. FISCHMAN
¿Aceptas el trabajo, Pepe?

Pepe sin dudarlo.

PEPE
Sí, claro, ¿Qué tengo que hacer?

SRA. FISCHMAN

¿Recuerdas esa base de la Fuerza Aérea que tú y tu padre construyeron para Castro en 1960?

PEPE

¿Te refieres a la de SAN CRISTOBAL?

SRA. FISCHMAN

¡Sí!

Tenemos que visitar e inspeccionar esa base con tu ayuda.

Pepe se da cuenta del peligro que entraña.

PEPE

Lo que me pides es un suicidio.

SRA. FISCHMAN

Créeme Pepe, esas no son nuestras intenciones.

En esta misión te escoltarán los mejores soldados que tiene los Estados Unidos.

Además, no creo que tengas ninguna otra opción, ¿no es así, Sr. Martínez?

La Sra. Fischman se levanta y le da la espalda a PEPE. Pasan varias pausas.

PEPE

¿Estás diciendo que nunca conseguiré las visas que solicité?

SRA. FISCHMAN

Déjeme ponerlo de esta manera PEPE...

¿Le gustaría volver a trabajar como camarero y seguir luchando, o le gustaría sacar a su familia durante esta vida?

La Sra. Fischman se vira hacia Pepe. Se está frustrando.

PEPE

Creo que sabe la respuesta de esa pregunta.

SRA. FISCHMAN

¡Bien! Entonces tenemos un acuerdo.

(una breve pausa)

Ahora hay una condición muy importante a nuestro acuerdo PEPE.

PEPE

¿Y cuál es esa?

SRA. FISCHMAN

Debes mantener nuestro pacto y acuerdo totalmente confidencial.

No hablará de esto con nadie, ni siquiera con tu mejor amigo Pablo.

Una vez más, Pepe se sorprende por la información que tiene la Sra. Fischman.

SRA. FISCHMAN

¿Tenemos un acuerdo, Sr. Martínez?

PEPE
Le doy mi palabra.

SRA. FISCHMAN
Bien, lo quiero listo en cuanto lo llame.

Le entrega un sobre que ha estado todo el tiempo encima de la mesa.

SRA. FISCHMAN
Lea esto cuando vuelva a su apartamento.

He conseguido empleo para usted y
Pablo.

Ahora debo pedirle que se vaya, tengo
otras cosas urgentes que atender.

La curiosidad lo invade. Está a punto de hablar cuando

SRA. FISCHMAN
Ya he dicho suficiente.

La Sra. Fischman apaga su cigarrillo en un cenicero que hay sobre la
mesa.

SRA. FISCHMAN
¿Estarás listo cuando te llame?

PEPE
¡Sí! Estaré listo.

El mayordomo trae el agua. Un primer plano del vaso mientras nos
disolvemos a

EXT. DÍA LA CHOZA

Otro día abrasador. Las olas de calor suben desde el suelo.

INT. DÍA LA CHOZA "EN PANTALLA 3 MESES DESPUES"

Alicia está sudando profusamente. Sufre un dolor evidente sujetándose el bajo vientre.

> ALICIA
>
> ¿Por qué siento estas contracciones?
>
> Mi bebé no se supone que nazca hasta dentro de un mes.

> ROSA
>
> Cálmate, tómalo con calma.
>
> Este calor puede ser abrumador.

Rosa seca el sudor de la frente de Alicia. Alicia respira profundamente. Intenta relajarse.

> ALICIA
>
> Rosa, necesito que me prometas algo.

> ROSA
>
> Ahora no Alicia, vamos, cálmate.
>
> Necesitas descansar.

> ALICIA
>
> Rosa por favor esto es muy importante para mí.

> ROSA
>
> Está bien cariño, ¿qué pasa?

ALICIA

Prométeme que no importa lo que pase,
tú te encargarás del bebé primero.

ROSA

¿Te estás volviendo loca?

Alicia agarra con fuerza el brazo de Rosa.

ALICIA

¡Escúchame!

Pase lo que pase cuidarás el bebé.

(una pausa)

Prométeme...

Rosa tratando de apaciguar a Alicia.

ROSA

Por supuesto que vamos a cuidar al bebé.

Basta ya de tonterías, hay que ahorrar tu
energía. Necesitas descansar.

Alicia aprieta con más fuerza el brazo de Rosa casi cortándole la
circulación.

ALICIA

¡Prométemelo Coño!

VARIAS PAUSAS

Alicia está pegada a Rosa esperando una respuesta.

ROSA

Sí Alicita… te lo prometo.

Alicia suelta el brazo de Rosa, se reclina en la silla y respira profundo…

Se abanica con un abanico de mano.

LA IMAGEN SE DISUELVE A NEGRO

EN PANTALLA, APRIL 1st. 1961

EXT. NOCHE HOTEL MIAMI BEACH FLORIDA

Pablo y Pepe atienden la barra en una discoteca. El local está lleno de mujeres. Suena el teléfono de la barra. Pablo contesta el teléfono.

PABLO

¡Aquarius Bar and Grill!

Hace una pausa para escuchar.

PABLO

Claro que sí, un segundo por favor.

Pablo se vira hacia Pepe.

PABLO

Pepe, tienes una llamada.

Pepe termina de preparar una bebida y se la sirve a un cliente. Se acerca al teléfono.

PEPE

Hola,

SRA. FISCHMAN

Hola Pepe soy yo.

Pepe apenas oye quién está al otro lado. La música está a todo volumen.

PEPE

¿A quién?

Pepe se lleva la palma de la mano libre y se tapa la oreja opuesta.

PEPE

¿Podría hablar un poco más alto?

SRA. FISCHMAN

Soy yo, Pepe. ¡Sra. Fischman!

PEPE

Muy bien, Sra. Fischman.

Lo siento por el ruido, es que estamos muy ocupados esta noche.

SRA. FISCHMAN

Es la hora Pepe. Tienes que estar en Nick 's Cabaret a la 1AM.

Dos de mis asistentes se reunirán con usted en la sala VIP.

Pepe mira su reloj.

PDV DEL RELOJ CUARZO – Son las 11:00 PM

PEPE

Muy bien, allí estaré.

SRA. FISCHMAN
¡No llegues tarde!

PEPE
Está bien, no se preocupe...

Pepe cuelga el teléfono. El bar está lleno de clientes.

PABLO
Vamos Pepe, échame una mano.

Pepe se apresura a ayudar a Pablo. Mientras preparan las bebidas.

PABLO
¿Quién era?

PEPE
Mi cita de esta noche.

PABLO
¿Una cita?

PEPE
Sí, ¿qué tiene de malo?

PABLO
¿Y Alicia?

PEPE
¿Qué, ahora eres mi consciencia?

(una pausa)

Pablo le mira extrañado.

> PEPE
>
> ¿Puedes cubrirme esta noche?

> PABLO
>
> ¿Qué estás diciendo?

> PEPE
>
> ¿Qué eres sordo?

> PABLO
>
> No puedo creerlo...

Pepe empuja a Pablo a tomar una decisión con el gesto de "¿Y bien?".

> PABLO
>
> ¡Está Bien!

> PEPE
>
> Gracias, sabía que podía contar contigo.

> PABLO
>
> ¿Tu cita tiene una hermana, una amiga...?

> PEPE
>
> Esta noche no, pero lo comprobaré.
>
> Esta chica es una verdadera belleza.

> PABLO
>
> Mejor que lo sea.

EXT. NOCHE EL TROPICANA NIGHT CLUB EN LA HABANA, CUBA

INT. NOCHE EL TROPICANA

Luis está solo sentado en una mesa disfrutando del espectáculo. Está a punto de terminarse un cigarrillo cuando por el rabo del ojo vislumbra a un hombre con un brazalete rojo y negro que le mira fijamente. En el brazalete se lee "26 de Julio". Luis reconoce el brazalete. Es idéntico a los brazaletes que llevan los escuadrones de la muerte castrista. Luis evita el contacto visual. Se seca los labios tras beber un sorbo de agua y llama al camarero. El camarero se acerca a la mesa.

LUIS

¿Dónde están los baños?

CAMARERO

Por el pasillo y hacia la derecha.

No puedes perdértelos.

LUIS

Gracias.

Tranquilamente, Luis se levanta de la mesa y camina hacia los baños.

INT. BAÑOS EN EL TROPICANA

Al entrar en los baños, un soldado que sale lo sorprende. Luis se recompone y entra. Se acerca a los urinarios como si fuera a bajarse la portañuela y orinar. Se para pacientemente ante el urinario. El último hombre se marcha. Inmediatamente, Luis se sube la portañuela y se acerca a la ventana del baño. Intenta abrirla. La manilla se rompe. Rápidamente, va a uno de los lavabos y coge un manojo de papel higiénico envolviéndolo alrededor de su mano derecha. Vuelve a la ventana y la rompe con el puño envuelto en papel. Se sube al filo del muro y salta hiriéndose en el proceso.

EXT. CALLEJÓN NOCTURNO

Luis aterriza en el callejón encima de varios latones de basura armando un jaleo terrible.

VOLVER AL SOLDADO DEL BRAZALETE

El ruido de los latones de basura alerta al asesino. Decide seguir a Luis a los baños.

INT. BAÑOS NOCTURNOS EN EL TROPICANA

El asesino entra en el baño buscando a Luis. Encuentra la ventana rota. Se da cuenta que Luis se ha percatado de su presencia. El asesino comienza su persecución tras Luis y sale corriendo del baño hacia el callejón en busca de Luis.

EXT. CALLEJÓN NOCTURNO

A estas alturas, Luis ya ha realizado una tremenda ventaja.

PUNTO DE VISTA (PDV) DEL ASESINO

Asesino mira hacia el callejón y ve a Luis.

Luis está a una manzana y media de distancia, apenas visible por el asesino.

CAMARA SOBRE LUIS

Luis se da cuenta que el asesino se está acercando. El pánico se apodera de él. Corriendo tan rápido como puede, Luis dobla la esquina y empieza a buscar un lugar donde esconderse. Intenta abrir varias puertas de edificios de apartamentos y luego de carros aparcados en la calle, pero todas las puertas están cerradas. Reanuda la carrera hacia otra calle cambiando su dirección.

A estas alturas, el asesino ya tiene la mirilla encima de Luis y está ganando terreno rápidamente.

CAMARA EN EL ASESINO

En una persecución implacable, el asesino atropella a los peatones derribando a varios de ellos.

DE VUELTA A LUIS

Luis dobla la siguiente esquina aparentemente dando vueltas en círculos. Ve

un pequeño café y decide entrar.

INT. CAFÉ NOCTURNO

Luis entra por la puerta principal y sale a toda prisa por la puerta trasera.

EXT. NOCHE PARTE TRASERA DEL CAFÉ

Al salir por la puerta trasera del café, Luis se fija en una tapa de alcantarillado que hay en la calle. La abre y baja rápidamente.

INT. DEL ACANTARILLADO UN AGUJERO EN LA TAPA

Al cerrar la pesada tapa del alcantarillado, se atrapa un dedo entre la tapa de hierro y el borde de acero, haciendo su dedo añicos. El dolor es insoportable. La sangre que brota de su dedo mancha su camisa y sus pantalones. Sin aliento y con el dedo casi desprendiéndose de su mano, consigue mantener la calma, muy tranquilo y totalmente quieto.

EXT. NOCHE CERCA DE LA TAPA DE ALCANTARILLADO EN LA PARTE TRASERA DEL CAFÉ

En cuestión de segundos, el asesino sale por la puerta trasera del Café. Se detiene un instante en busca de Luis. De repente, echa a correr de nuevo sin saber adónde se dirige.

INT. NOCHE EN EL INTERIOR DEL TÚNEL DEL ALCANTARILLADO

Luis temblando con miedo acaba de oír pasar al asesino y decide bajar por la boca de alcantarillado hasta el fondo. Al pie de la misma, intenta orientarse mirando a su alrededor. No ve nada porque la oscuridad es total, así que se mete la mano en el bolsillo y saca una caja de fósforos. Enciende uno, pero se apaga rápidamente. Se mete la mano en el bolsillo de la camisa y saca un bolígrafo. Del bolsillo de su traje saca un pañuelo y lo engancha al bolígrafo, envolviéndolo hasta que queda bien apretado. Enciende otro fosforo y prende fuego al pañuelo. La luz apenas ilumina el túnel.

Luis se orienta y se dirige hacia uno de los túneles. A medida que avanza por el túnel, Luis esquiva roedores y basura a cada paso. Pasa junto a una escalera que se dirige hacia arriba, luego pasa por otra escalera, y finalmente, se detiene antes la tercera escalera. Sube por ella y abre ligeramente para echar un vistazo. Al observar la zona, ve que no hay moros en la costa.

EXT. NOCHE A NIVEL DE LA CALLE JUNTO AL ALCANTARILLADO

Rápidamente, Luis sale, cierra la tapa del alcantarillado y camina a paso ligero por la calle.

EXT. NOCHE EN UNA PARADA DE AUTOBÚS

Luis llega y se sienta junto a varias personas que aparentemente esperan el autobús. Echa un vistazo a la gente que le rodea y se quita la chaqueta para mezclarse con la multitud. No ha pasado ni un minuto cuando varias personas se levantan del banco.

LUIS PDV

El autobús está a un par de manzanas recogiendo pasajeros.

CAMARA ENFOCA A LUIS

Respira aliviado. Cuando se levanta para subir al autobús, siente una presencia detrás de él. Sin previo aviso, sus rodillas se doblan cuando la estocada de un gran cuchillo penetra su espalda. La hoja del cuchillo sobresale por la parte delantera de su camisa, girando y retorciéndose a medida que el asesino lo mueve para garantizar el máximo daño. Luis está muerto, sólo que aún no ha caído. El asesino empuja a Luis hacia delante mientras saca el cuchillo. Su cuerpo sin vida cae delante del autobús que se aproxima. El conductor del autobús, incapaz de detenerse, atropella a Luis aplastando lo que queda de este joven confundido. El asesino se aleja mientras una multitud se reúne para presenciar lo ocurrido.

DISOLVER A

EXT. NOCHE ENTRADA PRINCIPAL DE LA BASE AÉREA HOMESTEAD FLORIDA USA

EN PANTALLA: ABRIL 15 1961 2:00 AM

Pepe llega en un taxi escoltado por dos hombres. Se bajan y se acercan a la verja.

PEPE
Mi nombre en clave es "Trueno"

GUARDIA

Espera aquí.

El guardia hace una rápida llamada telefónica y se dirige hacia Pepe.

GUARDIA

Espera en esa entrada. Te recogerán en
un minuto.

Los tres hombres se dirigen hacia las puertas de entrada. Ha pasado menos de un minuto cuando llega un policía militar y los recoge. Pepe se sienta delante.

EXT. NOCHE CON EL JEEP

El Jeep atraviesa una sección de la base donde se están llevando a cabo preparativos militares. Llegan frente a un edificio de dos plantas.

POLICIA MILITAR (MP)
Síganme, por favor.

El policía militar escolta a Pepe y a los dos hombres al interior del edificio.

EDIFICIO MILITAR NOCHE INT.

Pepe sigue al policía militar por la entrada principal y el pasillo. Llegan a unas puertas dobles. Al entrar, se sorprende al ver a Pablo en uniforme sentado esperándolo. Hay otros tres militares en la sala.

PEPE

¿Qué demonios haces aquí?

PABLO

Esperándote. ¡Soy tu cita esta noche!

PEPE

¿Eres del CIA? ¿Verdad?

Pablo asiente con la cabeza. Pepe un poco molesto.

PABLO

Pepe por favor entiende, nosotros teníamos que estar seguro de que podíamos confiar en ti.

PEPE

¡Maricón Coño! ¡Hijo de puta!

PABLO

Cálmate...

Deja que te presente.

Pablo se levanta y presenta a los oficiales presentes. Pepe estrecha la mano de cada uno de ellos.

PABLO
Este es el comandante Johnson, Teniente
Smith, y Sargento Carter.

Pepe se vira hacia Pablo.

PEPE
Confío en ti Pablo, no me falles.

PABLO
No te he fallado hasta ahora.

¿No es así?

(una pausa)

PABLO CONTINUA

Mira, no tenemos un minuto que
perder.

Te informaré en él camino.

Sígueme.

COMANDANTE JOHNSON

Buena suerte, hombres.

Pablo y todos los agentes saludan al comandante Johnson. Juntos ellos
salen y se dirigen a un helicóptero adyacente al edificio.

Los hombres suben al helicóptero de las Fuerzas Aéreas Americanas
listo para despegar. (una pausa) El helicóptero despega.

INT. HELICÓPTERO VOLADO NOCTURNO EN ALGÚN
LUGAR SOBRE EL MAR CARIBE

PABLO

Estamos en camino a reunirnos con un grupo de la Armada frente a la costa sur de Isla de Pinos.

PEPE

¿Un grupo de combate?

Pepe enarca las cejas.

PABLO

No hagas más preguntas.

Pronto conocerás los detalles de la misión.

CORTE A

EXT. NOCHE LLEGANDO A UN PORTAAVION DE EE.UU. EN EL MAR

Los cuatro hombres se bajan del helicóptero. Les espera un oficial. Les saluda y los conduce bajo cubierta.

INT. NOCHE PORTAAVION DE LOS EE. UU.

Otro oficial recibe a los cuatro hombres en la cubierta principal.

LT. SMITH

Bienvenido a bordo.

Están justo a tiempo, por favor síganme.

El teniente Smith les conduce al centro de operaciones, el corazón de la nave. El capitán Harper les espera.

CAPITÁN HARPPER
Señores, bienvenidos a la operación "90 Millas".

Pablo y los otros oficiales saludan al capitán Harper. Pepe les sigue.

CAPITÁN HARPPER
Tenemos un trabajo crítico que hacer y debemos cumplir nuestro horario.

(una pausa)

EL CAPITÁN HARPPER CONTINÚA
Escuchen, exactamente a las 3 de la mañana, vamos a reunirnos con el submarino U.S. Sea Wolf.

Subirán a bordo a las 3:15AM. El Oficial Clement de él Sea Wolf les proporcionará el resto de los detalles al embarcar. Sus equipos están listos abajo y el teniente Smith les mostrará dónde recogerlos.

El capitán Harpper mira su reloj de pulsera.

CAPITÁN HARPPER
Por favor, sincronicen sus relojes.

La hora actual es 2:14.40. ¿Alguna pregunta?

Sin preguntas.

CAPITÁN HARPPER
Buena suerte.

EXT. NOCHE LA CHOZA EN CUBA

(EN EL SONIDO) SE ESCUCHA A ALICIA LLORANDO Y A VECES GRITANDO

INT. NOCHE EL LA SALA: LA CÁMARA SE DESPLAZA DESDE LA PUERTA PRINCIPAL DE LA SALA Y LENTAMENTE ADELANTA HACIA EL DORMITORIO.

Alicia está LLORANDO de dolor. Ella está en la cama y apenas podemos ver lo que está pasando.

CÁMARA AVANSA LENTAMENTE Y SE ASOMÁ POR LA RENDIJA DE LA PUERTA DEL DORMITORIO

Alicia intenta dar a luz. Rosa la anima a respirar y a empujar con más fuerza. Oscar está inmóvil junto a Rosa, preocupado por el proceso en curso.

OSCAR

¿Qué pasa Rosa?

¿Va todo bien?

Rosa a los pies de la cama intentando ayudar a Alicia.

ROSA

Cállate Oscar. Todo está bien.

(una pausa)

Sigue empujando cariño, sigue empujando.

Alicia se esfuerza al máximo, pero las contracciones son escasas.

ENFOQUE EN ROSA

> ROSA
> Oscar rápido, tráeme más agua caliente
> y toallas limpias.

Oscar sale corriendo del dormitorio para coger lo que Rosa le ha pedido. Rosa cierra y tranca la puerta del dormitorio tras de él.

ENFOQUE EN OSCAR AL CERRAR LA PUERTA

Aunque Oscar se queda perplejo por el cierre de la puerta, el continúa como si nada.

INT NOCHE DORMITORIO DE ALICIA - UN MONTAJE

Alicia lucha por su vida y la de su bebé. Rosa está haciendo todo lo que puede.

DISOLVER A

INT DÍA AFUERA DE LA HABITACIÓN DE ALICIA

Han pasado unas horas. Óscar vuelve a llamar a la puerta del dormitorio. Al volver, se da cuenta de que un silencio inquietante se ha apoderado de la casa y que ya no se oye a Alicia decir nada. Oscar lleva más toallas y agua caliente y llama una y otra vez a la puerta del dormitorio.

> OSCAR
> Rosa, abre la puerta.
>
> Tengo más agua caliente y toallas
> limpias.

Finalmente, Rosa abre la puerta. Sale con un bebé envuelto en toallas. El vestido de Rosa está empapado de sangre y sudor. Rosa como un zombi.

ROSA

Alicia tuvo una niña.

OSCAR

¿Una niña?

ROSA

Sí, una niña preciosa.

Oscar, mirando por encima del hombro de Rosa, se da cuenta inmediatamente de que algo va terriblemente mal.

OSCAR

Rosa... ¿Qué le pasa a Alicia?

Rosa asiente con la cabeza, desesperada.

ROSA

¡Está muerta! No lo logró.

OSCAR

¿Cómo es posible? ¿Qué paso?

Rosa casi histérica.

ROSA

Intenté detener la hemorragia, Pero era
demasiado. No pude salvarla.

Oscar no lo puede creer y entra en la habitación de Alicia.

EL PUNTO DE VISTA (PDV) DE OSCAR

Alicia pálida e inmóvil en sábanas cubiertas de sangre.

Oscar no puede soportar el estado de Alicia y abandona el dormitorio.

VOLVER A ROSA

Oscar entra en escena. Se acerca a Rosa y la abraza a ella y al bebé. El intenta ser fuerte y los consuela. Al final, él también empieza a llorar descontroladamente.

LA CÁMARA RETROCEDE Y SE FUNDE A NEGRO

EXT. NOCHE FRENTE A LA COSTA DE CUBA EN LA CUBIERTA DE UN SUBMARINO

Pepe y Pablo se dirigen a la escotilla de la proa seguidos por el teniente Smith. De repente, intensos relámpagos iluminan el horizonte. Inmediatamente después se oyen explosiones no truenos. Al parecer, se está produciendo algún tipo de ataque y se oye en el fondo. Pepe y Pablo se miran.

PABLO
Es la invasión de Bahía de Cochinos.

PEPE
¿Los americanos?

PABLO
No. Se llaman "La Brigada 2506".

Son un grupo de 1.400 hombres entrenados por la CIA para esta invasión.

Pepe a sabiendas.

> PEPE
>
> Eso no es suficiente.
>
> Fidel tiene aviones Migs y decenas de miles de soldados.

> PABLO
>
> No te preocupes, los americanos proporcionarán apoyo aéreo durante la invasión y durante la limpieza después del desembarco.

Pepe aprieta su puño mostrando su exuberancia.

> PEPE
>
> ¡Sí!

> LT. SMITH
>
> Muévanse, no tenemos todo el día.

INT. NOCHE: SALA DE REUNIONES DEL SUBMARINO

Coronel Clement da la bienvenida al equipo.

> COL. CLEMENT
>
> ¡Buenos días! Soy el coronel Clement, bienvenidos al Sea Wolf. Exactamente a las 04:30 horas saldremos a la superficie 2 millas de la costa sur de Cuba cerca de la Playa Majana.

> PEPE
>
> La conozco bien.

COL. CLEMENTS

Por eso está aquí, Sr. Martínez.

(una pausa)

Ocho "Marines" más ustedes dos (señalando a Pablo y Pepe) desembarcarán llegando a la playa a las 04:50 horas. Su misión principal es determinar qué capacidad nuclear tiene Castro, si la tiene. Tenemos datos no confirmados que indican que Castro construyó una base de lanzamiento de misiles nucleares en San Cristóbal. Informarán sus encuentros inmediatamente y obtendrán fotografías que corroboren sus hallazgos. ¿Alguna pregunta?

LT. SMITH

Señor, ¿tiene las frecuencias?

Mientras el coronel Clements entrega un sobre al teniente Smith.

COL. CLEMENT

Deben evitar todo contacto con el enemigo.

PEPE

Excepto al sacar a mi familia. ¿Verdad?

El coronel Clement ignora la pregunta de Pepe.

COL. CLEMEMT

Los sacaremos de aquí a las 04:30 horas
del jueves.

Eso es aproximadamente dentro de 72
horas.

(Una pausa)

¿Alguna otra pregunta?

Pepe ignorado por COL. CLEMENT y preocupado por su familia empieza a hacer una pregunta cuando Pablo le retiene. Pablo hace un gesto para callar a Pepe.

PABLO

Sshhhh. Lo sabe.

No se hacen más preguntas.

COL. CLEMENT

Buena suerte caballeros.

El coronel Clement sale de la sala.

Pablo se dirige a Pepe

PABLO

¿Listo para salir?

PEPE

Misiles nucleares, ¿eh?

PABLO

No están confirmados. Por eso estamos aquí.

PEPE

Por eso estás aquí. ¿Qué pasa con mi familia? ¿Cuándo los sacamos?

PABLO

Después de terminar nuestra misión.

PEPE

Genial... ¡simplemente genial!

Pepe preocupado e inquieto.

PABLO

Deja de preocuparte. Tenemos tiempo de sobra.

DISOLVER A:

EXT. NOCHE LA COSTA SUR DE CUBA PLAYA MAJANA

A lo lejos se ve la costa de Cuba. La operación "90 millas" está en marcha. Dos balsas con cinco hombres en cada una despegan del submarino.

EXT. EN LA PLAYA MAJANA DE CUBA

Las balsas llegan sin ser detectadas.

LT. SMITH

¡Vamos, vamos, cada segundo cuenta!

Los hombres salen disparados de las balsas arrastrándolas hacia la playa junto a dunas de arena y rocas. Rápidamente entierran las balsas y el equipo sobrante. Se reúnen alrededor del teniente Smith. Este hace una señal con la mano para salir. Los hombres entran a la densa jungla tropical.

EXT. TEMPRANO POR LA MAÑANA. TOMA ESTABLECIENDO UNA TIENDA DE CAMPO EN CUBA

Se oye un gallo cantar al fondo. Óscar sale de la tienda con una bolsa de su compra. De repente, pasan dos camiones cargados de soldados cubanos. Oscar se esconde detrás de una casilla telefónica. Otros dos camiones del ejército pasan a toda velocidad. Uno con provisiones y el otro con un cañón Howitzer. Un joven cruza la calle corriendo y pasa junto a Oscar. Oscar lo detiene.

                    OSCAR
          ¿A qué viene tanto revuelo?

          ¿Qué es lo que pasa?

El joven frenéticamente

                    JOVEN
          ¿No has oído...?

          ¡Los americanos invadieron la Bahía de
          Cochinos!

El joven se echa a correr. Oscar no puede creer lo que oye.

                    OSCAR
          ¡Coño! ¡Ahora Si!

Óscar empieza a correr, agarrando la bolsa de la compra con una mano y equilibrándose con la otra.

EXT. DÍA LA CHOZA

Oscar entra por la puerta principal.

INT. DÍA LA CHOZA

OSCAR cierra la puerta con una patada. Emocionado, tira la compra al sofá.

> OSCAR
> ¡Rosa, Rosita tengo tremenda noticia!

Rosa sale del dormitorio.

> ROSA
> Cálmate, la bebé está durmiendo.

> OSCAR
> ¿Calmarme? ¡La invasión americana está aquí!

> ROSA
> ¿Qué estás diciendo?

> OSCAR
> Rosita, no estoy bromeando.
>
> Acabo de ver varios camiones de soldados y armas en camino hacia la Bahía de Cochinos.

> ROSA
> ¿La Bahía de Cochinos?

> OSCAR
> ¡Sí! Ahí desembarcaron.

Rosa extasiada.

                         ROSA
             ¡Gracias a Dios!

                        OSCAR
             ¡Sí! Nuestra pesadilla esta al terminar.

Rosa y Oscar se abrazan. Saltan por la sala como dos niños pequeños.

La bebé empieza a llorar.

EXT. DÍA EN ALGÚN LUGAR EN LAS SELVAS DE CUBA

LT. SMITH y los soldados americanos atraviesan la selva acercándose a la pequeña ciudad de San Cristóbal. Pepe y Pablo son los últimos del grupo y están a punto de cruzar una carretera principal cuando el ruido de vehículos pesados detiene su avance. Los hombres se congelan y se funden con el entorno.

PUNTO DE VISTA DE LOS SOLDADOS AMERICANOS

Los vehículos incluyen un TANQUE, UN CAMION ERNORME, un LANSADOR DE MISILE que transporta un COHETE LARGISIMO y varios otros vehículos de transporte de tropas. Los vehículos de transporte de personal van cargados con tropas soviéticas. El convoy pasa.

                         VOLVER A LT. SMITH

                      LT. SMITH
             ¡Mierda!

             Estos cabrones tienen cohetes nucleares.

SGT. CARTER

Sí señor, ese fue un SS-19.

¿Te fijaste en los vehículos con soldados?

LT. SMITH

Esos no son cubanos, me parecen rusos.

SGT. CARTER

Afirmativo, creo que eran tropas rusas.

LT. SMITH

¿Seguro sargento?

SGT. CARTER

Sí, señor, eran soviéticos.

Fuerzas Especiales.

El teniente Smith se dirige al cabo Williams que lleva el equipo de radio.

LT. SMITH

Cabo, transmita por radio un código 6

a submarino y usa el condigo secreto 4-D. ¡Ahora!

El cabo se pone hacerlo inmediatamente.

LT. SMITH

Espero que lleguemos a tiempo.

SGT. CARTER

Sí señor, yo también.

Pablo se vuelve hacia Pepe.

PABLO
No contábamos con esto.

PEPE
Diablos, todo el mundo sabe que hay tropas rusas en Cuba de hace meses.

PABLO
Me refiero a los misiles nucleares.

LT. SMITH
¡Corten el Chisme!

Muévanse. Nos quedaremos ocultos hasta que oscurezca.

EXT. DÍA EL CUARTEL GENERAL DE LA CIA

INT. DÍA CUARTEL GENERAL DE LA CIA

Un oficial uniformado camina enérgicamente por el pasillo con un sobre en la mano izquierda. La cámara le sigue de cerca. El oficial atraviesa unas puertas dobles y entra en una sala de conferencias. Está presente la plana mayor del ejército estadounidense y el jefe del Estado Mayor. Está en proceso una reunión en mesa redonda donde se discute la situación en Cuba.

INT. DÍA CIA CUARTEL PRINCIPAL. SALA DE CONFERENCIAS

AIRFORCE COL. EDWARDS
El apoyo aéreo programado ha sido cancelado por el presidente Kennedy.

> GENERAL INGLE DE INFANTERÍA DE MARINA
> Los hombres en la playa no tienen
> ninguna oportunidad de triunfar
> a menos que reciban apoyo aéreo
> inmediatamente.

El oficial que ha traído el sobre se lo entrega al jefe del Estado Mayor (JCS - Joint Chiefs of Staff). Éste lo lee.

> JCS
> Señores.

> (un pausa)

> Acabamos de recibir nueva información
> de nuestro equipo en la isla.

> Inteligencia indica, que a menos hay una
> división de tropas soviéticas desplegadas
> cerca de la Bahía de Cochinos.

> Además, tenemos confirmación visual
> de que existen misiles nucleares SS-19
> soviéticos en Cuba.

La sala se queda en silencio.

> AIRFORCE COL. EDWARDS
> ¿Dijiste que la confirmación visual ha
> sido obtenida?

> JCS
> ¡Afirmativo! Eso es precisamente lo que
> he dicho.

> AIRFORCE COL. EDWARDS
> Recomiendo que pospongamos la intervención militar hasta que podamos evaluar mejor la situación.

> GENERAL INGLE DE INFANTERÍA DE MARINA
> Estoy de acuerdo. Además, debemos notificarle al presidente inmediatamente.

JCS coge el teléfono rojo que tiene delante.

> JCS
> Se trata de un asunto de seguridad nacional. Necesito hablar con el presidente inmediatamente.

EXT. NOCHE LA CIUDAD DE SAN CRISTOBAL

Pablo, Pepe y el resto del equipo llegaron bien y sin ser detectados. Desde las afueras de la ciudad se ven las luces de la base aérea. El grupo se instala mientras el sargento Carter explora la base con sus binoculares.

> SGT.CARTER
> Señor, será mejor que eche un vistazo a esto.

El sargento Carter entrega los binoculares al teniente Smith. Pablo y Pepe están junto al teniente Smith mientras mira por los binoculares.

> LT. SMITH
> ¡Hijo de puta!
> Parece que también tienen misiles SAMS.

SGT. CARTER
Teniente, ¿ve esas lonas camuflajeadas a
unos 100 metros al este de los Cohetes?

El teniente Smith mira por los binoculares y enfoca a su derecha.

LT. SMITH
Sí, parece que están cubriendo algún tipo de lanzador. Tenemos que averiguar qué demonios hay bajo esas lonas.

SGT. CARTER
Sólo hay una manera de averiguarlo.

Deja de mirar a la base y se da la vuelta.

LT. SMITH
Si esos son misiles de largo alcance, estamos en tremendo problema.

(una pausa)

Bien, vamos a entrar.

Sargento Carter, tome a PEPE y PABLO
y cubran el terreno alto en el lado oeste
de la base.

Quiero fotos de toda la instalación.

SGT. CARTER
Sí, señor.

El teniente Smith se gira hacia los demás hombres.

LT. SMITH
Bob, Jerry, ¡el momento a llegado!

Averigüemos qué hay debajo de esas lonas.

Mantengan los ojos y los oídos abiertos.

(una pausa)

Si la cosa se pone fea, nos encontraremos de vuelta por la carretera principal inmediatamente. ¿Alguna pregunta?

(otra pausa)

¡Rock & Roll!

EXT. NOCHE EN LAS AFUERAS DE LA CIUDAD

El teniente Smith y seis de sus soldados se abren paso a través de la maleza hasta llegar a la base. Lenta y metódicamente penetran el área siempre manteniéndose en las sombras y lejos de la luz de la luna. Finalmente, llegan al perímetro de la base. La maleza que rodea el perímetro ha sido recortada creando un campo de exterminio de 30 yardas. En este campo de exterminio sólo crece 5 cm de hierba y los reflectores escudriñan periódicamente la zona en busca de indeseables. El teniente Smith se dirige a uno de sus hombres.

LT. SMITH
Bien, mide la frecuencia de los reflectores.

Bob cronometra los reflectores.

BOB
Escanean la zona cada dos minutos.

LT. SMITH señala a los dos primeros hombres que penetrarán la base.

LT. SMITH
Tienes 2 minutos. ¡Listo! ¡Vayan!

Justo cuando las luces terminan de barrer la zona, dos de los soldados corren a través del perímetro hasta la valla principal. Con un par de cortaalambres se abren paso rápidamente y se esconden detrás de unos barracones. Antes de desaparecer, le hacen una señal al teniente LT. Smith para que los demás se unan a ellos.

LT. SMITH
Muy bien! Bob, Joe, su turno.

Bob y su compañero siguen idénticamente el mismo camino hasta la valla, sólo que Joe tropieza y cae. Las luces que escanean sistemáticamente la zona casi pillan a Joe al descubierto. El teniente Smith y los dos hombres restantes toman posiciones para asegurar su salida. Los cuatro soldados en la base se abren paso hasta la lona. Bob y Joe entran.

INT. NOCHE DENTRO DE LA LONA

Varios generadores están funcionando y están enchufados a un panel de control. El panel tiene un mapa geográfico de los Estados Unidos. Una serie de luces rojas brillantes iluminan las ciudades de Miami, Washington DC y Nueva York. Varias luces ámbar se encienden y apagan en la base del panel.

BOB
¡A la mierda con esto!

JOE
No puedo creer esta mierda.

Los hombres están aturdidos. Varios lanzadores de misiles nucleares de largo alcance están cargados y aparentemente listos para disparar. Joe saca rápidamente su cámara y hace una toma tras otra de los misiles, los lanzadores y el panel.

EXT. NOCHE FUERA DE LA LONA

Los dos soldados americanos que vigilan la entrada a la lona se dan cuenta de que varios soldados rusos están saliendo de sus cuarteles y se dirigen hacia la lona. Los dos soldados americanos alertan a Bob y Joe para que salgan. Los soldados soviéticos entran en la lona. Bob y Joe consiguen salir de la lona sin ser detectados haciendo un agujero en la parte trasera de la lona. Bob y Joe se reúnen con los otros dos soldados y salen de la base sin dejar rastro.

EXT. NOCHE AL OTRO LADO DE LA BASE

CÁMARA ENCUENTRA A PABLO, PEPE Y SGT. CARTER

Ese equipo inspecciona la zona desde la orilla de la maleza, justo fuera de la zona de exterminio. Con los ojos y los oídos bien abiertos.

SGT. CARTER
Saquemos fotos de las tropas soviéticas.

Pablo señala un árbol alto con vista sin obstrucción a la base.

PABLO
Sargento, ¿ve ese árbol?

SGT. CARTER
Sí.

PABLO
Con el lente telefoto yo puedo conseguir
todas las fotos que quieras.

El sargento duda un momento.

SGT. CARTER
También será un blanco fácil si algo va
mal.

PABLO
¿Tienes una idea mejor?

SGT. CARTER
¡Muy bien, hazlo!

Cubriré tu flanco izquierdo.

(una pausa)

Pepe cubre el otro lado.

Pepe mira a Pablo un poco preocupado.

PEPE
No estoy seguro de que sea una buena
idea.

PABLO
No mevengas con tonterías. Usa ese rifle
si es necesario.

SGT. CARTER
Tienen 10 minutos.

Pablo se vuelve hacia Pepe.

PABLO

¡Vamos!

Pepe y Pablo se dirigen en una dirección mientras el sargento Carter se dirige en otra.

ACERCAMIENTO AL SGT. CARTER

SGT. CARTER
¡Que Dios nos ayude!

El Sgto. Carter se instala en un tronco hueco en el suelo preparándose con una buena línea de fuego.

EXT. NOCHE JUNTO A UN PINO ALTO

Pepe y Pablo llegan al árbol. Pablo señala varios arbustos altos.

PABLO
Instálate allí.

Cúbreme el trasero.

PEPE
Ten cuidado.

PABLO
Para avisarme sólo silba como un Sinsonte. (un pájaro cubano).

Pablo enseña a Pepe a silbar. Pepe sonríe y le responde con un silbido idéntico. Pablo, satisfecho, empieza a trepar el árbol.

ENFOQUE DE PABLO

Lentamente y sin hacer ruido, Pablo se sube al árbol hasta un lugar desde el que tiene una vista panorámica de toda la base. Rápidamente coge su cámara y enfoca la base. Con la cámara toma una foto tras otra.

DE VUELTA A PEPE

Abajo, Pepe tiene los ojos bien abiertos y suda a mares. Mientras se acomoda entre varios arbustos, siente que su propio corazón late como un tambor. De repente, Pepe oye a un par de soldados cubanos que hablan y caminan hacia él. Pepe (nervioso) intenta silbar, pero no le sale nada. Lo intenta una y otra vez, pero sus labios están secos y le entra el pánico, así es que no sale ningún sonido. Mira a Pablo. Sin pensarlo, coge una piedra y se la lanza a Pablo.

ENFOQUE EN PABLO

PABLO reacciona al golpe de la piedra y deja de tomar fotos.

CERCA DE DONDE CAE LA PIEDRA

La piedra rebota en varias ramas antes de caer al suelo.

CERCA DE LOS DOS SOLDADOS CUBANOS

El ruido de la piedra al caer ha alertado a los soldados de la presencia de alguien más en el área. Se detienen y desenfundan sus armas. Uno le hace una señal al otro: "tú ve por ahí, yo iré por aquí".

VOLVER A PEPE

Mediante señas con la mano, Pepe avisa a Pablo de la llegada de 2 soldados.

VOLVER A PABLO

Guarda la cámara y saca su cuchillo.

EL PUNTO DE VISTA DE PABLO

Puede ver a los dos soldados que se acercan a Pepe desde distintas direcciones, pero aún no puede hacer ningún movimiento. Uno de los soldados cubanos que camina hacia Pepe pasa justo por debajo de él.

VOLVER A PEPE

Pepe oye llegar a los soldados y se queda inmóvil.

CERCA DEL SOLDADO CUBANO N.º 2

Sin saberlo, flanqueando a Pepe y a unos 10 metros de distancia, el soldado comienza a sondear los arbustos con su bayoneta.

VOLVER A PEPE

Al darse cuenta de que está rodeado, hace el primer movimiento. Ataca al soldado que tiene más cerca y lucha por arrebatarle el fusil. El soldado va por su pistola, pero Pepe lo derriba antes de que pueda sacarla de su cartuchera. Continúan forcejeando.

ENFOQUE AL SOLDADO CUBANO N.º 1

Oye el forcejeo y se apresura a ayudar a su compañero.

VOLVER A PABLO

Pablo agarra una rama y la utiliza para lanzarse desde lo alto del árbol encima del soldado N.º 1.

ENFOQUE A PEPE

Pepe recupera control de la pistola y dispara una bala contra el soldado. Sin previo aviso, suenan más disparos y se desata el pandemónium. Luces se encienden y se enfocan a PEPE desde todas las direcciones, iluminando el cielo nocturno. Las balas pasan zumbando a su lado. El sonido de una sirena aumenta el caos. Pepe entra en pánico y sale corriendo hacia Pablo.

CON PABLO

Ha golpeado al otro soldado hasta dejarlo inconsciente y se está levantando del suelo. Pepe entra en escena.

PEPE
¿Creo que la he cagado?

PABLO
Olvídalo, vamos.

Ambos salen corriendo del encuadre.

EXT. NOCHE LA ENTRADA A LA BASE

Una serie de equipos de búsqueda se reúnen junto a la entrada principal de la base. Tanto las tropas soviéticas como las cubanas se movilizan organizando equipos de búsqueda. Todos los equipos de búsqueda tienen Perros K-9. Los equipos de búsqueda salen de la base en dirección a Pepe y Pablo.

ENFOQUE A PABLO Y PEPE

Abriéndose camino por la selva corriendo más rápido de lo humanamente posible.

EXT. NOCHE CON LT. SMITH, BOB, JERRY Y LOS OTROS HOMBRES EN LA SELVA.

Un reflector encuentra a LT. Smith.

> LT. SMITH
> ¿Qué demonios...?
>
> ¡Muévanse!

Los hombres arrancan corriendo hacia la carretera principal. Mientras corren a toda velocidad.

> LT. SMITH
> ¿Willie viste lo que empezó este caos?

> WILLIE
> Todo lo que oí fueron disparos.
>
> (una pausa)
>
> De pronto se desató el infierno.

> LT. SMITH
> Date prisa y envía por radio la clave roja.

> WILLIE
> ¿Qué código uso?

LT. SMITH
Olvídate del código. ¡Hazlo!

Willie, corriendo a toda velocidad, gira el radio y transmite el mensaje.

EXT. NOCHE AL LADO DE LA CARRETERA

Bob y Joe llegan primero a la carretera principal. Están sin aliento. Pueden

oír vagamente el ladrido de los perros en el fondo. Entonces llega el sargento Carter.

JOE
¡Dios mío sargento!

¿Qué paso?

SGT. CARTER
Pablo y Pepe deben haberse enredado
con una patrulla.

El teniente Smith llega con Willie y los otros hombres.

LT. SMITH
¿Dónde están Pepe y Pablo?

SGT. CARTER
Deben de estar al llegar.

Los ladridos de los perros son cada vez más fuertes y cercanos.

BOB
Si no nos vamos ahora mismo todos
seremos picadillo.

>   LT. SMITH
> Tranquilo Bob...
>
> Esperaremos 1 minuto...
>
> entonces nos vamos de aquí.

Los hombres se colocan espalda contra espalda protegiéndose los flancos.

ENFOQUE A PABLO Y PEPE CORRIENDO A TODA VELOCIDAD POR LA SELVA

Mientras corren.

>   PABLO
> Extraño estar sirviendo mesas en el hotel.

>   PEPE
> Era más fácil no.
>
>   (una pausa)
>
> ¿Creo que vamos en la dirección equivocada?

>   PABLO
> Tenemos que desviar a los perros para ganar tiempo.

DE VUELTA A UN EQUIPO DE BÚSQUEDA SOVIÉTICO

En plena persecución, sueltan a los perros. Los K-9 despegan como un rayo. Los soldados los persiguen en la Selva.

VOLVER A PABLO Y PEPE

Atraviesan un barranco y un arroyo. Al otro lado del arroyo se detienen y vuelven hacia la carretera principal. Pablo se da la vuelta para ver cómo va Pepe. Pepe parece seguirle el ritmo.

VOLVER A LT. SMITH Y EL EQUIPO AMERICANO

El teniente Smith mira su reloj.

LT. SMITH

Vamos Pablito...

No me falles ahora.

(varias pausas)

Mierda... Hemos esperado suficiente.

¡Vámonos!

Justo cuando se preparan para evacuar, Pablo entra como un bólido. Pepe está unos metros atrás. Ambos agitados. Pablo sigue sujetando la cámara y la levanta.

PABLO

¡Tengo las fotos!

LT. SMITH

¡Bien!

Bob... dirígete a la playa.

Un helicóptero de fabricación soviética vuela casi rozando las copas de los árboles. Todos caen al suelo excepto Pepe, que no mueve un músculo. A todo pulmón.

PEPE

¿A la playa?

¿Dónde coño crees que van?

Pepe mete una bala en el directo de su rifle. Apuntando al teniente Smith, parece dispuesto a disparar a la primera persona que se dirija hacia la playa. Todo el mundo se paraliza.

PABLO

¿Estás loco?

PEPE

No, pero tu si estas loco si crees que yo
voy a dejar a mi familia atrás.

LT. SMITH

Nos van a matar a todos.

El sargento Carter empieza a moverse. Pepe reacciona. Directamente al Sargento Carter.

PEPE

¿Quieres ser el primero en morir?

El sargento Carter retrocede. Los K-9 están cada vez más cerca.

LT. SMITH

Mira Pepe podrías matar a dos o tres de
nosotros, pero te garantizo que uno de
nosotros te mata a ti.

Las tensiones aumentan. Sin duda, un momento desafiante.

PABLO
No lo hagas. Esto es un suicidio para
todos incluyendo tu familia.

Desesperadamente

PEPE
¡Es mi única oportunidad de salvarlos!

De repente, el helicóptero vuelve a pasar, pero esta vez más cerca y con
un faro cegador que ilumina la zona.

LT. SMITH
Escúchame Pepe, si tienes un deseo de
muerte está bien. Pero soy responsable
de estos hombres y no voy a dejar que
los maten.

(varias pausas)

Sin previo aviso llega un K-9 que se abalanza sobre el grupo y ataca a
Pablo. Pepe le vuela la cabeza al perro con 2 tiros. La situación permite
a los soldados apuntar con todos sus rifles directamente a Pepe. Para
complicar las cosas, empieza a llover.

LT. SMITH
¡Vete! Salva a tu maldita familia.

Nos vamos. (Se dirige a sus soldaos)

Vámonos.

Pablo se vuelve hacia el teniente Smith

PABLO
Me quedo con él.

LT. SMITH
¿Vas a desertar con tu amigo?

PABLO
¿Y su familia?

LT. SMITH
¿Qué de ella?

Esto no es un debate, es una orden.

¡Muévete!

Pablo no sabe qué hacer.

PEPE
No tienes razón para quedarte. ¡Vete!

El teniente Smith, Pablo y sus hombres desaparecen en la selva todos en la misma dirección. Pepe sale disparado en la dirección opuesta.

DESVANECE A NEGRO

EXT. DÍA LA CHOZA

Varias gallinas deambulan frente a la CHOZA. Ha dejado de llover y la mañana está llena de vapor.

INT. DÍA EN LA SALA

Rosa está empaquetando sus pertenencias personales al igual que Óscar, metiéndolas en una bolsa de lona. Está ansiosa por abandonar la CHOZA y volver a su casa de La Habana. La bebé está en el sofá envuelta en un edredón. Rosa termina de llenar la bolsa.

ROSA
Me pregunto cómo ira la invasión.

OSCAR
Es increíble, ¿verdad?

Rosa se acerca a la puerta del dormitorio y lentamente la abre.

EL PUNTO DE VISTA DE ROSA

El cuerpo de Alicia yace en la cama cubierta por una sábana.

ROSA
¿Qué hacemos con Alicia?

Oscar se da la vuelta. Duda un momento.

OSCAR
Necesitamos....

¡¡¡KAAABOOMMMMM!!! UNA EXPLOCION

La puerta trasera de la CHOZA se abre de golpe. Pepe entra furioso apuntando con su rifle a todo lo que se mueve. Oscar y Rosa no pueden creer lo que ven. Rosa corre hacia Pepe. Lo abraza y lo besa. Pepe le corresponde. Oscar está en estado de shock.

PEPE
Mamá, como te he extrañado.

ROSA
Yo también hijo, yo también.

Pepe mira a Oscar por encima del hombro de Rosa. PEPE le hace una señal a PABLO para que se acerque. Pepe se separa de Rosa para abrazar y darle las gracias a Oscar. Se abrazan fuertemente.

PEPE

¿Cómo te lo puedo agradecer?

OSCAR

Tú hubieras hecho lo mismo por mí.

Rosa, Pepe y Óscar se juntan en un abrazo los tres. El llanto de un bebé interrumpe la celebración. A Pepe se le iluminan los ojos. Se le dibuja una sonrisa en la cara.

PEPE

¿Es ese mí…

ROSA

Hija.

El llanto procede del sofá. Pepe se acerca a su hija recién nacida.

ROSA

Alicia la llamó Lucía.

PEPE

¿Dónde está Alicia?

Un silencio inquietante cubre la habitación. Rosa se acerca a Pepe. No encuentra palabras para decírselo. Pepe percibe problemas. A riesgo de ser redundante, se vuelve hacia Rosa.

PEPE

¿Dónde está Alicia?

Rosa empieza a llorar. Se abraza a Pepe. Pepe mira a Oscar.

PEPE
¿Qué le pasa? ¿Dónde está?

Oscar desesperado.

OSCAR
Murió dando a luz.

Pepe está DEVASTADO. Explota en un ataque de ira.

Desafiante ante Dios y toda la creación Pepe estalla.

PEPE
Oh Dios, ¿Cómo puedes hacerme esto?

¿Por qué me has abandonado? ¿Por qué?

¡Nunca he pedido nada!

¿Por qué a ella? ¿Por qué la abandonaste
a ella?

Si existes, ¿cómo pudiste permitir que
esto sucediera?

¿DIME CÓMO? ¿POR QUÉ?

Pepe rompe a llorar histéricamente.

PEPE
¿Por qué yo, Dios mío? ¿Por qué Alicia?
¿Por qué?

Pepe llora desconsoladamente por Alicia. Oscar abraza a Pepe intentando consolarlo. Rosa también intenta calmar y consolar a Pepe. Pepe con un dolor atroz mira al bebé.

OSCAR

Tu hija nació ayer.

PEPE

¿Dónde está Alicia?

Con algunas dudas.

OSCAR

Está en el dormitorio.

Inmediatamente, Pepe se da la vuelta y se dirige hacia la puerta cerrada del dormitorio. Con duda y con cuidado, la abre.

EL PUNTO DE VISTA DE PEPE

Lentamente, el cuerpo de Alicia se revela en la cama cubierta con una sábana.

INT. DÍA LA CHOZA EL DORMITORIO

En silencio, se acerca a ella. Con cuidado, baja la sábana y deja al descubierto el rostro de Alicia. Está pálida y sin vida. Pepe cae de rodillas y se derrumba de nuevo. El dolor es desgarrador... demasiado para soportarlo.

DESVANECE A NEGRO

INT. DÍA EN LA SALA DE LA CHOZA

Óscar y Rosa están sentados en el sofá con la recién nacida en el regazo de ella. Pepe cierra la puerta del dormitorio y entra en la sala. Su aspecto lo dice todo.

ROSA

¿Quieres algo de beber?

Pepe asiente con la cabeza. Rosa le da la niña a Oscar y va a buscar un vaso de agua. Oscar mira a la niña de Pepe.

OSCAR

Lucía va a ser una hermosura.

Pepe se acerca a Oscar. Oscar le da la bebé a Pepe. Un momento interesante, un momento que nunca se olvida. (Varias pausas)

De repente, KAAABOOMM... tanto la puerta delantera como la trasera de la Choza se abren de golpe. Pablo entra por la puerta delantera con su rifle M-14 cargado y preparado. El sargento Carter entra por la puerta trasera apuntando su fusil. Todos se quedan paralizados. La bebé se sobresalta y empieza a llorar.

PEPE

¡Dios Mio…!

PABLO

No pensaste que te dejaríamos atrás, ¿verdad?

El teniente Smith entra tras el sargento Carter. Bob y Joe entran detrás de Pablo. Pepe mira fijamente al teniente Smith.

LT. SMITH

¿Qué coño estás mirando?

Pepe esboza una sonrisa mientras Óscar, Pablo y el resto de los hombres se echan a reír.

OSCAR
Tu ves Rosita, te dije que los americanos
nos habían invadido.

PEPE
No tan rápido Oscar.

No tan rápido.

OSCAR
¿Cómo que no tan rápido?

PEPE
Mil cuatrocientos cubanos invadieron la
Bahía de Cochinos, no los americanos.

LT. SMITH
Y hay muchas posibilidades de que la
invasión sea un fracaso.

OSCAR
¿Por qué? ¿Que quieres decir?

LT. SMITH
Todo nuestro apoyo se ha paralizado
indefinidamente gracias a las fotos que
tomamos.

OSCAR
¿De qué estás hablando?

LT. SMITH
Lo siento. El resto es confidencial.

El llanto de la bebé se hace más fuerte. El teniente Smith mira su reloj.

LT. SMITH
No tenemos mucho tiempo.

PABLO
Pepe, retrasamos nuestro encuentro 48
horas.

¿Están todos listos?

Pepe asiente.

PEPE
Estamos listos.

OSCAR
¿Y Alicia?

PEPE
Viene con nosotros.

PABLO
¿Dónde está?

PEPE
Está en el dormitorio.

Pablo y Pepe van al dormitorio. Oscar, Rosa y los hombres se preparan para partir.

INT. DÍA DORMITORIO DE ALICIA

Pablo entra y ve un cuerpo cubierto en la cama. Vuelve a mirar a Pepe. Pablo, perplejo, se acerca al cuerpo y levanta la sábana. Pepe emocionado.

PEPE

No tenía por qué morir.

Varias pausas.

PABLO

Pepe no podemos llevarla.

PEPE

No me iré sin ella.

PABLO

El teniente Smith nunca lo permitirá.

Pondrá en peligro toda la misión.

PEPE

Estás perdiendo el tiempo. ¡Ella viene con nosotros!

Pablo siente el dolor de Pepe y nota su mirada y determinación. Pasan varias pausas.

PABLO

Vamos, dame una mano.

Pablo empieza a envolver el cuerpo de Alicia en más sábanas. Pepe, con los ojos vidriosos, ayuda a Pablo en el proceso.

DE VUELTA EN LA SALA DE LA CHOZA

Pablo y Pepe entran en la sala. Pablo lleva el cuerpo de Alicia envuelto en sábanas y mantas. Pepe lleva los fusiles y una mochila.

PABLO

Estamos listos.

LT. SMITH

¿Qué eso...?

PABLO

Alicia necesita nuestra ayuda.

PEPE

Nuestro trato era traer a mi familia.

El teniente Smith mira perplejo y confuso al sargento Carter. El sargento Carter parece entender la petición de Pepe. Asiente al teniente Smith comunicándole su deseo de ayudar a Pepe. El teniente Smith cumple el trato.

Con orgullo.

LT. SMITH

Vámonos, ¡muévanse!

Uno a uno, abandonan LA CHOZA.

DISOLVER A

EN PANTALLA "ABRIL 1976 MIAMI FLORIDA ESTADOS UNIDOS"

INT. DÍA LA BIBLIOTECA (El mismo lugar donde comenzó la historia)

Lucía llora. La consuela PEPE. Juan sostiene una foto de Alicia y tiene los ojos vidriosos y llorosos. Rosa abre la puerta de la biblioteca y se asoma al interior.

> ROSA
> ¿Es una fiesta privada?

> PEPE
> No mamá, por favor entra.

ROSA capta el ambiente.

> ROSA
> Supongo que por fin le contaste a Lucía
> toda la historia.

> PEPE
> Sí.

> LUCIA
> Ya era hora, abuela.

PEPE a punto de desplomarse

> PEPE
> Pienso en ella todos los días.
>
> Todavía me duele como si fuera el
> primer día.

> ROSA
> No hay nada que lamentar.
>
> Hiciste todo lo que pudiste.

Pepe mira a Lucía. Sin palabra sentimos el amor y el cariño que se profesan. Pepe coge la mano de Lucía y se sienta a su lado.

PEPE

Lucy, tu madre quería que tu fueras siempre fuerte e independiente como ella.

LUCIA

Pero yo lo soy, papá.

Varias pausas

PEPE

Ella tenía mucha fe en América.

De alguna manera sabía que si perseveras, ¡tus sueños pueden hacerse realidad aquí!

Lucía se seca las lágrimas de los ojos.

LUCIA

Lo haré papá, Haré que se sienta orgullosa de mí.

Suena el teléfono. Rosa contesta.

ROSA

¿Hola?

A Rosa se le iluminan los ojos. Una hermosa sonrisa se dibuja en su rostro. Podemos oír vagamente a la persona que llama del otro lado.

EL MAYORDOMO
¿Lo dejo entrar?

ROSA
Por supuesto.

Rosa cuelga el teléfono.

PEPE
¿Quién era?

ROSA
El Mayordomo, acabamos de recibir un
Fed Ex.

PEPE
Bien, ya basta.

Volvamos a la fiesta.

En unos segundos se abren las puertas de la biblioteca. Entran Pablo y Oscar. Con las manos cargadas de pastelitos y regalos. Los dejan en el escritorio.

PABLO
¿Qué pasa, Socio?

¿Has trabajado en algún hotel últimamente?

OSCAR
Oye, te estás poniendo viejo.

¿Qué le ha pasado a tu cintura?

Pepe y Rosa se recuperan de su tristeza. Reciben a Pablo y Óscar con los brazos abiertos. Lucía y Juan hacen lo mismo. Lucía empieza a abrir un regalo.

PEPE

Ahora si…

¿Mira a estos dos criminales?

Rosa y Pepe se burlan de Pablo y Oscar. Comparten un afecto especial, un sentimiento de auténtica amistad. Todos se sientan,

PABLO

¿Qué te parece?

PEPE

¿Sobre qué? ¿De que estas hablando?

OSCAR

Coño Pepe, ¿no lees los periódicos?

PEPE

He estado tan ocupado últimamente que apenas tengo tiempo para ver las noticias.

PABLO

Pues mira esto.

Pablo despliega una revista que ha traído y la tira encima de la mesita.

PDV LA PORTADA DE UNA REVISTA

Es un ejemplar de una revista popular. La portada tiene una foto de Fidel Castro. Parece cansado y agotado. Los titulares dicen,

"INTENTO DE ASESINATO A FIDEL CASTRO - CASI EL FIN DE UNA ERA"

PEPE
Demasiado poco y demasiado tarde para
todo el daño que ha hecho.

PABLO
Cierto Pepe... Pero no es demasiado
tarde para nosotros.

PEPE
Gracias a Dios!

Pepe, Óscar y Pablo disfrutan de un momento de libertad rebosantes de orgullo y alegría libre del comunismo Castrista.

EL FIN

CRÉDITOS DEL VÍDEO

Después de más de sesenta años en el exilio, la mayoría de los cubano-americanos siguen compartiendo la misma esperanza y los mismos sueños de que algún día ellos también puedan regresar a su patria "una Cuba libre".

NOTA

Pepe murió de diabetes en 1997.

Pablo se retiró supuestamente de la CIA. No se sabe su ubicación.

Oscar murió de un ataque al corazón en 1980.

Rosa murió de cáncer en 1995.

BIOGRAFÍA

Jose Luis González nació en La Habana, Cuba el 15 de septiembre de 1952 en una familia de clase media.

Jose Luis emigro a Miami, Florida el 2 de noviembre de 1960, cuando apenas tenía 8 años con su hermana, su padre Hilario González Gia y su madre la doctora Edilia González Cruz- Álvarez. Ninguno de ellos hablaba inglés, ni tenían familia o amigos en los Estados Unidos.

Pasaron aproximadamente 3 meses mudándose de hotel a hotel, mientras que su padre trabajaba muy duro para pagar por su comida y refugio, hasta que lograron encontrar un apartamento que decía "Se Renta" pero No a "Negros, Cubanos o inquilinos con mascotas".

Sufrieron muchas injusticias, pero nada de eso los hizo descartar el sueño americano "Vivir en Libertad".

Jose Luis se graduó de Miami Senior High School, (el bachillerato) en donde se destacó como atleta y alumno. En el 2012 Miami Senior High lo invito' a pertenecer al "Salón de la Fama" por sus logros.

También se graduó en el 1975 de la Universidad de Miami, con su maestría en contabilidad donde atendió con una beca universitaria jugando Football americano. Gracias a sus habilidades de jugar Football, Jose Luis fue firmado por el equipo profesional de los Oakland Raiders en el año 1975.

Desde 1975 a 1978 Jose Luis jugo futbol profesional americano representando a varios equipos incluyendo los Philadelphia Bell y los Philadelphia Eagles de donde se retiró finalmente en Septiembre del 1978.

En 1978 Jose Luis empezó su carrera contable con Ernst & Ernst donde aprendió mucho. Jose también trabajo con Deloitte & Touche y Grant Thornton por más de una década, Esta experiencia fue importantísima para ayudar a Jose Luis llegar a su próxima etapa. En 1984 Jose Luis se convirtió en un Contador Público Certificado, llevándolo a la posición de CFO en distintas empresas públicas y privadas americanas.

Su amor por el arte lo convirtió en el productor ejecutivo de películas como Shadow Force con la participación de Dirk Benedict y también escribió, produjo y dirigió la película The Last Semester en 1999.

En su actual faceta de escritor, Jose Luis está lanzando su primer libro " Ninety Miles" (Noventa Millas) el cual es un libro basado en una historia real de amor en la época de la revolución cubana y todo el entorno y personajes reales que acontecían en ese momento.

SINOPSIS NOVENTA MILLAS

Basada en hechos reales que abarcan cuarenta años, esta historia trata sobre la lucha incesante de una familia en busca de la libertad; los "Siete Fundadores", del círculo íntimo de Fidel Castro y su Partido Revolucionario Cubano; y una aventura épica impulsada por una apasionada relación amorosa ambientada en la Cuba pre y posrevolucionaria de 1959.

La historia de amor es el principal impulso de este libro. Pepe, el único sobreviviente del círculo íntimo de Fidel Castro escapa varios intentos de asesinato y se ve obligado a dejar a su familia y a su prometida (Alicia) en Cuba. Alicia, que lleva un hijo nonato de Pepe, oculta su embarazo para garantizar la salida de Pepe inmediata a un lugar más seguro, los Estados Unidos. Después de una angustiosa fuga a Callo Hueso (Key West), Pepe recibe la noticia del embarazo de su prometida y comienza un largo y peligroso viaje para salvar a Alicia y a su criatura por nacer. Pepe aprovecha la oportunidad para regresar a Cuba como agente de la CIA en una ultra encubierta y clandestina operación llamada "90 Millas". Esta operación se lanzó justo antes de la invasión de Bahía de Cochinos el 17 de abril de 1961. El objetivo de "90 Millas" era determinar el alcance de las capacidades militares de Castro, es decir, la capacidad nuclear.

El llamado Gran Círculo Interno de los Siete era un grupo de hombres que ayudaron a organizar y financiar el Partido Revolucionario Cubano incluso la Revolución Cubana. Estos hombres proporcionaron todos los recursos necesarios para la revolución de Castro. Jugaron un papel decisivo en el derrocamiento de Batista, el dictador reinante de la isla de Cuba. A los dieciocho meses del ascenso de Castro al poder, seis de los 7 hombres del Gran Círculo Interno habían desaparecido o habían sido asesinados metódicamente por asesinos desconocidos.

Esta historia también descubre la verdad sobre la crisis de los misiles de octubre en 1962. El gobierno estadounidense (principalmente la administración Kennedy) ignoró los informes sobre el fortalecimiento militar de Castro. Además, altos funcionarios del gobierno conocían y tenían pruebas de la existencia de armas nucleares en Cuba mucho antes de los infames Misiles de Octubre en el 1962 y el sobrevuelo del avión U-2 de la Fuerza Aérea de los Estados Unidos.

Hay muchas facetas de esta historia. Una trágica historia de amor con el telón de fondo de la Revolución Cubana. Una aventura increíble y una mirada a la búsqueda de libertad de una familia cubana. Y una parte de la historia de Estados Unidos nunca antes conocida.